BABYSITTER BEAR

BODYGUARD SHIFTERS #7

ZOE CHANT

Babysitter Bear
© 2021 Zoe Chant, all rights reserved.

This book is a standalone with an HEA, but includes characters from the earlier books. Here are those books in order if you'd like to read them:

1. Bearista
2. Pet Rescue Panther
3. Bear in a Bookshop
4. Day Care Dragon
5. Bull in a Tea Shop
6. Dancer Dragon

There is a convenient boxed set of the first four books.

DAN

This couldn't possibly be the place. Could it?

Dan Ross stood in ankle-deep snow beside the rural road, looking across snow-covered pastures to a rambling farmhouse with smoke curling from a fireplace chimney. There was a collection of outbuildings, all with neatly shoveled paths, and an honest-to-goodness barn with an actual horse browsing on hay, inside a wooden pole fence that wrapped around the barn.

On a post by the driveway, a mailbox shaped like a barn read THE RUGERS.

Apparently this was the place, even if he hadn't thought a guy like his old buddy Derek would live on a farm in a million years.

He adjusted his duffel over his shoulder. It contained all his worldly possessions, mostly just a collection of spare clothes and a few books he was reading; he'd learned to travel light in the Army. He curled his gloved hand through the duffel strap. His other hand—a pair of metal clamps half-hidden in the sleeve of his military surplus coat—rested lightly against his thigh.

Inside him, his bear seemed to stir, rousing a little at the smells of pine and woodsmoke on the clear sharp breeze.

Woods? Run? Hunt?

His bear was a simple animal with simple pleasures. He *wished* he could let it run and hunt. He just didn't have a clue what would happen if he shifted into a bear with only three legs and he wasn't ready to find out.

He hadn't shifted since losing his arm, two years ago.

He'd hitchhiked out here on a farm truck after taking a bus to Autumn Grove, the nearest town. The small town was unexpected enough. He knew Derek lived somewhere kinda rural, but he hadn't been prepared for the little brick downtown with its handful of shops.

This, though ...

Standing there in the cold wind, Dan took out his phone. He hesitated. He was right here at the top of the driveway. He may as well just walk down and knock on the door.

Still, after a minute, he played back the saved message that Derek had sent him some months back, even though he already knew it by heart.

"Hey, Danny-Boy," Derek's voice said, and Dan couldn't help smiling.

"Yeah, up yours, Derek," he muttered at the phone.

The message continued, Derek's gruff voice speaking as if out of the past. It was strange listening to it here, looking down at the little farmhouse rather than sitting on a bed in one of a number of shitty motel rooms.

"Remember how we used to talk about setting up our own business when you got out of the service? I know that was years ago, but guess what. I'm finally doing it. Me and Ben Keegan from the old days got together and we're running our own private security company for people like us."

There was a slight, meaningful hesitation on that last

part. Shifters were what he meant, Dan knew; the secrecy habit was too deeply ingrained to talk about it, even on a voicemail message.

"So anyway," Derek went on, "I'm reaching out to some of the guys I know from the old days. See if anyone's interested. We're just getting off the ground and we don't have much business yet, but hell, even if you don't need a job, let's get together just for old time's sake. I'm living in a town called Autumn Grove, and you're probably laughing right now because I was never a settling down in small towns kind of guy. But things change, you know? I'm gonna run out of message here, so I'll just text you my address and you can call or stop by. Assuming you're even in the same part of the country as—"

The message cut off.

Dan hesitated for a long moment with his thumb over the call button, then put the phone back in his pocket.

"Yeah, it's a nice thought, Derek," he murmured. He looked down the driveway again. "But we haven't seen each other in a long time, and there might be a few things you don't know about me. I don't think they hire a lot of one-armed guys to run security detail."

Especially a one-armed shifter who doesn't shift.

Still ... he'd come all this way. If Derek was going to turn him down, maybe it would be harder to do it in person than over the phone.

He started walking slowly down the driveway. His low-topped town boots slipped and slid on the snow. With every step, he thought once again that he'd made a mistake. What was he *thinking*, dropping himself into the middle of the family life Derek had built for himself here?

He came to a fence and a gate, made of heavy steel poles. It stood open, but there was a security camera mounted to the top of one of the poles. Dan smiled a little.

Okay, that was the first thing he'd seen so far that felt like Derek.

The horse raised its head, noticing him. It was a small black-and-white pony with a blue blanket wrapped around its roly-poly body. It gave a loud snort.

"Yeah, thanks, buddy," Dan said. "Same back atcha."

The driveway curved into a large, plowed-out parking area in front of the house. There were several vehicles parked there: a practical all-wheel-drive Subaru SUV, a big black truck, and a low-slung shape with a canvas cover draped over it and snow on top of that; from the shape it looked like some kind of classic muscle car. That was Derek's for sure, but much better for cruising on summer highways than driving in the country in the winter.

Dan took a deep breath and mounted the steps to the porch. There was a cat at the door. As far as he could tell, it was an ordinary cat, not a shifter, a small gray tabby. It looked up at him and let on a small peeping *miaow*.

"You too, huh?" Dan said, and knocked.

There was no answer. When he listened, he could hear noises inside: voices, and a sudden crash.

His entire body tensed. Were they under attack? Maybe that was why the gate was open.

He dropped the duffel on the porch and tested the doorknob. It turned easily.

Braced for trouble, Dan opened it.

The cat uncoiled from its crouch and shot inside, just as something brightly jewel-colored sped outward past Dan's leg.

"Catch her!" someone yelled from inside.

Dan spun around and grabbed whatever-it-was on pure instinct.

He found himself holding a tiny, bright purple dragon. It was so colorful, so shiny, and above all so *small* that it looked like a toy. But it was clearly alive. Its little claws dug into his wrist, and it stared up at him with glittering golden eyes.

"Uh, hi," Dan said.

It put out a tiny tongue and licked his wrist.

"Where is she? Skye? Oh, thank God." The door was pushed the rest of the way open, and a man in a blue, open-necked shirt stepped outside. Not Derek: he was shorter and slighter, with a few strands of gray salting his dark hair. He had a slightly wild-eyed look about him. "That's a, uh—pet—just give her to me, please."

"Here." Dan held out his arm and the little dragon leaped eagerly to cling to the other man's denim shirt. Dan frowned at him. There was a sense of familiarity about him. Then it clicked, all of a sudden. "Ben! Hey!"

Ben's wariness abruptly relaxed into friendliness, the recognition of one shifter for another. "Oh, hey! Dan! Wow, it's been ages. Derek said he'd sent you some messages but hadn't heard back."

"Yeah, I've been ... busy," Dan said. He was still staring at the dragon, which was now nuzzling against Ben's face. "Is that a dragon?"

"This is my daughter, Skye," Ben said proudly. "Er, normally she's not quite this—purple. She's going through a phase. It's good to see you! Come on in."

He held the door, and Dan retrieved his duffel and stamped the snow off his boots. The farmhouse was just as warm and cozy inside as it looked from the outside, with kids' toys scattered all over the place and a playpen in the corner. Dan felt terribly out of place. He didn't belong here. He shouldn't have come.

"Derek!" Ben called. The dragon had wound herself around his neck like a scarf, gleaming in the lamplight. "Check out who's here, man!"

The only response was a thump and a high-pitched banshee wail of "Noooooooo!"

"You guys aren't under attack or anything?" Dan asked cautiously. Ben didn't seem alarmed.

"Sort of," Ben said wryly. "We're outnumbered too. But at least they're not armed." And with that cryptic comment, he led the way into the kitchen.

If the living room had been a bit untidy, the kitchen looked like a hurricane had gone through it. The table was strewn with baby things as well as an open laptop and a folder of papers. Derek Ruger, all six and a half muscular feet of him, was trying to fill a bottle with a very small baby tucked up against his shoulder and a dark-haired little girl clinging to his leg and crying.

Derek looked exactly the same as he had back in their service days, which was what made it so incongruous seeing him draped in little kids.

The baby was in a pink onesie and looked very young. The toddler had a sparkly unicorn shirt half on and half off, and a winged pony toy clutched in one fist. There was a box of crackers scattered around her feet; it looked like they had been attempted as a bribe and then rejected.

"Honey," Derek was saying, while trying to juggle the bottle and the baby, "you're going to have to put down Rainbow Sparkle Magic so I can put your shirt on."

"No!" the little girl sobbed, clutching the toy to her chest protectively, as if he'd suggested stuffing the pony down the garbage disposal.

"Honey, your arm won't fit through the sleeve like that. It's not physically possible."

"You need a hand there?" Ben asked, trying to choke off a laugh. "Hang on, let me get Short and Scaly settled—no, sweetheart, not up there," he added, catching Skye as she tried to leap for the top of the refrigerator, tiny wings churning.

Dan cleared his throat. "I'm pretty good with kids. Can I try?"

"Be my guest," Derek said, and then did a double-take. "Whoa, Dan! Man, it's great to see you! What are you doing here? You never called me back. I wasn't even sure if I had the right number."

"Yeah, sorry about that. Guess I had my own stuff going on for a while there." Dan went down to one knee and smiled at the little girl. "Hi, kid. I'm your dad's friend Dan. What's her name?" he asked, glancing up at Derek.

"Mina," Derek said. "Short for Jimena." He swiveled his leg so that Mina was facing Dan. "Honey, say hi to Dan."

Mina squeaked and buried her face in Derek's leg. The half-on, twisted-around sweatshirt dangled from her arm like a butterfly's partly shed chrysalis.

"Hi there," Dan said. "Are you shy? Me too." He covered his eyes with his good hand. The other—the metal clamp hand—was still half hidden in the sleeve of his coat. "Where's Mina? Oh no, I guess she's gone. I can't see her at all."

There was a tiny giggle. Dan jerked his hand down.

"Oh, there she is!"

Mina shrieked and hid behind Derek's leg.

"Is this your pony friend?" Dan asked, and Mina gave a little nod. She was an utterly adorable kid, maybe two or three, with huge dark eyes. "I love ponies. Can I see him?"

Mina hesitated and then lurched away from Derek's leg and held him out.

"Wow, what a beautiful pony," Dan said, cupping his hand under the pony without trying to take it. "What's his name?"

Mina mumbled something that sounded like "mmmmsparklymagic."

"Wow. Here, let me give you a hand with your shirt, okay?

Turn," Dan said, and she obediently swiveled and presented an arm. "I'll just hold your pony friend for a minute to keep him safe, and then give him back."

"Holy shit," Derek said from above him. "Cow, I mean. Holy cow."

"Dan's always been kind of a kid whisperer, hasn't he?" Ben said. Dan glanced up while pulling Mina's shirt onto her other arm. Ben had Skye wound around his arm like some kind of sparkly ornament, holding her wings down with one hand while she tried to scrabble free. "Remember how kids were always all over him? Village kids, orphanage kids, it didn't seem to matter if he spoke the language or not."

"It's not magic or anything," Dan said, embarrassed. "It's not that hard." He tugged down the shirt and gave Mina back the pony, which she snatched out of his grasp. "There, that's better, huh?"

"I've been trying to get that shirt on her for an *hour*," Derek said.

"Well," Ben said, "if it makes you feel any better, she'll probably be out of it in a few minutes. At least if she's anything like Skye." He rubbed the top of the baby dragon's head with his thumb.

"Can't dragons take their clothes into a shift?" Derek asked.

"They *can*, sure. If they're wearing clothes to begin with."

"Ah."

Mina had now decided that Dan was her new favorite person. She offered him a soggy cracker.

"Uh, thanks, sweetheart."

"Sorry for the reception, but now you know what it's like around here," Derek said. He had the baby tucked in the crook of his muscular arm with the bottle in her mouth. "This is Lulu, and you already met Mina. Damn, it's been a long time, man! We've got a heck of a lot to catch up on. Coat hook's by the back door, coffeepot over there, cups above the sink. Help yourself."

Dan hesitated; he had been trying to put this moment off as long as possible. Might as well get it over with. He stripped out of the beat-up old Army coat and hung it where Derek had indicated.

Underneath, he was wearing a T-shirt with the straps of the prosthesis over the top. The prosthesis was the old-fashioned kind, probably unchanged in general style since the 1950s: a plastic flesh-colored forearm and elbow, a pair of metal clamps for grasping and manipulating objects, and straps that let him use his shoulder muscles to open and close the graspers. He had a fake hand that went in place of the clamps, but he hated wearing the damn thing because it was next to useless for picking things up.

He took a deep breath and turned around to see them both looking at him.

"What?" Dan said. "Never seen a guy hang up a coat before?" He went over to the coffeepot. "Things have changed a bit since you saw me last."

"I guess so," Derek said. "Shit, man."

Dan shrugged and got himself down a coffee cup. He used the prosthesis to open and close the cabinet door, trying to be casual and feeling a little like he was going through some kind of test, a job interview of sorts.

And also just showing the other guys that he could still do everything he used to do.

As best he could, he generally tried not to buy into any of that bullshit about only being half a man or whatever. He was still the same man he'd ever been; he was just a one-armed version of himself.

But he also wasn't the kind of guy who was cut out for sitting at a sedentary desk job.

And there were very few employers who were willing to

consider a one-armed man for any kind of physical work when there were plenty of two-armed men who wanted the same jobs. To most human employers, he couldn't explain that shifter strength and durability helped make up for it; he could sling around bags of cement one-armed that would have taken normal men two good arms to carry. But how could he tell an ordinary human boss that he was twice as strong as a normal man and his bones didn't break as easy? They could look right at him and see that he wasn't suited to work in a warehouse, do security work, go into law enforcement.

His therapist at the VA had tried to talk him into retraining for a new career. But there wasn't anything he wanted to do. Or more accurately, there was just one thing he wanted to do: work with his hands. And he couldn't do that anymore.

This was his last chance. At least here, among other shifters, he didn't have to justify his strength and skill.

And he'd procrastinated about as long as he could by stirring milk into his coffee. Dan looked over at the other two. "So this isn't how I was expecting my job interview to go, but ... are you still hiring?"

A moment of blankness passed over Derek's face. "Oh, right. Yeah. The job."

"Fuck, man," Dan snapped. Ben covered Skye's ears, although since she was dragon-shaped, not much ear was visible anyway. "I mean ... damn!" Okay, so he hadn't been around little kids in a while. "If you don't want to hire a one-armed guy, just say so."

"Wait, wait, hold on. That's not actually the problem." Derek took a seat at the kitchen table, in front of the open laptop, and adjusted the baby in his lap. "The bodyguard agency is kind of a ... a work in progress, I guess you could say."

"The problem is we haven't got enough work for even one bodyguard right now, let alone three," Ben said. "And I think you can see why." Skye had crawled up on his shoulder and was chewing on his hair.

"We used to have Gaby's mom living with us and looking after the kids, but she met a guy at seniors' bingo night who was up from Florida visiting his grandkids," Derek explained. "So now she's down in Orlando most of the time. It's made getting the business off the ground a little bit tricky, since both of our mates work."

The stubborn hope that Dan had been clinging to all the way out here began to crack and fall apart. "Guess I should've called ahead," he said, trying to make a joke out of it.

"I'm really sorry, man. Wait ..." Derek rotated in the chair, trying not to disturb the baby falling asleep in his arms. "Please tell me you didn't quit your day job."

"I was looking for a change anyway," Dan not-quite-lied. It wasn't quitting if he hadn't had a job to begin with. He'd been knocking around between short-lived security gigs, whenever he could get a bar owner or event manager to give him a chance as a bouncer, but even that work had dried up lately.

Ben gave him a look, and Dan remembered that Ben's panther let him know when people were lying.

Oops.

"Crap," Derek said. "Listen, dude, we might be able to figure out something, like a trial basis kind of thing ..."

Dan stiffened.

"I don't need charity," he said, his bear bristling.

"It's not charity," Ben said quickly, moving in to defuse the situation. "Actually, what we've both realized lately is that neither of us is that good at the administrative side of things. You used to do the supply-clerk thing in the Army, didn't you? Filing, typing—"

Dan was already vigorously shaking his head. "Typing's not my thing these days," he said, gesturing with the metal clamp.

"Website building?" Ben tried hopefully.

"What about babysitting?" Dan asked.

It was meant to be a joke, but by the time he said it, he had already realized that he meant it. And at the looks on their faces, he felt something new—a cautious dawning of hope.

"Yeah, I—*wait*," Derek said. "Are you offering?"

Dan shrugged. "I came here looking for a job. I'm not too picky about what the job actually is. I can't do data entry worth a damn." He gestured with the clamp again. "But I can cook and change diapers."

"*Can* you?" Derek asked. "I don't mean to offend here, seriously. But I've got all I can do keeping up with with these two with a pair of working hands."

"I can brush my teeth, zip my fly, and tie a necktie, so I think I can handle a baby," Dan said. A baby's diaper was a delicate task, but after some of the exercises the physical therapist had put him through, he was confident he could do it.

Especially if the alternative was being homeless.

Derek and Ben shared a look.

"How are you with baby dragons?" Ben asked.

"Well, let's find out." Dan reached out his flesh-and-blood hand. Skye immediately jumped from her father's shoulder to Dan's arm and scrabbled up to curl around his neck.

"Job interview done," Derek said. "You're hired."

PAULA

"You QUIT?" Paula said in desperation and disbelief.

She hip-checked her way into the diner's kitchen with a stack of dirty plates in each hand, her shoulder tilted up next to her ear to hold her phone.

"I'm sorry!" said the voice of the diner's one and only (and now former) full-time waitress, sounding a little desperate herself. "I was going to tell you, I swear! It's only, I hadn't heard back from the other job and I thought I didn't get it and then I did get it and they pay more than you do—"

"So you just decided not to come in to work instead."

The kitchen was sweltering, the cook busily slapping scrambled eggs onto plates. Paula slid the dirty plates one armload at a time into the dishwasher.

"I'm *really* sorry," the ex-waitress was saying. "Um, can I come in on Friday and collect my last paycheck?"

"Sure," Paula said. "Why not. You can bring back your DeWitt's Diner T-shirt at the same time. And now we're in the middle of the breakfast rush so I have to go."

She very carefully hung up instead of throwing the phone across the room.

"Lost another one, huh?" said the cook, Mitch, without a break in the quick slap of spatula on griddle as he somehow balanced a dance of hash browns, eggs, and pancakes without ever mixing them up or getting pancake batter in the scrambled eggs.

Big, tattooed Mitch had been Paula's first hire after she inherited the place from her parents only to have their long-time cook retire for health reasons immediately after. She had hired him mainly because she was desperate, but at this point it was hard to imagine the diner without Mitch and his always entertaining, dubiously authentic stories of his misspent youth.

"Third one in a month," Paula groaned. "It's not even worth training people at this point." She checked her phone. Other than the waitress, there were no recent calls or texts. "Mitch, *please* tell me you've seen my son today."

"Sorry, Miz DeWitt. Nope."

Paula sighed and sent yet another text. *Austin! You're supposed to be helping out in the diner before school! Did you make your sister's lunch like I asked?*

No answer. She looked toward the back door of the diner and thought briefly of running across the alley into the house where she had grown up, and now lived with her two kids, to roust her son and get her daughter ready for the day.

Even more longingly, she thought of not having to get up at four-thirty to get ready for the morning rush at the diner. Just having leisure time to spend with her kids. Not *working* all the time.

"They're getting restless out there," Mitch said. "Order up!"

Paula groaned. She slapped a smile on her face, grabbed the freshly loaded plates and headed out to the dining area.

"Miss, I don't even have a glass of water yet," someone

complained as she whisked the plates to the appropriate table.

"I'll be with you in just a minute, sir."

She left dishes piled on the end of an unused table while she frantically scribbled orders. Swooping back into the kitchen, she was just in time to see a small, bright-green-clad figure come banging through the door that led out to the alley, along with a rush of cold wind.

"Mommmm!" Lissy's little face was bright pink from cold under her spring-leaf-colored hat. "I need lunch money!"

"Your brother was supposed to make your lunch."

"Uh-uh," Lissy said. "He just went to school."

Paula cursed under her breath. "Here," she said, and grabbed a grilled cheese sandwich that Mitch had just smacked off the griddle. "Ow! Hot!" She stuffed it into one of the bags they kept around for carry-out orders, and looked around wildly for something from the general fruit-and-vegetable category. The only thing in sight was a pile of tomatoes. She put one of those in too, along with a cup of yogurt, and thrust it into her daughter's hands, then herded her through the kitchen and out into the dining area. "Do you have your boots? Where's your book bag?" Lissy's hair didn't look like it had been brushed, but at this point Paula was willing to let it go. The school bus stop was visible through the café's front window, and there was a flash of yellow. "There's the bus. Hurry!"

Lissy ran off, banging through the door onto the snowy sidewalk as the school bus's red stop lights began to flash.

The dining room full of customers spontaneously applauded.

"Thank you," Paula said modestly. There were times when she really appreciated the camaraderie of living in a small town.

"Miss, I asked for a warmup on my coffee ten minutes ago," came from a corner.

On the other hand, there was always someone like that.

∽

It wasn't until a couple of hours later, when the breakfast crowd had drained out, that she finally got a chance to sit down and rest for five minutes. Mitch had very generously skipped his morning break to help her clean up the dining area, and she flipped the sign to CLOSED to give herself a few minutes to cram some leftover scrambled eggs into her mouth and text her teenager again.

Austin, when you get this, CALL YOUR MOM.

She had always promised herself that she wasn't going to do to her own kids what her parents had done. She loved her parents, but had deeply resented spending her teen years at mostly unpaid labor in the diner. She had *loathed* the diner, from the smell of grease to the cracking of her skin after a day spent with her hands immersed in dishwater. There were a number of reasons why she had fled for the big city as soon as she graduated from high school, but getting away from the diner was definitely part of that.

She never wanted her kids to feel that way.

And yet, here I am. Running the diner just like my parents did. Roping my son into doing my chores.

Paula sighed and rubbed her forehead. Then she composed another text.

Sweetheart, I'm sorry. It's been a rough morning. I depend on you a lot and I know that. Just tell me if I'm piling too much on.

She stared at it, then deleted the last two sentences and just sent the apology.

The bell at the front door jingled, and Paula looked up. She hadn't bothered to lock the door, figuring that she didn't need to scare off customers if someone was determined enough to get past the CLOSED sign. This was the dead time between breakfast and lunch, so it wasn't all that likely for anyone to come in anyway.

And yet here someone was. Paula didn't dislike very many people, but she took an instant dislike to this guy. He just looked ... *creepy*, was the word that came to mind. He didn't look like a trucker or a farmer or even a tourist, the usual types of single guys that they got in addition to the family dining crowd. He would have been almost instantly forgettable if she'd looked at him in a crowd on a city street—dark suit, slicked-back dark hair, sunglasses—but here, he stood out. He glanced around the interior of the diner. His eyes were hidden behind the sunglasses, but there was still something about the way he was looking around that she didn't like.

"Sorry," Paula said. "We're closed."

That too-curious, somehow *vicious* gaze came to rest on her. Instead of leaving, he came in and closed the door behind him.

Paula stood up slowly. She kept her hand on her phone. Mitch was just in the back; if she shouted for help, he would hear her.

"I said we're closed," she repeated, and took a side step to the mop bucket. "If you'll excuse me, I have a lot of cleaning up to do—"

"Mrs. Raines?" the stranger said, and Paula's stomach did an unpleasant swooping thing.

She had never used her married name in Autumn Grove. Here, she was one of the DeWitts (*you know, Martha and John's daughter*), the DeWitts who ran the diner. Austin and Lissy still technically had their dad's last name for official school purposes, but they were "the DeWitt kids" everywhere else.

There was no good reason why a stranger should come in here calling her by her ex-husband's name.

"Do you know Terry?" she asked, but—stupid question; of course he did. A better question was why he was here. "Are you a lawyer?" Maybe her ex had finally gotten it together on child support.

"Terry?" Sunglasses laughed. "That's funny. Is that what you call him?"

Her stomach did the awful swooping thing again.

For her entire disastrous marriage to Terry Raines, she had suspected, and then known for sure, that he was lying to her about something big. Marriage-destroyingly big. She just had never known what it was.

She had sometimes imagined fancifully that Terry was living some kind of double life. Now she was slapped in the face with the worst kind of confirmation. He hadn't even told her the truth about his *name*.

"What's his real name?" she asked in a voice that didn't sound like her own.

The stranger pushed his sunglasses on top of his head. That was no improvement. His eyes were the strangest color she'd ever seen, almost gold.

"Why don't you just tell me where he is, Mrs. Raines. Our business is with him, not you."

"I don't *know*," Paula said shortly. "I haven't heard from him in over a year. If you find him, tell him he owes child support and there had better be a present in the mail for Austin's next birthday."

"Who's Austin?" the stranger asked, and Paula froze with her hand clutching her phone.

Whoever this is, he doesn't know about the kids.
He's no lawyer.

What the hell was Terry mixed up in? Mafia? Loan

sharks? Whatever it was, she wanted no part of it. Especially not with the kids to worry about.

She dropped the phone into her apron pocket and whipped the mop out of the bucket. In high school, for a brief period, she had been a baton twirler. Now she spun the wet mop in a perfect two-finger twirl that would have impressed even old Mrs. Karluch, their gimlet-eyed baton-twirling instructor. It just barely missed the ceiling lights, sent a spray of bleach water arcing across half the tables, and came to rest pointing at the stranger's face.

She had the pleasure of seeing him stumble away until his back slammed into the door. Apparently he hadn't expected the little ex-wife to come bearing a loaded mop.

"Get out of my diner," Paula said.

He wiped mop water off his cheek with the back of his hand. "We're not done talking, lady."

Paula kept the mop aimed at his face. "Yeah, we are. Terry's problems aren't my problems. Not anymore."

"You think so?" His tone was nasty, and it began to sink in on Paula that—once his initial shock had worn off—someone who was used to hassling people for money might not be put off by a small woman armed with a mop soaked in bleach water. "Let me tell you how it is. You're going to help us get in touch with—"

"I haven't talked to that deadbeat in over a year." Paula tried to keep a quaver out of her voice. She could see the gold-eyed stranger getting bolder by the moment.

Now he reached out, gripped the mop just behind the head, and moved it away from his face. Paula struggled to keep hold of the mop as it was moved against her resistance. She didn't have a chance. He was shockingly, terribly strong.

"Maybe we should go somewhere private and talk about this some more," he said.

From behind Paula, a voice said, "I think I heard the lady tell you to leave."

Mitch was standing in the kitchen doorway. He was holding one of the big knives from the kitchen. He held it down against his leg, but he held it in a way that suggested he knew a few things to do with it. As usual in the overheated kitchen, he wore nothing on top but a sleeveless, sweat-damp T-shirt, half tucked into his stained jeans. His bare, hairy arms were all muscle and covered in crudely inked tattoos, a skull and a rose and the name Veva and some cartoony dinosaurs. Paula had long suspected that they were jail tattoos, but didn't really want to ask.

"She said get out," Mitch added. "Just in case you missed it."

In his other hand, he was holding a damp cloth. With his eyes fixed on the stranger, he began to carefully polish the blade of the butcher knife.

Paula's eyes nearly popped out of her head. She edged out of the way to make sure she wasn't between them. The stranger was looking at Mitch now instead of her, and his hand had slipped off the mop head. She gave it a fierce thrust, poking him in the face with the wet mop end.

He made a noise like "Blargle!" and stumbled into the door.

"Out!" she snapped.

He wrenched the door open, scrubbing at his face. "We're going to find him with or without your help," he said coldly, and slammed the door behind him with a loud clash of bells.

"I don't care!" Paula yelled after him. "Terry can drive off a cliff for all I care!"

Terry ... or whatever his real name was.

Her knees wobbled. She swayed against the counter, and lowered the mop for support.

"You okay, Miz DeWitt?" Mitch said.

"Uh ... yeah. I'm okay. Thank you. Also," Paula added, "remind me not to get on your bad side."

Mitch grinned. "If he comes back, ma'am, just you let me know."

"Okay," Paula agreed. "Sure. Thanks."

Mitch gave her a nod and went back to the kitchen.

Paula returned the mop to the bucket and went over to peek cautiously out the door. The sidewalk was clear; there was no one in sight except a boy shoveling snow outside the hardware store.

That weirdo hadn't had a weapon. He wouldn't come back, would he? Maybe once he thought about it, he would realize that there was no point in going after her for Terry's debts or present whereabouts.

A quivering feeling of weakness went through her, as if in counterpoint to her furious strength a few moments before. She had to raise her hand to her face to make sure she wasn't crying. Her eyes felt hot and prickly.

Damn Terry. He just had to keep finding new ways to screw up her life. Her biggest regret was marrying that loser—or would have been, at least, if it hadn't resulted in two beautiful kids. She wouldn't undo Austin and Lissy for the world.

And honestly, Terry hadn't been an awful husband. He was a decent father to the kids, too, when he was around. But he was a pathological liar, and apparently it went deeper even than she had realized.

She was done with men. Absolutely done.

With a deep sigh, she got a bleach rag and went to wipe the mop water off her recently cleaned tables.

He won't come back. I'm sure he won't.

Because I don't know what I'm going to do if he does.

DAN

Waking up early had never been a problem for Dan. He'd struggled more at adapting to a night work schedule at his various post-service bouncer jobs. Even when he went to bed at 2 a.m., he tended to pop awake by 5:30 or 6, rain or shine, winter or summer.

But it was someone moving around out in the main part of the house that woke him this time. He jolted out of a restless sleep to find himself wide awake and sitting up, adrenaline pumping through his body. For a disorienting moment, he didn't have any idea where he was, and then he remembered. He was in Derek's spare bedroom, and this was his first full day taking care of Derek's kids.

Light showed in a strip under the door. There was no clock in the room, but he tapped his phone and checked the time. 3:50 a.m. Either there was an intruder who had turned on the lights, or someone in the household was an even earlier riser than Dan himself.

He got up and put his pants on, not bothering with the prosthesis. He went quietly out into the main part of the house. If it was an intruder, he didn't want to give himself away.

The living room was very quiet and dark. The light was coming from the kitchen, where he heard soft clinking and then a voice muttering quietly.

Dan arrived in the doorway and found a smallish woman with her hair pulled back in a dark ponytail, bent over and rummaging through a cabinet.

Ah. This must be Derek's mate Gaby. He hadn't actually met her yesterday. She had come home while he was out with Derek in the barn, being shown the animal-related chores, and by the time they were back in the house, Gaby was upstairs taking a nap. According to Derek, she worked extremely early hours at the bakery these days and was sometimes in bed as early as 7 p.m.

"Where did I put that pastry cutter?" Gaby muttered under her breath. "Come on, it's gotta be here somewhere." She straightened up, still carrying on her inner monologue. "I can always ask Mom where the—AAAAAAAA!"

Dan jumped back. "Sorry!" he said hastily.

Gaby clapped a hand over her mouth. She held very still. Dan started to open his mouth. Gaby shook her head vigorously and pointed a finger toward the ceiling. Confused, Dan stood still too, and then he heard a faint, wailing cry from upstairs.

"Uh," he said sheepishly. "Sorry."

"I'm the one who woke her," Gaby said. She swiped a hand across her hair, smoothing it back into the ponytail. She was small but very intense. "Do you always sneak around? I'm guessing you're Dan. Derek told me about you." Her gaze dropped to the stump of his right arm. Her eyebrows went up a little, but she didn't say anything, which was almost worse than if she had.

"Uh, yeah," he said, feeling intensely self-conscious. The

baby was still crying upstairs. "Listen, I'll get that. I think it's my job now. Okay?"

Gaby hesitated, then nodded, but as he went upstairs, he was aware of her quiet, padding footsteps following him. He liked that about her. He wouldn't have wanted a stranger picking up his baby unsupervised the first time, either.

Derek's tour of the house yesterday had included the upstairs, but in the dark Dan had to pause for a moment, even with acute shifter night vision, to remind himself where everything was. The wailing came from a bedroom to his left with an open door. At the end of the hall, the master bedroom door was cracked open. From behind it, there was rustling, and Derek groaned sleepily, "I'm up, I'm up."

"Don't worry about it," Dan said quietly, not wanting to wake up the other kids. "I'm on it."

"He's on it," Gaby echoed, sounding a little baffled, as a drowsy-looking Derek appeared in the bedroom doorway in boxers and a football T-shirt.

Dan went into the baby's room. A nightlight shaped like a butterfly glowed dimly in the corner. By that light and his own night vision, he found his way to the crib. Lulu, in a white onesie covered in blue flowers, had kicked off her covers and was thrashing and crying.

"Hush, baby," Dan murmured. He had a moment of low-key panic when he wasn't sure if he could pick her up one-handed, or if he trusted himself to pick her up that way without dropping her. But then it passed. He had handled belligerent drunks one-handed. He'd learned to shave and brush his teeth and take the lids off of jars. He could handle one not-very-big baby.

He dipped a hand under her and scooped her up, bringing her against his shoulder. It worked beautifully. He used the stump of his other arm as a light prop for extra security, but didn't really need it. It was years since he'd held a baby, but his body still knew exactly what to do. He cuddled her against his shoulder, and her crying settled down into tiny hiccups and then silence.

Turning around, he saw Derek and Gaby in the doorway, Derek with his arm around his mate's shoulders.

"Yeah," Gaby said after a moment. "I think this is going to work out just fine."

∼

GABY HAD to head off to work, and Derek went back to bed. Lulu cried every time Dan put her down, so he carried her with him while he moved around in the Rugers' kitchen, starting coffee and familiarizing himself with the kitchen's contents.

It was strange to be in someone else's kitchen like this. He reminded himself that this was his job now. At least until the security agency got off the ground and they had to work out some other arrangement. Not exactly how he would have seen his life going, but right now, with Lulu's soft little baby head nestled under his chin, smelling of powder and baby shampoo, he would take this in a heartbeat over being a bouncer at some hole-in-the-wall nightclub run by a douchebag.

He had to put Lulu down in order to actually *do* anything, in his one-armed state. He took her back to the guest bedroom with him, turned on the light, and laid her on the bed. Lulu lay there, kicking her legs, and stared at him with her wide-eyed milky baby stare while he put on his prosthesis.

It was a fairly quick process now that he'd done it so often: a little baby powder on the stump to stop it from chafing, a soft stump sock to cushion it, and then the stump fit into a plastic socket above the prosthetic arm's elbow joint, and the control straps went around his upper body.

Those straps could ache and dig in after a long day of picking things up. When he had mentioned this to his physical therapist at the VA, she had said wryly, "I know it's not quite the same thing, but let me tell you how good it feels to take an underwire off after a sixteen-hour workday. It never gets fun, but you can get used to it." And then she showed him some little adjustments to take the pressure off the straps when he needed to rest the skin underneath. And she was right, he had gotten used to it and hardly noticed the pressure of the straps anymore, except at the end of the day when he was tired anyway.

Lulu watched the whole thing with her fist jammed into her mouth.

"What do you think, kiddo?" he asked her, and scooped her up again.

She snuggled against his shoulder and looked around, kicking her legs a little.

"Right. Let's go make some breakfast."

In the living room, he found a playpen and slid it into the edge of the kitchen, where he laid her on a blanket. She was perfectly calm, he found, as long as she could see him. It was only when he got out of her sight that she started to fuss and cry.

He had coffee ready and breakfast cooking by the time Derek and the other kids came downstairs.

"Wow," Sandy said. The kid was nine, big-eyed and adorable and just starting to get gawky. "You're like a male nanny."

"Alejandro Diaz Ruger," Derek began sternly.

Dan found himself grinning. "It's all right, I don't mind. That *is* what I am."

"Can I look?" Sandy asked, and when Dan nodded, he

came over to examine Dan's prosthesis. Dan showed him how the clamps—technically a pair of curved metal hooks—opened and closed. "Whoa. *Cool*."

"Don't bother the man if he tells you to stop, Sandy," Derek said. He was carrying a sleepy Mina against his shoulder, her legs in little unicorn-covered tights dangling on either side of his thick forearm. He went over and fetched a piece of toast from a plate where Dan had been buttering them.

"I really don't mind," Dan said. And it wasn't just talk. He had found that he preferred kids' honest curiosity to the way that adults edged around the topic of the prosthesis and didn't really want to bring it up. "So what kind of things are you into, Sandy? You like sports?"

Sandy lit up. "I'm on the softball team."

They chatted about sports while Dan finished making breakfast and set the table. Derek settled Mina in her highchair and kept casting glances at Dan bustling around the kitchen.

In the playpen, Lulu began to fuss.

"She might be hungry," Derek said. "Sandy, go get one of your sister's bottles, okay?"

Sandy dashed off. While he was gone, Derek remarked, "You know, I gotta say, I had to ease into all of this myself. Didn't have a clue about it in the beginning. I wasn't expecting you to be a natural like this."

"Told you I was good at it."

Derek laughed. "You know, I think Gaby's right, but then, my mate's a smart lady. This is gonna work out fine."

∾

It was a Saturday, so they had a leisurely morning. Sandy

worked on a bit of homework while Dan did the dishes and Derek put Lulu down for a nap.

It was so homey and domestic that Dan could almost forget, for whole minutes at a time, that this wasn't *his* home. It was someone else's borrowed domesticity that he was enjoying.

He gave in, for a few minutes, to imagining that his mate was here. That this was his house, his kids.

But no, that didn't feel right. It *wasn't* his house and it *wasn't* his kids. He was a guest in someone else's warm, cozy family life. And as much as he appreciated them welcoming him in, he could never forget that they weren't *his* family and he didn't belong.

"Whoa," Sandy said from the doorway, and giggled.

Dan looked around. "What's up, kiddo?"

"I was looking for Dad. I couldn't figure out this math problem." Sandy waved the math page in the air, but his gaze was fixed on Dan's prosthesis. "Sorry, I didn't mean to laugh, just—what's that for?"

"Oh, right, that." Dan looked down at the prosthesis. "It keeps it dry."

He had found a pair of heavy-duty dishwashing gloves under the sink and stuck one of them over the end of the prosthesis. This wasn't something he'd learned from his physical therapist; it was a trick he had figured out himself the first time he had to try to figure out how to do something in the sink without soaking the clamps. Just because the prosthesis could get wet didn't mean it was good for it to be submerged for long periods of time.

"Oh. That makes sense. I'm sorry I laughed."

"Don't be," Dan said. He grinned, and flicked the rubber glove, making the bright yellow fingers wobble as if they were full of Jell-o. "It looks completely ridiculous, you're right. Hey, forget the math. C'mon over here and help me dry. That part's still hard."

"Dad never dries the dishes," Sandy said, but he grabbed a dish towel and joined Dan at the sink.

"Yeah, well, I'm the nanny, so—" *So I don't get to half-ass it*, was on the tip of his tongue, but then it occurred to him that the kind of friendly trash-talking he was used to doing with his ex-military buddies might not go over so well to a nine-year-old. "So it's my job to do that part too."

"You want me to do your job?" Sandy said. "Do I get paid?"

"You've got the makings of a great lawyer in your future," Dan said, and handed him a dish.

He was a little surprised at himself, finding how easy it was to smile at the kids and settle into an easy rapport with them. Derek had a really great little family here. Dan hoped that Derek knew how good he had it. But of course he did; Derek wasn't a guy who would ever take his family for granted.

"Is it really called that?" Sandy asked. He stared at the plate Dan handed him and then began to scrub it clumsily with the towel. "A nanny, if it's a guy."

"Why not? I don't think there's a specific guy term. You could call me an au pair," Dan added, dredging up the term from some news story he'd seen. *Au bear*, he added in his head, with a grin he kept to himself.

"Manny," Sandy said.

"I'm *not* calling myself a manny, you can bet your bottom dollar on that."

Sandy giggled. "We could make up a word for it."

"Like what? Like ... doodle-lally?"

Sandy snort-laughed. "I'm not gonna tell the kids at school you're our doodle-lally."

Dan nudged him. "You got a better word, then?"

"Ummmm ... well, Dad calls himself the chief cook and bottle-washer, sometimes."

"Does that make me the assistant cook and bottle-washer?"

"You're right," Sandy said. "That's not better." He hesitated, looking down at the cup he was drying, and placed it beside its fellow cups. "Do you have kids?"

"No," Dan said, with a fierce twinge. "Not any of my own."

"How did you learn to do all of this, then?"

"Hey, these are useful skills for any man to have. You should learn them too." When Sandy looked skeptical, Dan went on, "Listen, I bet your mom is *so* glad that your dad knows how to do all of these things."

"She had to teach him," Sandy said.

"Well then, he's a good student, and imagine how happy your future girlfriends will be when they don't have to teach you because you already know."

Sandy made a face at the mention of girlfriends. He was quiet for a little while, drying dishes, in the pensive way of a kid with something on his mind. Finally he said, "Derek's not my real dad. I mean, not my birth dad."

"Oh," Dan said. He hadn't known that. Although thinking back on it, he should have realized. Derek hadn't had a kid back when Dan had known him, hadn't even had a family on his radar. "Do you think of him as your dad anyway?"

"I guess he is. I don't really remember my real dad. He died when I was just a baby. Mom says I don't have to call Derek my dad if I don't want to, but ..." He lifted a narrow little shoulder in a shrug. "I got used to it."

"Ah, well, I guess he thinks of you as his son too," Dan said, looking down at the kid's bristling dark hair, with a cowlick that stuck up in the back. He felt completely out of his depth; he hadn't anticipated having a conversation this emotionally complicated with a nine-year-old.

But sometimes kids just hit you with stuff like that out of the blue. He found himself saying, "You asked how I learned all of this. It was in foster care, actually. Taking care of littler kids. I never knew my dad, either."

"What happened to him?" Sandy asked, looking up quickly.

"He died. Both of my parents, a very long time ago."

"Oh," Sandy said, and grinned hesitantly, a gap-toothed grin with a missing baby tooth at the edge. "I guess that's something we have in common."

"It sure is, kid."

He tried not to let the melancholy feeling drag him under, not on a bright Saturday like this, with the sun glittering on the snow outside. Together, he and Sandy cleaned the kitchen, not talking much. Sandy showed Dan where to put things away, and Dan set him to mopping down the top of the stove.

"Wow," Derek said from the doorway. "You've got him doing chores already."

"It's not *chores*," Sandy declared promptly. "Dan's showing me how to do stuff. Dad, what do you call Dan?"

"What?" Derek said blankly, looking mildly panicked.

"He asked me earlier if I was a nanny," Dan said.

"Oh. Uh."

"I told him we should make up our own word for it. Or," Dan said, shrugging as he folded a dish towel with quick flicks of his good hand, "we could just go with nanny. It's probably not going to do much for me on the dating front, but you never know."

"Are you wearing a dish glove on your, uh—"

"It keeps it *dry*, Dad," Sandy declared with the confidence of a kid who had learned a new fact and needed to share it.

"Right," Derek murmured. "Listen, Dan, I was thinking— when the girls are up from their nap, do you want to take the kids into town for a while? You can get to know the place a little, and Sandy can show you where everything is. You can get lunch for them—I'll pay for it, obviously—and pick up a few groceries that we need. If you're good with that."

"Sure," Dan said, easygoing. Why not? This was his life now. There were worse things; he had just been through a few of them. And he wouldn't mind looking around the cute little downtown that he had briefly glimpsed when the bus dropped him off.

His bear seemed eager at the idea of looking around the town. Dan wasn't sure why, but he decided to roll with it. Maybe just being out of the city and closer to the woods was making his bear more active.

∼

DEREK GAVE him the keys to the family's all-wheel-drive, winter-capable Subaru. "You ever drive one of these before?" Derek asked.

"I know how to drive, man. I even know how to drive in snow. And if that's a sideways way of asking if I can drive at all," Dan said, "the answer is yes."

"I wasn't trying to—" Derek began uncomfortably.

"If you want to know if I can do something, just flat out ask, okay? The answer is probably yes. Yes, I can drive. I can wash dishes. I can button my shirt. I learned to do all of this stuff at the VA. I don't mind being asked. Just don't make a big deal about it."

"Yeah, don't make a big deal about it, *Dad*," Sandy called from the entryway, where he was putting his coat on.

"Well, that's me told then," Derek said. He was down on one knee, getting Mina into her cute little pink coat. "Do you want to take the baby? You don't have to. I can keep her here with me; just one kid isn't going to be that much of an issue for getting work done."

From what Dan knew about babies, that probably wasn't true. "Nah, I can take her, if it's okay to take her out in the cold. I don't know how cold-proof babies that little are."

"She's fine. You can switch the car seat to carry her around and put a blanket over her, or use the front carrier." Derek looked up. "Uh, you haven't ever put a baby in a car seat, have you?"

"I have a big girl seat," Mina declared. Her fist was firmly clenched on her Sparkle Pony again, making it difficult to get through the sleeve of her coat. "Lu has a *baby* seat."

"Yeah, I'm gonna need a crash course in this," Dan admitted.

So Derek walked him through Car Seats 101, and they packed up a bag of things for Lulu and got her into a warmer onesie too. By the time they were done with all of this, Dan was starting to feel like he was getting outfitted for a mission to the North Pole rather than taking three kids shopping for the afternoon.

"Yeah," Derek said at the look on Dan's face, buckling Lulu into her car seat through the SUV's open back door. The air was sharp and cold, probably right around freezing; the sun was warm on their shoulders, but there was a slight breeze with a bite to it. "Welcome to my world. You don't have to jump in on the deep end here, you know. You can just hang out around the house today and go into town later."

"*I* want to go to town," Sandy declared.

"Pal, until you have a driver's license, that's not your call."

"Nah, I'm up for it," Dan said. "It'll be good to get out a little and see where things are."

"It's easy to get to, anyway." Derek straightened up and pointed. "You probably know this since you came out here yesterday, but just turn right on the road and it takes you straight into downtown. Parking's free, so you can just find a space and then walk around. The supermarket is on the edge of town by the highway. Sound good?"

"I've got this," Dan said, as much to himself as Derek.

For all his reassurances to Derek, he actually *hadn't* driven much since losing his arm, let alone in the winter. But the pavement was clear and dry, and he parked in one of the mostly empty parking slots downtown, outside a sign that said DeWitt's Diner with a pair of crossed utensils. His bear took notice of that too.

You're always hungry, aren't you? Dan thought at it.

But it *had* been a while since breakfast.

"Can we get cheeseburgers?" Sandy asked.

"Sure," Dan said, struggling with the buckles on Mina's car seat. "If you give me a hand unstrapping your sister here."

Soon he had Mina out of her seat, and the handles of Lulu's car seat looped over his prosthesis. The day was continuing to warm up, and some of the snow was melting along the sidewalk. He was glad now that he hadn't let himself stay inside all day. It was a gorgeous day for being outside and looking around the pretty little downtown. The sky was vividly blue overhead. During the entire time he had been getting the kids out of the car, only one other vehicle had passed.

"Cheeseburgers, cheeseburgers," Sandy chanted. He raced ahead to hold the door of the diner for Dan, who had both hands full with the little girls.

A bell on the door tinkled when they walked in. There were bright-colored plastic tables and chairs, and an old-fashioned counter with stools and a board behind it where the day's specials were written, next to a wide-open window showing a glimpse of gleaming silver appliances in the kitchen.

"Be right with you!" a woman's voice called from somewhere in the back, and deep inside Dan, his bear stood up and paid attention.

Sandy had plunked himself down at a booth by the window. Dan found plastic menus in a rack by the counter and scooped up a couple of them before shepherding Mina over to join her brother. He set the baby carrier beside himself on the seat, checked to make sure Lulu seemed to be happy (she was fast asleep with the pacifier in her mouth) and slid a menu across to Sandy.

"I already know what I want," Sandy said impatiently, pushing it aside. "We've been going here since forever. Can I play my game?"

"Yeah, well, it's my first time, kid, so just give me a minute. What game?"

Sandy showed him a handheld plastic device.

"Sure, but you have to stop playing it when the waitress comes to take your order, okay?"

"Mmmmmkay," Sandy said, bending over the device.

Mina squirmed in her seat and then reached for a handful of sugar packets. Dan started to reach across to stop her, forgot he was using the prosthesis, and knocked over the little table-mounted rack holding ketchup and napkins. The ketchup bottle rolled across the table. Dan lunged and caught it with his good hand just as it slipped over the edge of the table. Mina, shocked, started to cry, which woke up Lulu, who also started to cry.

At that moment, the swinging doors to the kitchen opened, and an angel came out, wearing an apron and carrying a coffeepot.

She was perhaps in her mid to late thirties, about Dan's age. Her hair was a spill of brown curls with blonde streaks, pulled back in a messy bun while straggling curls escaped around her face. A spray of freckles spattered her perfect round nose.

And Dan's bear, with impeccable timing, lurched up from deep inside him. *Mate!* it cried joyfully, the reverberations ringing around his head.

Dan's hand opened. The ketchup bottle slipped from his fingers and smashed on the floor.

Mina stopped crying for a shocked instant and then wailed louder, almost drowning out Lulu.

This was off to a perfect start.

PAULA

"SHIT," said the unbelievably handsome stranger who had just dropped a full bottle of Heinz 57 on the linoleum floor that Paula had thoroughly mopped last night.

Then the hot stranger, in visible panic, whirled around to the two kids across the table from him. "I need both of you to forget that you just heard me say that."

Wait a minute, those were the Ruger kids. Sandy was in Lissy's fourth-grade class. Paula couldn't remember his little sisters' names off the top of her head, but she definitely recognized the family. Except for the guy. She would definitely remember if she'd seen *him* before.

Meanwhile, she was just standing here staring at him. From his perspective, it must look like horror at the ketchup mess, not the impressed kind of staring at his shoulders and cheekbones and—ahem. Paula got herself together and marched across the floor with quick taps of her sensible waitress shoes, stepping around the shattered bottle. At least she had a well-established procedure for this sort of situation. Order of priorities: calm down customers, take order, clean up mess.

"Don't worry about dropping things," she said with a bright, professional smile. "Happens to me all the time. Hi, Sandy."

"Hi, Mrs. DeWitt," Sandy said without looking up from his game.

The little girl—Mina, right, that was her name—was still sniffling. "Awww, don't cry there, sweetheart." Paula had *loads* of experience at calming down restless, upset children. She reached into her apron pocket and scooped out a rolled-up placemat, a mini box of crayons, and a cheap plastic toy dinosaur. "Do you want this, honey? Here you go."

She put these in front of the little girl, who subsided to faint whimpering and reached for the colorful toy. Meanwhile Hot Stranger had taken the baby out of her carrier and was jiggling her against his broad chest, which made him about a thousand times hotter.

"Look, ma'am—miss—" His eyes flicked down to her name tag. "—Paula, I'm really sorry about the mess. Just point me to a mop and I'll clean it up."

"You don't have to," she said, turning over his cup. "I'll get it in a minute. Coffee?"

"Yes, please. Look, let me clean it up for you. I'll feel terrible if I don't."

There was a fierce intensity to the way he said it, making her take a second look at him.

She was still having to work on trying not to stare. Guys who looked like that didn't walk into small-town diners every day, or *any* day. He had a firm square face, dark hair growing out of a short cut, and the most intense brown eyes she'd ever seen. There was a dusting of stubble across his chin, like he hadn't shaved that morning; it might have looked scruffy on someone else, but on him, it only emphasized the sharp, clear planes of his face.

She ought to say no. There was no way that letting the

customer clean up a mess was going to get her a decent tip. Or any tip. But all of a sudden she didn't give a damn about the tip. She just wanted to see more of him.

"If you insist, I'd sure appreciate the help," she said.

He put the baby back in her carrier and stood up, turning out to be taller than she'd realized. A slight flush touched his to-die-for cheekbones when he saw the extent of the mess. Up close, she realized that there were amazing dark lashes framing those incredible eyes.

"Kids, stay where you are, there's broken glass all over the floor."

"Here." Paula whipped a dish towel out of her apron pocket. "I'll get the kids' orders while you get that."

He was actually lifting it out of her hand before she quite registered that he hadn't taken it with a regular hand, but rather, a metal clamp half-covered by the sleeve of his coat. By that time, he was already crouched on the floor, collecting the glass.

"So are you a friend of Derek and Gaby Ruger?" she asked, taking a step to the side to get out of his way of his way.

"He's our manny," Sandy said, and Hot Guy looked like he wanted to sink into the floor. His shoulders practically went up around his ears. Very nice shoulders, Paula couldn't help noticing, even in the old military-surplus coat he was wearing. "And I want a cheeseburger and a Coke, please."

"Gotcha, and Mina is probably going to want the chicken fingers like usual?" Mina was paying no attention, focused on scribbling on the placemat and part of the table. "Do you know what she wants, Mr.—I'm sorry, I didn't ask your name."

"Chicken fingers sounds good to me." He looked up from collecting broken glass in the rag. "I mean, for her. Not me. And it's Dan. My name, that is."

What a nice name. What a strong, manly, comforting

name. A woman could wrap up in that name, and oh no it had been a really long time since she had even thought about men after Disaster Ex-Husband Terry; what was she even *thinking*?

She took a few more steps back to get a little psychological distance as well, which unfortunately meant she was now taking their order from behind the next table over. She felt ridiculous. It was a good thing there was no one else in the diner at the moment.

"Well, Dan, I'm Paula—" Which he already knew. Right. "—and welcome to Autumn Grove." She took a deep breath and tried to claw her way back to some dignity. "Would you like to try our specialty, the Double DeWitt Burger? It's our specialty. Two patties of fresh local beef, cooked your way, all the trimmings." She tried not to stare at his shoulders flexing under the coat.

"That sounds great, ma'am," he said, and smiled at her as he straightened up. It was a dazzling smile that made her stomach swoop and her knees go weak. "So I, uh_—" He had a handful of ketchup-sodden rag wrapped around the remains of the bottle. "Point me to the trash, and I'll grab a mop."

Not exactly how her ideal conversation with her dream guy was supposed to go. Paula dropped the order pad into the pocket of her apron and held out her hands.

"No, you're going to get all—"

"I've been covered with worse," she said, taking it from him carefully. His hands brushed hers: warm fingers, cool metal clamp. The sexual charge at his touch was unmistakable. Oh God. He just got sexier the closer she got. "Mop and bucket and other cleaning supplies are behind the counter. I'm just going to—kitchen—" And with that, unceremoniously, she fled.

"So what happened out there?" Mitch asked as she

dropped rag, glass, and all into the trash and then ran her hands under the sink.

"I have no idea what you're talking about."

Mitch grinned. "Your face is red, Miz DeWitt."

Paula wiped her wet hands on her apron and slapped the order up on the board. "I'm taking a short break. I'll be back in just one minute."

She fled for the loading door that led to the alley. The door opened on a blast of cold wind and dazzling brilliance, the sun glinting off the snow on the back of the Petersons' auto-yard shed. Paula stepped out into the alley, ignoring the wind cutting through the light sleeves of her blouse and raising goosebumps on her legs under her waitress skirt. She closed the door behind her and took a few deep breaths.

She was a middle-aged, divorced mother of two. She was too old and too jaded and most of all, too *sensible* to be mooning over a sexy stranger.

But what a stranger to moon over. She could still hear the deep, growly vibration in his voice, shivering all the way down to her toes.

Stop it. There has got to be a reason why a guy like that is taking care of the Rugers' kids instead of married with kids of his own.

She'd already had to deal with one fixer-upper. She didn't need another.

Even if he was absolutely gorgeous.

DAN

He had found his mate and chased her away by dropping a full bottle of ketchup on her floor and then dumping most of it into her hands. She had vanished into the kitchen and hadn't come out, not even to bring Sandy his Coke.

Inflicting three screaming kids on her probably hadn't helped either.

Well ... two screaming kids, neither of which was screaming now. Mina was coloring happily and Lulu had fallen back asleep. Sandy was engrossed in his game. Still bundled in his coat, he looked like a hunched-over little monk at the table.

"You sure you wouldn't be more comfortable with your coat off?" Dan asked, mopping industriously.

"Nope," Sandy said. Only the tip of his nose was showing and the game was three inches from his eyes.

"Watch your sisters while I put this back, okay?"

"Mmm-hmm."

Dan kept an eye on them anyway while he returned the bucket, mop, and paper towels where he'd gotten them from. He washed his hand in the bathroom with the door open—it was a small unisex bathroom that opened off the main dining area—and then went back to the table.

Still no mate. If he hadn't had the kids to keep an eye on, he would be tempted to go into the back and see if he had upset her.

Don't be ridiculous. She didn't act upset. She's just busy. Also, having a total stranger chase her into the kitchen is probably not going to make the best impression.

Then the swinging doors opened and his angel in a waitress apron breezed out again, and all rational thought flew out of his head.

She was carrying a large plastic cup in one hand and a small plate in the other. "I'm sorry this took so long, honey," she told Sandy, putting the cup in front of him. She set the plate of chicken fingers in front of Mina, which involved leaning over the table. A wave of her perfume came with it, something light and fresh and sweet. "The burgers will be up in a couple of minutes. Anything else I can get for you folks?"

"You could sit down and talk for a minute," Dan suggested. His bear was nearly paralyzed at her nearness, and he couldn't believe his own boldness. "Not if it'll get you in trouble at work or anything. But I'm new in town, and ..."

He floundered, running out of things to say, but she was smiling, really smiling, crinkling up her eyes and turning his chest inside out. "No boss to worry about. I own the place."

"That's amazing," Dan said honestly.

Her cheeks turned pink. "Amazing is a bit strong for it. I grew up working at the diner and inherited it from my parents when they retired and moved to Florida."

"So you've been running or helping run a successful business for decades. That's even more amazing."

Now she was even pinker. It contrasted beautifully with her blue eyes and curls. "I thought I was the one who was supposed to flatter *you*, if I'm angling for a good tip. Not to give away trade secrets or anything."

"I wasn't angling. Just telling the truth."

"Well, one thing I can tell you for sure, Dan the Manny, is that we're happy to have you here in Autumn Grove."

The bell at the door tinkled. Paula turned toward it, a bright, welcoming smile settling onto her face. It didn't seem any less genuine than her usual smiles, and Dan thought that she seemed like a natural to run a small-town diner like this. She clearly liked her customers, and liked people in general.

Then the welcome smile dropped off her face, replaced by shock and anger—and fear.

A bolt of shock went through Dan, too. He had to clutch at the edge of the table. He had heard that part of the mate bond was knowing when your mate was in distress, but he hadn't expected it to kick in this early or this hard.

"Excuse me," Paula said in a low, distracted voice. Clutching her waitress notepad to her chest like a shield, she marched toward the door, back straight, to confront whoever had just come in.

Dan hastily twisted around in his chair.

The guy in the doorway was trouble. Dan knew that at a glance. He knew the type. The guy was nondescript-looking, almost professionally so, dark-haired and greasy-looking with a bit of a slouch. Sunglasses hid his eyes.

"I told you to leave," Paula snapped in a low, tense voice. "And Mitch told you to leave too. How *dare* you come here while I have customers!"

"And I told you we'd talk again, Mrs. Raines," the stranger replied. His voice was pitched low, but Dan's shifter hearing easily caught it.

"Leave or I'm calling the police," Paula demanded, still trying to keep her voice down.

"Really? You want to get the police involved, and explain all of this to them and your neighbors?"

With his mate's distress vibrating down his every nerve ending, Dan had only one option.

"Sandy, stay with your sisters," he told Sandy quietly, and got up just as Sunglasses gave Paula a little push. She staggered backward.

Dan saw red. Literally.

It was all he could do to keep his bear from erupting into a wall of protective teeth and claws right there in the diner. As it was, he barely remembered crossing the diner floor, until his one good fist closed on the front of Sunglasses' jacket.

"Hey!" the man barked, jerking backward.

He was strong enough to pull free of Dan's grip, which should have held him like a steel clamp. The jacket tore slightly from the pressure.

This guy's a shifter, Dan thought, startled.

The shifter looked shocked too. Then his gaze went to Dan's right arm and the metal clamps. His eyes narrowed.

"Who's going to make me? You and what army? I'm supposed to be afraid of a one-armed—ack!"

Dan seized him by the collar, in a tighter grip this time, and jerked him closer.

"I used to work as a bouncer. I know how to take out the trash. Do you want this man to leave, ma'am?" Dan asked Paula.

Paula swallowed and nodded.

"I ... uh, yes," she said. "Yes, please."

"Could you watch the kids for me for just a minute?"

Paula gave a jerky little nod. "Yes," she said, her voice growing stronger. "Yes, I can do that."

"Thanks. Come on, friend."

Shifting his grip expertly, Dan frog-marched Sunglasses

out onto the sidewalk. The other man writhed furiously, but he was unable to use his full shifter strength to tear out of Dan's grip without shredding his own jacket, and apparently he was unwilling to do that.

Rather than stopping on the sidewalk, Dan marched him down the row of businesses. Passing pedestrians and shoppers behind plate-glass windows stopped to stare at them. Cars slowed down too. This was clearly the most interesting thing anyone in Autumn Grove had seen all day.

"This is humiliating," Sunglasses said between his teeth. "Let me go."

"Not until they get a good look at you."

"What they're going to see is *you* manhandling me—ow!"

Dan pushed him around the corner and into the relative privacy of the alley behind the block of businesses. The businesses along Main Street backed onto the alley, and a wooden privacy fence shielded the backyards of the adjoining row of houses from the alley's trash cans and loading doors.

Now Sunglasses was starting to look nervous. "Look, it's just business, what I got going on with the merry widow in there. It's not personal. I don't know what your stake is in this, or *what* you are, but I don't mean her any harm."

"She seemed pretty upset." Dan gave him a hard shake. "Why are you hassling her?"

"Ow! Let up! It's not about her. It's about her ex."

"So why bother *her* about it?" Dan demanded. "Leave her alone."

Sunglasses pulled away, and this time Dan let him go. The sunglasses had slipped down his nose, revealing a flash of startling gold eyes. Whatever kind of shifter he was, Dan didn't think it was anything he'd seen before.

"How is it any of your business?" Sunglasses asked. He

straightened his lapel and pushed the sunglasses up his nose, hiding his hawk-gold eyes.

"Because I don't like seeing a lady bothered," Dan said quietly. He leaned in very close, letting his bear rise to the surface, so the other man could see it in his eyes. "I'm a bear, a big fucking alpha grizzly. You want to mess with that?" Dan pushed him hard, so that his back slammed into the wall. "Yeah, I didn't think so. I'm a problem you *really* don't want to have. Get out of here, and if I see you in town again, now or ever, and *especially* if I see you anywhere near Paula, we'll have this chat again, okay? Except I won't be as nice."

Sunglasses made a low growling sound, and there was a moment when Dan thought the other shifter was going to call his bluff. But then Sunglasses pulled away, and scrambled away down the alley, his dress shoes slipping on the ice and snow.

Dan followed him out to the street, and watched him get into a car and drive away, hightailing it for the highway. Taking a deep breath, he walked back up the street to the diner and went inside.

Paula and the two older kids were plastered to the window. They all spun around to look at the door when he came in.

"Thanks for watching them," Dan said mildly. He went back over to his table. "Sandy, Mina, sit down, don't stand up on the seat. It's rude."

They both plunked obediently down. Sandy was wide-eyed. "Wow, you just walked that guy out of here like on a TV show! Who was he?"

"No one you have to worry about," Dan told him, and turned to Paula. "I told him to leave. Looks like he followed orders, but if he comes back, let me know, okay? I told him I wouldn't be as nice the second time around. And that's a promise I mean to keep."

Paula flushed. "You don't need to get involved with my problems."

I already am. I was the first time I saw you. Now and forever.

Again ... not helpful.

"Nobody should get away with that," he said. "I'll be happy to throw him out again, harder this time."

Paula looked dubious. "You don't even know me."

It was technically true, and yet not. It was as if he had met her in some other life, a long time ago. His soul knew hers.

But that was another thing he couldn't just blurt out.

"I know enough," he said. "I know you're a busy, successful businesswoman who doesn't need to deal with this kind of sh—er, crap. And you shouldn't have to handle that kind of thing on your own."

He had said something wrong. It was like a shutter came down behind her eyes.

"I've been handling things on my own for a long time," Paula said. "I'm just going to check on your order."

"Paula—wait—Sandy, watch your sisters!"

Leaving Sandy making a put-upon sighing noise behind him, he hurried after her. She wasn't running away, as such, and she turned around before she got to the kitchen, holding her waitress pad clasped to her chest.

"I didn't mean to imply you can't deal with it by yourself," Dan said quietly. "Obviously you can. It's just ... sometimes a little help is nice. That's all."

Paula's harder expression melted a little. The corner of her mouth quirked up.

"And I do appreciate it. Really. You get used to doing things on your own, sometimes it's hard to cope with someone telling you they have your back."

"Boy, do I know *that* feeling," Dan said, heartfelt.

They shared a moment's commiserating smile. The eye contact deepened. Her eyes were amazing, a thousand shades of blue, like all the summer skies he'd ever seen, rolled into one—

"Order up!" the cook yelled. Dan jumped, and Paula took a quick step back. The cook looked around from setting plates in the window and added with a scowl, "This guy bothering you, Miz DeWitt?"

"No, Mitch, I'm fine." Paula scooped up the plates and turned to Dan, smiling. "And sometimes it's easy to forget how many people actually *do* have your back. Let me just carry these to the table for you."

"I can give you a hand if you want."

She handed off one of the plates. "Now I really *am* risking my tip," she said, laughing.

For a tip, how about my entire heart? My home, my house, everything I am ...

Which brought him up short. What did he have to offer a mate right now? He was living in a friend's spare bedroom, watching someone else's kids.

Paula stopped, frowning at him. "Are you all right?"

"I'm fine. I just ..." He almost backed off. Almost. He had so little to give a mate. But if he ran away, he could give her nothing at all. "I'd really like to ask you out for coffee sometime. If you want to."

There was that shutters-going-down expression again. Paula looked down at the plates in her hands.

"It's not that easy," she said. "I mean, you seem nice. Really nice. And you helped me a lot just now—"

"I didn't help you out to get you to go on a date with me," he said, horrified.

"No, no, it's not that I thought you did." She looked up again, eyes wide and wary. "It's just that ... I have kids, I don't think I mentioned that. I'm a single mom. I can't rush into anything. You have to understand that."

"I do," he said quickly. "It was just a thought. Never mind, no worries."

He started to turn away.

"Wait!" she said, and he looked back, hope rising in his chest.

Paula took a quick breath. "Tonight there's a kind of a thing, I mean it's not really a thing, it's just that me and some of the other parents from my daughter's class are taking our kids to the indoor mini golf course up by the highway. Do you want to maybe meet us there? You can bring your kids, I mean the Rugers' kids, and I'll bring mine. The kids can shoot a few holes, and we can—talk. Because I'd like to talk more."

Dan's bear was paying attention with every fiber of its being.

"Just two adults taking the kids somewhere," Paula added.

"Definitely."

"Not a date."

"For sure," he agreed. "Not at all. Two adults."

"Yep." She smiled at him again. She smiled a lot, it seemed. It settled very naturally onto her face, as if not smiling was the unnatural state for her.

If he hadn't already been gone the moment he looked into her eyes, he was certainly gone now.

"Tonight," he said, and he found that he was grinning so hard it felt like his face would split in two.

PAULA

Since she currently had no full-time staff and no part-timers she trusted to leave in charge, Paula had started closing the diner in early afternoon, after the lunch rush died down. Afternoons were always dead anyway, and they never had much of a dinner crowd. She didn't serve alcohol, and most people preferred to go to the bar and grill, or La Taquerita, the one Mexican restaurant in town.

This meant she could be home when the kids got off school.

It also gave her far too much time to dither over her not-a-date with Dan.

Were earrings too much? Half the time she didn't even bother putting studs in her nominally pierced ears. She couldn't even remember the last time she had bothered to wear one of the handful of nice dangly earrings she owned.

What about makeup? When she had time, she dabbed on a bit of lipstick and mascara for work (fair or not, it noticeably kicked up her tips) but she didn't always have time for it. Was the red too much, she wondered, or the understated coral ...

"Mom," Austin said in horrified disbelief, wandering past the open bathroom door, "are you *really* getting dressed up to go to The Big Putz?"

"Don't call it that or you'll get your sister started," Paula said, holding one of the danglies in front of her earlobe.

Austin had perfected the art of the exasperated teenage huff, and he did it now. "Mom, do I have to go? Can't I stay home? I'm fifteen; I don't need a babysitter. *Please*. It's so boring."

Normally, she would have let him. But there were extenuating circumstances.

"Mrs. Chang said you've been cutting American History all week."

Austin froze, and in the mirror, Paula glimpsed him looking abruptly guilty, as if she'd caught him doing something much worse than skipping class. She turned around to get a better look at his face, but he was already scowling, the vulnerable moment gone.

"So?" he said. "I'm getting good grades on the tests."

"You can't just decide not to go to class, Austin, it doesn't work that way. Where were you instead?"

"Just ... hanging out!"

"With who? Do I need to tell your friends' parents that their kids are cutting class too?"

"Everyone does it!" Austin said belligerently, tucking his hands under his arms.

"That may be, but you're going to stop immediately or I'm grounding you."

Austin looked suddenly hopeful. "If I'm grounded, does that start tonight?"

Paula felt outmaneuvered. It had been so much easier to deal with the kids when they were younger. "No. You're going to Sir Putts-A-Lot with us and that's final."

"Mom!" Austin protested, just as Lissy wailed from down

the hall, "Moommmmm! I can't find my golf shoes! The froggie ones!"

"You don't need special shoes to play mini golf, dumbass!" Austin yelled back. "That's bowling!"

"Mommmm!"

"Austin James DeWitt Raines, don't call your sister a dumbass."

"Or what?" Austin demanded. "Or you'll make me go mini golfing?"

"You're going to Sir Putts with your sister and me, and that's that."

Austin stomped off and slammed his bedroom door.

Paula wondered how much of a power struggle she was going to have getting him out of the house. She might have to leave him behind after all. Why didn't kids come with a convenient manual?

"I need my frog shoes!" Lissy wailed.

Paula went with the dangly earrings. This was the closest thing to a date she'd had since Lissy was born. Even if it didn't go anywhere, she might as well have some fun tonight.

Kids or no kids.

～

EVEN AT 6 p.m. on a winter night, the parking lot of Sir Putts-A-Lot was half full. Through the early winter darkness, Paula scanned the lot for vehicles she recognized, which was at least half of them. There was Maybelle Hartz's little Toyota truck, and the Kozlowskis' minivan, and that brand new Range Rover that was apparently Doug Espinoza's idea of a midlife crisis machine.

It occurred to her that she had no idea what sort of vehicle Dan drove. She spotted the Ruger family Subaru hiding behind Ed Johnson's big white truck, and felt her heart clutch with a strange mix of relief and regret. He was here! And he'd brought the Rugers. That was good, right? Not a date. Definitely.

"Mom?" Lissy called from the door.

"Coming!" She gave up her car search and hurried to the door, waving to one of the Kozlowskis—she could never remember all their names.

Inside, the building's cavernous open space echoed with shrieking kids' voices. As always, in all weather, it somehow managed to be both stuffy and drafty at the same time. Plywood barricades painted to look like brick roughly cordoned off an area near the door for a front desk and some long laundromat-style racks for coats. Paula collected the kids' jackets and let them go on ahead while she hung them up.

"Paula?"

She wasn't prepared for the thrill that went through her at the sound of Dan's voice, but she certainly appreciated it. Turning, she saw him with Sandy. Both of them still had their coats on.

"You came," she said, beaming. "Do you want to ditch your coat? You'll probably get too hot once you start moving around."

"I wasn't sure if there was a coat check desk or something," Dan said.

"Oh, no, there's no desk or anything. Just hang it up on the rack. It's not like you won't recognize your own coat later."

Dan laughed a little. "This *is* a small town," he said, mostly to himself. He shrugged out of his coat; underneath, he had on a plaid shirt that hugged his muscular chest. Lucky shirt. "Yeah, sure, why not. Can I take yours, kid?"

Sandy stripped off his parka and Dan draped it over his arm—the artificial one. Paula was definitely *not* staring, but she was curious. She hadn't gotten a very good look at his arm earlier. He moved so naturally that she never would have noticed it if not for the visible metal of the clamp end.

"Where's the rack?" Dan asked.

"Oh. Right. Over here."

"Mooooom!" Lissy yelled from the front desk, her voice cutting through the echoing hockey-arena cacophony of voices and clattering golf balls.

"Coming!" Paula yelled back. "My public awaits," she said to Dan. "Who else is here?"

"I don't know anyone but you," Dan said.

"No, I meant—didn't you come with the Rugers?"

"Just Sandy," Dan said.

"I saw their car outside—"

"Oh, yeah. I borrowed it for the evening. Gaby and Derek are staying in with the girls."

"*Mom!!*"

"Hold your horses!" Paula called back. Lissy, she saw, had located two of the other little girls from her fourth-grade class, both of them clutching bright-colored golf clubs. Lissy was showing off her light-up frog shoes, a Christmas present this past December and currently her pride and joy. "Well, in that case, do you two want to play against us?"

"Sure," Dan said, with an easy grin that curled her toes.

Paula paid at the desk, passing their ball and putter to a deeply unimpressed-looking Austin to hold, and bought some concession tickets to get hot dogs and Cokes for the kids.

"Hey, I'll get yours too," she said to Dan over her shoulder.

"You don't have to."

"It's my treat. Small-town hospitality. Kids," she said, "this is Dan. He's new in town. These are my children, Austin and Lissy. Say hi to Dan, kids."

Neither of them was paying much attention. Lissy was

still focused on her friends. Austin looked like he thought he was a martyr going to the rack.

"You know, I don't even think I even know your last name," Paula said, slightly embarrassed.

"Ross," Dan said.

Ross. Paula was *not* doodling little hearts around that name in her head. Definitely not.

They gathered their equipment and went on inside, past the barricades and into the wide-open space of the building's interior. Banks of overhead fluorescent lights lit it up like a box store, and underneath, Astroturf spread out in a maze of holes and obstacles, ramps and bridges.

The general theme, in keeping with the name of the place, was Ye Jollie Olde Medieval England. There were miniature castles, plastic knights on horseback, and a fake mill with a slowly spinning water wheel where you had to putt the ball into a cup on the wheel.

All of it looked like it had been built in someone's backyard workshop, which was probably true. The castles gave the impression that they might fall over if you pushed on them, though Paula knew from experience that the plywood structures were sturdy enough for children to climb on.

Some of Lissy's classmates were trying to get their ball past a slowly opening and closing drawbridge over a water trap. As usual, several balls floated in the water. There was a pool skimmer with a laminated printer-paper sign taped beside it reading, FISH YOUR BALLS OUT - THE MGMT. Someone, probably around Austin's age, had spray-painted over the first two words so it read, instead, BALLS OUT - THE MGMT.

She was starting to regret inviting Dan here, but it was too late.

"Want to do the yellow course, kids?" she asked.

"Is that the one with the dragon?" Lissy said. "*Yeah!*"

"Joy," Austin muttered under his breath, slinking along behind them.

Paula squeezed his arm and pressed half the concession tickets into his hand. "Here, you can stuff down as many hot dogs as this will buy, or whatever else you want. Do you need some change for the arcade games?"

Austin made a grumbling sound that might have been "Yes."

"This building has been here forever," Paula explained to Dan as she dug into her purse. "It started out, I think, as some kind of combination drive-in and roller rink, back in the fifties. It might even have been here before that."

"I *wish* we had a roller rink," Austin muttered. "At least that would be sort of fun."

"You like roller skating, champ?" Dan asked him. "When I was a kid, I used to love skateboarding."

Austin gave him a look of deepest exasperation.

"Here," Paula said, giving him the quarters. "Stay in sight, please."

Austin grunted and slouched off in the direction of the concession stand with its adjoining bank of retro arcade games. It was a general hangout area for older siblings and parents taking a break from all the preteens on the golf course proper.

"I'm sorry about him," Paula said. "He wanted to stay home. I hoped he'd have fun, but ..." She shrugged with a rueful smile. "I guess I wouldn't have wanted to go mini golfing with my mom when I was his age, either."

"Mommmm," Lissy moaned, tugging at her arm. Paula gave her the ball and let her line up the first shot on the yellow course.

"So you were telling me about the history of the building?" Dan prompted, while the kids played through the first few yellow-flagged holes and the two of them followed behind.

Paula winced. "I'm sorry. What a thing to dump on you the minute we walked in. I must be boring you horribly."

"Not at all," he said, and sounded sincere. "I really love that this town's history is so real to you, that it's so much a part of your life."

"It's not a very exciting history," Paula said. "So yeah, this is one of those buildings that keeps changing hands while various businesses start up and fail. When I was a kid, there was a bowling alley here. Oh gosh, what was it called? Something that makes Sir Putts-A-Lot sound classy ... oh yeah, it was All About Bowl. It was *the* teen hangout spot. Mostly for lack of competition, I guess."

She smiled, remembering the loud clash of balls and pins, the deafening chatter of teens trash-talking each other; this place had always had the absolute *worst* acoustics, and generally smelled of mold.

"Then, let's see, after the bowling alley closed, they did the 4H livestock auctions here while they were renovating the fairgrounds. And I think there was a paintball place for a while, but I never went there. I had moved away by then."

"You moved?" Dan asked, surprised. "I thought you had lived here your whole life. I mean, from what you said about helping your parents run the diner."

"No, I went away to school." And met Terry. And got married. That was definitely a can of worms she did *not* plan to open on a first not-a-date. "What about you?" she asked hastily. "City boy all your life?"

"Pretty much," Dan said with another of those self-effacing, effortlessly charming smiles. "Grew up all over—Atlanta, Chicago, a few other places."

"Oh, military brat?" she asked.

"Foster kid."

Shit. "Sorry."

"It was a long time ago." His smile was a little sad. "But, yeah, after that, I went into the Army."

"Do you mind if I ask how you, um ..." She couldn't think how to ask what she really wanted to know in a way that wouldn't be potentially offensive. *How did a guy like you end up working as a male nanny?* No, no, no. She tried to rephrase it. "Have you been doing this for long?"

"Miniature golf?" he asked, looking blank.

"No, I mean the—watching the kids thing."

"Oh," he said, surprised. "It's kind of a—complicated situation."

"Yeah, I don't know anything about those sorts of situations," Paula said. She glanced around in search of Austin, but there was no sign of him. So much for "stay in sight."

She shot him off a brief text: *Where R U?*

Mom!!!! Im in the bathroom!!!!!!

Sorry!! she typed back, and sent a blushing-face emoji.

why are you like this, Austin sent back.

"Everything okay?" Dan asked as she put the phone away.

"Yeah, it's fine. Just being a mom."

The course had been generally sloping upward for the last couple of holes, a plywood ramp covered in scratchy, lurid green Astroturf. Now they were on an overpass looping across the floor-level section of a different, blue-flagged course.

"Well, this seems safe," Dan remarked, looking down through the scratched Plexiglass barriers at other families playing through the course beneath them.

"Oh yeah, totally," Paula said. "One of these days it's going to collapse beneath the weight of a sixth-grade class and they'll be sued out of existence. In fact, that's sort of what happened to the paintball place, from what I heard."

"Yeah?"

"Yeah, someone got a concussion and they were slapped with a bunch of lawsuits."

"That doesn't really seem like the business's fault."

"It is when part of an obstacle course falls on someone's head."

"Oh," Dan said. "It's not the same owners, though, is it?"

"I don't think so. But you never know."

"Mom!" Lissy said. She held out the putter. "Do this one for me. It's *hard*. I always lose my ball."

"It's not *that* hard," Sandy said, waiting his turn with his club resting on his shoulder.

They were facing a ramp leading down. There was a series of small zigzag obstructions and, at the bottom, a witch's cauldron tipped over on its side, on a jerky conveyer belt that slid slowly back and forth. The objective was to get the ball into the cauldron. A recorded witch's cackle played at intervals.

"Lissy's right, this one is terrible," Paula said, but she gamely placed the ball at the top of the ramp. "You have to walk all the way down the ramp and get your ball if you miss, and it's really hard to get it in. Whoever designed this hole is evil."

"I can give it a shot if you want," Dan said.

"No!" the kids chorused at once. "You're on the *other team*," Lissy added in a horrified voice.

Dan smiled and raised a hand good-naturedly. He took a step back.

"Don't yell at me if we have to go down there and collect your ball a dozen times," Paula said.

She carefully tried to line up her shot. Embarrassingly, considering how many times she'd brought the kids here, she was not good at mini golf. Usually these evening games were an opportunity to stroll behind the kids and talk with other parents, or go hang out at the concession stand and enjoy half a cheap beer out of a plastic cup, while one of the other parents took one for the team and watched the kids.

This ball was *so* going off the ramp.

"It's all about timing," Dan said quietly.

He had moved up beside her. She was acutely aware of him, even though his plaid-shirt-clad elbow wasn't quite touching hers. He was looking down the ramp, studying the cauldron intently.

"If you let the ball go when the hole is lined up, you'll miss. The bumpers slow it down, so by the time it gets to the bottom, the hole isn't there anymore."

"Like—now?" Paula asked, and started to pull back the club. "Oh ... no." The witch's cauldron moved on, with a tinny cackle, before she could tap the ball. "I see what you're saying, but how do you figure out when to let it go?"

"May I?" he asked, and lightly laid his hand over hers.

"Yes," she breathed.

His hand was incredibly warm. She had never been so conscious of another person's presence. Every light brush of his skin against hers felt freighted with meaning.

"Watch it move for a minute." His head was next to hers, his neck and shoulders bent over to accommodate their height difference. His breath stirred her hair. "You have to get a feel for how fast it's moving."

It was safe to say she was no longer concentrating on the cauldron. He had a scent: soap and aftershave and the heated, slightly spicy smell of his skin. He was barely even touching her—they were in public, surrounded by kids, *her* kids no less ...

"Now!" he said abruptly, his hand brushing her skin.

Galvanized as if by electricity, her fist jerked on the club. The business end of the club glanced off the ball, which rebounded off a bumper and bounced back and forth down the ramp.

Paula thought it was going to miss. By all rights it should have missed. The cauldron was all the way off to the side when her ball began its trip down the ramp. But the timing was perfect. Just as the ball reached the bottom of the ramp, the cauldron finished its jerky, stop-and-start journey into place. The ball plunked into the cauldron's carpeted interior.

"Ahahahahaaaaaaa!" the recorded witch's voice cackled. "Bubble, bubble, toil and trouble!"

"This is *super* cheating," Sandy complained.

"Here, kiddo, I'll do ours," Dan offered. He held out a hand for the club, then took the ball.

Lissy gave a loud gasp. Her eyes went round as saucers. "What happened to your *hand*?"

Lissy hadn't even noticed, Paula thought, surprised. But then, Dan moved the prosthetic so casually that your attention wasn't drawn to his hands unless he specifically did something with them.

"Honey, don't stare," she said quickly.

"It's okay." Dan held up the metal hand with the colored ball clasped between the two clamps. He smiled reassuringly at Lissy. "It's just how my hand is. Want to see it in action?"

Lissy nodded.

"Hold out your hands."

She held them out, cupped together. Dan opened the clamps, and the ball plunked into her palm. Then he nipped it up neatly again, just as if he was picking up something with regular fingers. This time Paula saw that he rolled his shoulders under the shirt, a quick thrusting movement.

"How do you brush your teeth?" Lissy asked.

"Just like you do, except with my other hand."

"How do you tie your shoes?"

"Lissy, honey, please let Dan take his shot," Paula put in. "He can answer your questions after." She gave Dan an apologetic look, but he only shrugged a little and smiled. He lined up the shot one-handed, and sank it perfectly.

∼

THE TWO TEAMS ended up tied, although on several holes, including the final one—a dragon's head that opened and closed its mouth—Dan had taken the swing for both kids. Lissy, who had always been incredibly competitive, wanted to play another round to determine the winner. Sandy, more easygoing, just shrugged and said he didn't mind if she won. He was a sweet kid, Paula thought. Not many boys his age would have been that mellow about losing to a girl.

"Sorry, kids," she said, ruffling Lissy's hair. "Mom's got an early day tomorrow. Let's go use up the rest of our concession tickets, why don't we? You want a hot dog or nachos, Liss?"

This turned out to be the distraction she had hoped for. The kids ran ahead, and she and Dan trailed along behind.

"I'm really sorry about her giving you the third degree," Paula said. "You know, about the arm."

"I don't mind talking about it. Kids are curious." He gave her a sideways glance, inviting and a little shy at the same time. "Are you curious?"

"I guess I am," she said.

He brushed the back of her hand with the clamps, and when she turned her hand over, he laid the clamp-hand in her palm. Paula stopped walking, entranced by how the curved metal pieces fit together, easily able to clasp objects between them.

She curled her fingers carefully around the metal, as if she was holding his hand. Dan made a small sound, a slight inhale, and she felt him tense a little.

"Sorry!" she said, relaxing her grip. "Did that hurt?"

"No ... no." His voice was soft. Glancing up, she saw him looking down at her hand—their hands—with a strange intensity in his soft brown eyes. "It *can't* hurt. There's nothing to hurt. It's just that people don't normally ..."

"Touch it?" she asked gently.

He smiled. "People can be weird about it. Kids are actually better than adults, usually. They go ahead and ask the questions that adults don't want to ask."

"Like?" she asked.

"Like how it works." He rolled his shoulder, and she jerked a little in surprise as the clamps opened and closed. "My shoulder muscles operate a pulley system."

Paula couldn't help grinning in delight. "That's so cool," she said. She curled her hand around the clamps again. They were slightly warm now from her skin. "Ingenious, actually. But don't they have better ones now? Like, electronic ones that look like real hands."

"They do," Dan agreed. "I got to try out a bunch of different kinds at the VA hospital. And honestly, some of the modern ones are really amazing. But when it comes right down to it, I don't think I want a hundred thousand dollar piece of hardware attached to my shoulder. They need batteries and break a lot. This kind is cheap, relatively speaking, and almost indestructible. I can get it wet or dirty, and just wipe it down and it's good to go. If something does break on it, I can fix it myself, or pretty easily find somewhere that can repair it."

"Mom!" Lissy bellowed from the concession stand. "Whaddya want on your hot dog?"

"Don't yell!" Paula yelled back, and then rolled her eyes at herself, and grinned at Dan. "What do *you* want, nachos or hot dogs?"

"You're the expert. Which would you recommend?"

"They're both pretty awful, to tell the truth. I usually try to steer the kids toward the hot dogs. By concession standards, they're almost healthy, especially if you count ketchup as a member of the vegetable food group."

They rendezvoused with the kids at the concession stand. At some point Austin had rejoined the others. He had a tint to his cheeks and snowflakes in his hair, suggesting he'd recently been outside. However, she didn't see any sign of reddened eyes or anything else that might make her think he had been smoking or drinking with older teens. She decided not to nag about breaking the "stay in sight" rule. He was here now, so she wasn't going to get fussy if he wanted to go out for a little fresh air.

Hot dogs, nachos and Cokes were passed around, and they went and found an open space at the long picnic-style tables against the wall.

"Thanks for dinner," Dan told her. "Next time I pick up the tab."

"The important thing is that it's a dinner I don't have to cook," Paula said between bites of her hot dog.

"Do you come here often?" Dan asked. Paula cracked up and so did he, while the younger kids shared eye-rolling looks of exasperation and Austin looked like he wanted to sink into the floor. "You know what I mean."

"Yeah, I do. I'd say we come down here a couple times a month in the winter. It's a good way to get out of the house and let the kids have fun while the grown-ups talk."

"For certain values of fun," Austin muttered, and stuffed half a hot dog into his mouth.

"So what do you like in school, Austin?" Dan asked.

Austin only grunted.

"He's really good at math and science," Paula said. She ruffled Austin's hair before he could escape. "I bet he's going to be a famous scientist and make important discoveries."

"I like animals!" Lissy announced, wiping at a dollop of ketchup on her nose.

"That's not a school subject, dummy," Austin said.

"Austin," Paula sighed. "Please don't call your sister names."

"What are you going to be when you grow up?" Dan asked Lissy.

"A zookeeper," Lissy said promptly. "Or a farmer. Or the person that names the colors of paints. Or a falcon tamer—"

"You're forgetting the most important one," Paula said, suppressing a smile.

Lissy bounced in her seat. "Oh, oh, oh! I'm going to train dogs for blind people!"

"Someone came into her school last month and gave a talk about training service dogs," Paula explained. "They had some young dogs in training for the kids to pet."

"Puppies," Lissy said rapturously. "Mom, can we get—"

"No," Paula said. "For the nine hundredth time, we can't get a dog. Finish your hot dog."

"I don't want to eat a *dog*!" Lissy said, with a bright look in her eyes.

"More for the rest of us, then," Dan said, and, grinning, he leaned over the table and pretended to take the last remaining bite. Lissy squealed and stuffed it into her mouth.

"Don't eat mine!" Sandy protested, and swallowed so much hot dog at once that he almost choked. Dan patted him on the back.

He really was good with kids, Paula thought. Austin didn't seem to be warming up to him, but, well ... it was the age more than anything.

And she really, really liked him. She couldn't remember the last time she'd had this much fun at mini golf.

Or the last time she'd met someone she liked this much.

The mood was relaxed and pleasant as they got the kids

BABYSITTER BEAR

back into their coats and walked out to the parking lot. Paula gave Austin the car keys so the kids could run on ahead to unlock the car and get in out of the cold. Sandy hung back inside, talking to some of his classmates.

She and Dan were, for the moment, alone just outside the door.

"So, I don't know if most people's idea of a good time would be mini golfing with a bunch of kids," Paula said. "But you were great."

She was embarrassed immediately. *You were great.* It sounded like something you'd say to a kid after their soccer team lost.

But Dan only smiled. "You were too."

They standing very close together. Red and blue light from the neon marquee sign on the front of Sir Putts-A-Lot's warehouse-like facade flickered on his hair.

"I," she said, and then completely forget what she was going to say.

There was a light dusting of stubble on his chin, framing that incredible bone structure. It looked like Dan was one of those guys whose beard got completely out of control if he didn't shave twice a day.

He had a full mouth, wide and sensual. Just from looking at it, she could sense how the warm heat of those lips might feel on hers.

"I," she began again, faintly.

Dan leaned in. His lips brushed hers, hardly even enough to be called a kiss—but it was electric; it lit her up from the top of her head to the soles of her feet.

The door banged as Sandy came racing out.

Dan jerked back a little; Paula did too. She felt as if she was recovering her footing after nearly slipping off a ledge—a wonderful, wonderful ledge.

"I have to go," she said, breathless.

"Yeah. Me too." But Dan kept his hand on her arm, strong and warm even through her coat and his glove. "Do you think I—do you think we could—what are you doing tomorrow?"

Her heart raced. Not stepping back from the ledge after all. It was right there under her feet. Her toes were curled over the edge.

"I can call you?" she asked. It came out more questioning than she meant it, but he pulled out his phone. He unlocked it and handed it to her. It took her a moment to realize what he wanted; then she entered her number.

It's really been way too long since I was on the dating scene.

She held out her phone and he entered his number for her.

Now that she no longer had to deal with the warmth of his hand on her arm, the heat in his eyes, she felt a little more in control of herself. The ground was stable and secure again. But the ledge was still there.

"It's hard to make definite plans," she said. "There's work and Lissy's after-school activities, and just a *lot*." A thought occurred to her. "Oh, hey, the winter carnival is next weekend. If we don't see each other before then—"

"That sounds great," he said, and smiled in a way that heated her all the way through. "I've never been to a small-town winter carnival."

"Don't get your hopes up. It's just a bonfire and a skate pond. And the whole town's going to be there."

"Better yet. I can get to know some more people. I'm pretty isolated out at the Rugers' ranch."

"I'd love to introduce you around," she said. Her cheeks were hot. That ledge was very close. There was a part of her that desperately wished he'd just take the decision away from her, take her in his arms, pull her close and—

"Mom!!" from the car.

Dan smiled, and Paula laughed ruefully. "This weekend," she said, and was caught off guard when he reached out, trailing his gloved fingers through hers.

Reluctantly, they parted. She went to her car; he went to his. Paula kept looking back and so did he. Finally she had to force herself to get into the car. Austin had started the engine before sliding over to the passenger seat, but the ancient heater was spitting out ice-cold air as it slowly warmed up.

"Sorry kids, I didn't meant to leave you freezing out here."

Austin grunted and slouched down in his seat.

Lissy draped herself over the back of Paula's seat. "Mom, is that guy your boyfriend?"

Austin made a choking sound.

"He is another adult," Paula said firmly, "that I have a nice adult friendship with. I will tell you guys if that changes. Trust me, you'll be the first to know. Now put your seatbelt on."

But she thought about him all the way home. Nice adult friendships were all well and good, but it wasn't friendship that she felt when Dan's heated gaze met hers. And there was a part of her that fervently wished she wasn't going home alone tonight. She wondered if Dan was thinking the same.

DAN

There was a text on Dan's phone when he got up the morning after the mini golf outing.

Hey, just wanted to tell you I really had fun last night.

It had been sent at 4:45 that morning.

He looked at it before his morning shower, and after showering, and while he brushed his teeth. Then, cautiously, he texted her back.

Me too.

Of course he second-guessed himself right away. That was too simple, too plain. He should have said something nice. He should have mentioned her hair, or the way she looked. *You looked good last night*—that would make her happy, right? Because she had looked amazing, and she deserved to hear it.

Or would that be too much?

He could send her another text. But maybe *that* would be too much.

But maybe she'd think he was dismissing her, brushing her off with two little words.

It was ridiculous. He felt like a teenager with his first

crush. He remained in an agony of indecision and doubt all through making breakfast for the kids until finally another text came in.

OH GOOD, I really hoped I had your number right, or else I just said that to a perfect stranger.

Followed immediately by two more texts:

I don't text people much, at least people I haven't known my entire life.

This IS Dan, right? I hope this is Dan and not the waitress who quit last week and is probably getting a restraining order against me right now.

He found himself grinning stupidly. Even in texts, she was adorable.

Yes, it's Dan, he texted back. After a moment, he added, *I don't text people much either.*

Okay, wow, that was about the stupidest thing he could possibly have said there.

"Dan!" Sandy yelled from the table, two feet away. "The eggs are burning!"

"Damn," he muttered, and swooped in and rescued the eggs. "You don't have to scream, kid. I'm right here."

His phone chimed, but he couldn't look at it for whole minutes because he was too busy scraping eggs and sausage onto plates and mixing up cereal for Mina. When he looked again, there was just a smiley face icon.

But it was the start of a nonstop text flurry. It took less than two days to run through his entire allotment of texts on his ultra-cheap phone plan so that he was forced to upgrade to a better plan with unlimited texts.

They texted each other random comments throughout the day. It didn't matter if it was big or small.

Mina just glued herself to the cat. I felt you should know.

When Lissy was about that age, she covered the kitchen floor in baby oil so she could have sliding races with her cousin. Consider yourself lucky.

And:

Lissy told me a joke today. It's really terrible. Do you want to hear it?

Sure, he texted, in between diapering Lulu and trying to stop Mina from climbing on the baby's crib like a jungle gym.

Why is the baby strawberry crying?

I don't know, why?

Because her parents are in a jam.

It took him a minute to find an adequately appalled-looking emoji on the phone's selection.

I KNOW!!! Paula texted back. *Pretty great, huh?*

Sometimes it was a little, everyday observation:

This guy has been sitting at the corner table in the diner reading the paper & nursing one small black coffee for FOUR HOURS. I think he's a spy.

Sometimes it was something more serious ... more or less:

Mina drew all over herself and the floor with markers. That comes off, right?

Use baby oil. Or any kitchen oil will work. She's quite the artist, sounds like.

Yeah, he texted back, *if the canvas is herself or the walls or one of the cats.*

Hey I bet painting on cats is a great gimmick. A big gallery in New York will probably give her a solo show.

And sometimes it was quietly wistful.

Go outside, she texted him late one evening.

He was, for a change, by himself. The Rugers were watching TV in the living room. He had retreated to his room to have a little alone time, where he was lying on the bed, reading a mystery novel off their bookshelves. A heavy reading habit was something he'd picked up in the Army and had let lapse since he got out, but he had picked it back up again since he had come to stay at the Ruger farm. The isolated location and their groaning, overloaded bookshelves had made it easy to pick the habit back up as if he'd never stopped.

He didn't usually get texts from Paula this late. She went to bed early, and evening was also her dedicated kid-time, which he tried not to interrupt.

He rolled over and texted back, *Is this the start of another of Lissy's joke?*

No, I'm serious. Go outside.

He hesitated. He was very comfortable, enjoying the temporary solitude, and didn't really want to either interrupt the Rugers' family evening, or get the kids' attention.

But Paula hardly ever asked for anything.

He could have just asked why, but he decided to play along with the mystery. He got up, tucked his phone into his pocket, and quietly went through the house. Getting to his coat would have meant going through the living room and potentially resulting in everyone asking him where he was going, so instead he went to the back door and shoved his feet into a slightly too big pair of Derek's shoes.

He stepped outside into the chill night.

It was very cold, especially in a thin shirt. He wasn't wearing his arm, and hadn't bothered pinning up the sleeve just for lounging around in his bedroom, so the loose fabric hung limp against his side.

Being outside at night really made him aware of how far out of town the Rugers lived. From the front porch you could see some of the neighbors' lights through the bare trees, but back here there was nothing but darkness behind the house. The moon either hadn't risen yet, or was at its darkest phase, but the snow was faintly luminous in the starlight, enough to pick out the slender trunks of the trees against a white backdrop.

His bear stirred in him, restlessly straining with the pull of the night. It was a silent, wordless yearning, a primal urge to shift and run.

Resisting his shifts was something he'd grown used to, but it was harder tonight. He had to push his animal back into place by force.

Run, his bear said plaintively. *Hunt. Free.*

Not tonight.

One of these days he was going to have to figure out what it was like being a four-legged animal with only three legs. You couldn't keep your shift animal suppressed forever. No one could.

But this night, despite his bear's restlessness, he felt a still clarity, a sense of contentment that he didn't want to ruin by disturbing his carefully sought-after mental equilibrium.

There was a sharp burr from the phone in his pocket. He pulled it out. In the timeless stillness of the night, he had, for a moment, actually forgotten why he'd come out in the first place.

Are you outside? the text read.

Yes, he texted back. *Why?*

Look up.

He did.

The sky was clear like he hadn't seen it in years. Not since deployment. In desert places, sometimes the sky was like this. He had never realized, or perhaps he had forgotten, that this many stars existed.

Are you looking?

I'm looking, he texted. *Wow.*

See that sort of blotchy stripe down the middle of the sky?

Yeah?

That's the Milky Way, Paula texted. *You can't see it all that often. The sky has to be really, really clear.*

Are you looking at it now? he asked.

Yes.

It was strange, the kinship of doing the same thing at the same time in different places. He could almost feel her there beside him. Could almost see her, looking up at these exact same stars from just a few miles away.

I could go over there, he thought.

The possibility dangled before him, tantalizing. He could picture himself walking around to the front of the house, shivering a little in the cold—as he was starting to do now. Crunching across the trampled, frozen slush in the yard, unlocking the Subaru and warming his hand over the heat vents. Driving into town, to Paula on her porch, looking up at the stars. She could take his hand, take him inside ...

He tingled all over at the possibilities of where that might lead.

His hand hesitated over the buttons. *Can I come over?* He had only to ask.

Then Paula's next text chimed in: *Okay, I'm freezing my patootie off out here. Bed now. Early day.*

Yeah, he texted back. The disappointment was keen, but at the same time there was a pleasant anticipation, a Christmas-morning kind of eagerness. Some things were better for waiting. Not seeing her for so long made the entire idea of it desperately pleasing. Right now he felt that he could have basked for days in a single look from her clear blue eyes, drowned in the smell of her hair. He was drowning just thinking about it, in the most pleasant possible way.

I'm really looking forward to this weekend, he texted.

There was a pause that went on long enough for him to wonder if she'd gone to bed, but maybe she was just going inside and taking her coat off, because just when he was about to go inside himself, she texted back, *Me too.*

As it turned out, even if Paula hadn't invited him to the winter carnival (although he couldn't wait to see her again), Dan wouldn't have had a choice anyway. The kids were wildly excited. There was not even a question of not going.

Somehow it hadn't actually occurred to him that it was going to be a family outing until Gaby stamped into her boots and started bundling Mina into a puffy snowsuit.

"I can take them, if you want a quiet afternoon to yourselves," Dan offered.

He'd started to feel comfortable at the Ruger house to an extent that he wouldn't have thought possible just a week or two ago. He was learning the ropes of both the barn chores and the household routine. The pets had warmed up to him—there were actually four cats, though most of them lived in the barn and were half-wild, glimpsed only from a distance. And the kids had decided he was their new favorite thing, an entire adult of their very own that they could pester as much as they wanted.

Gaby glanced up, smiling, from zipping up Mina's snowsuit. "It's fine. The Keegans will be there too, and I haven't seen Tessa in a while. Mina loves playing with Skye."

"Skee!" Mina declared, as she looked up from fiddling with her snowsuit's dangly wrist snaps.

"In fact," Derek said, turning around from putting ice skates in a bag, "if you want the day off, this would be a good time for it."

"He's right," Gaby said. She fluffed Mina's hair and stood up. "You don't always have to be on duty. You could just have an evening to yourself, drink some beer, watch TV, maybe even go out to a bar or something if you want to."

Dan laughed. "What, and miss the biggest thing to happen in Autumn Grove for the entire month of January? I'd have to be out of my mind."

What he really would have missed, of course, was Paula's

warm smile and sparkling eyes. He was wrong, the texts were no substitute. Just the idea of seeing her today was driving him out of his mind.

"There's not going to be room in the Subaru for all of us," Derek said.

"Dan can drive my car," Gaby suggested. "Sandy could go with him. You want that, Sandy?"

"Yeah!" Sandy enthused.

Driving Gaby's little hatchback on the icy winter roads was more challenging than the all-wheel-drive Subaru. Dan followed Derek and Gaby, since he had no idea where they were going, fielding Sandy's enthusiastic chatter until they turned off the main highway past a sign reading GARBER PARK.

In the late afternoon sunshine, it was abundantly clear that this was, indeed, one of the town's big events. The small parking lot had already overflowed, and there were cars parallel parked on both sides of the winding road leading into the park. Dan shimmied into a parking spot a few cars down from the Subaru.

He found a text from Paula on his phone. *We're here! Come find us on the sled hill!*

"Where's the sled hill?" he asked Sandy as they got out.

"Oh, *man*," Sandy said. "Let's go there first!"

Gaby and Derek were still going through the complicated process of unpacking the kids from their car seats.

"Go on in," Gaby called, waving at them. "We'll meet you later. It's not a big place."

They walked along the edge of the road into the park. The sun was warm enough to melt the snow on the road, although snowbanks lay white and deep on either side. Dan pushed back the hood of his coat.

A banner flapping in the clear winter sunshine read WELCOME TO THE GARBER PARK WINTERFAIR! Dan could see why Paula had told him not to get his hopes up. As far as actual events, there didn't seem to be a whole lot going on. Most of the activity was centered around an honest-to-goodness outdoor skating pond, looking like something out of a painting circa 1850. There was a bonfire crackling cheerfully, a hot cocoa and cider booth, and a couple of game booths put together out of painted plywood. There were two food trucks in the parking lot, one selling hamburgers and corn dogs, the other offering Greek food. Each had a small line.

On the whole, it looked like people were making their own fun. Just about every family in Autumn Grove must be here: building snowmen, playing with dogs, having snowball fights. There appeared to be an enormous, grand-scale snowball fight and snow-fort building exercise going on in a wide-open field behind the skate pond; this was where it looked like most of the teens and college kids were. Dan wondered if Austin was among them.

Sandy dragged him past the little family groups and clusters of friends chatting with each other, which seemed mostly to fall out along age and male/female lines. The sled hill was visible from a distance, through the scattered trees, at the edge of the snowball-fight field. At the bottom, there was a big pile of plastic sleds and a pink-cheeked young woman with a clipboard signing them out.

Dan scribbled his name, and Sandy made off with a bright orange sled, scrambling up the hill across the packed-down snow. Dan lagged behind while he worked one-handed to secure a mitten over his clamps to keep the snow off. He rubber-banded it in place around what would be the wrist if he had one.

"Dan!" cried a voice that he would have known anywhere. That voice could have awakened him out of a sound sleep. He would have known it in a crowd of a hundred thousand people, let alone the couple dozen on the sled hill.

Paula was waving to him from halfway up the hill, pulling a sled with Lissy flopped on it.

"Here," she said as he approached. "You can help me pull the thousand-pound weight back there."

She was wearing a colorful knit cap pulled down over her ears, her hair springing out underneath in a profusion of wavy blonde-streaked brown curls, and the same coat she'd had on at the mini golf place. It was quilted, purple and green and red, with flowers around the collar that made Dan think of gardens and summer.

Lissy, belly down on the sled, was dressed all in green and wearing a hat that looked like the top half of a frog's head, complete with great sewn-on googly eyes.

"I see you caught a frog," Dan said. He took the rope Paula handed him.

"A frog with two broken legs," Paula said cheerfully. She looked energized, her eyes reflecting the blue of the sky and her face flushed from exertion and cold.

"I'm *not* a frog," Lissy yelled from the sled.

"Frogs are her favorite thing in the world right now," Paula explained as they climbed. "I had no idea that so many different products existed in the world with frogs on them. She has a frog backpack, a frog binder for her homework, frog shoes, a frog bedspread, a cup shaped like a frog—what are you looking for?"

"Sandy," Dan said.

The nine-year-old had completely vanished among the other little kids, a bunch of fast-moving splashes of color on the snowy hillside.

"Isn't that him?" Paula asked, pointing.

It was. Sandy had somehow, in the time it had taken Dan to get halfway up the hill, climbed all the way to the very top, past the flattish staging ground where parents were lining up toddlers on an assorted variety of sleds and up another little hill until he was just an orange dot.

Dan knew that he would have thought nothing at all of flinging himself down a hill like this when he was Sandy's age. It wasn't even dangerous; the slope was pretty gentle and there were no trees on the hill itself. Still, it seemed a lot steeper when there was a friend's borrowed kid at the top of it.

"He'll be fine," Paula said, seeing Dan's expression. "We used to sled on this hill all the time when I was his age. It's way safer than it looks from here, trust me. There's literally nothing to run into."

"I'm not worried, just keeping an eye out," Dan said, and hoped that Derek and Gaby didn't pick that exact moment to show up.

With a scream of "Look at me, Dan!" Sandy flung himself belly-first onto the sled just as they reached the flatter part of the hill. The sled launched itself like an orange rocket and shot past them, trailed by Sandy's shriek of delight. It tore down the hill, past other family groups straggling upward and one sled that had flipped over and deposited its riders (a small child and a parent) in a snowbank.

"Okay, I changed my mind," Dan said. "That looks fun. I think we should get the next ride."

Lissy sat up with a shocked and scandalized, "What?!"

Paula broke into a grin. "I think you're right. We *did* pull the sled up the hill, after all."

"Nooooo, me!" Lissy wailed. She flopped over the side of the sled and was clearly determined to make herself as heavy as possible.

"You can pull us up afterward," Dan said, sharing a grin with Paula.

"Noooo!"

BABYSITTER BEAR

Overhearing them, a nearby mom thrust out a purple sled. "If you need another, do you two want to use this one? We pulled it all the way back up here, but I think she's done for the day." She nodded to a child younger than Lissy, maybe four or five.

Dan had actually been joking ... mostly. But Paula took the sled and raised her eyebrows at him. "How long has it been since you rode on one of these?" she asked him, holding it up.

It was purple, flimsy plastic, about four feet long. "I don't think it's big enough, is it?" he asked dubiously.

"I've ridden down this hill with the kids about ten thousand times, so they can definitely take my weight, at least." Her smile faltered. "I mean, I know you were kidding. I just—"

"I wasn't entirely kidding." Dan took the sled. "Man, it's been ages since I've been on one of these."

"Whereas I am a certified expert by this point," Paula said, her warm grin popping out again. "First you lay it on the snow."

"Thanks, I got that part." Dan laid the sled down. He felt weirdly self-conscious. True, there were parents here and there on the hill who were sledding too, but most of them had toddlers in the sled with them.

"I can do it with you," Paula offered. The warmth in her smile had lit a spark that was growing rapidly into a flame. "If you need an expert."

"I think I could really use that," he said, slightly breathless. The look in her eyes made it feel like something was filling up his chest, pressing out the air.

Paula crouched down on the snow. She was wearing snowpants, leg-hugging pink ones peeking out from under the coat. They were caked with snow.

"Okay, let's see," she said. "With the kids I'd sit in the back with them in front, but it'll probably work better with you behind me."

Dan climbed into the sled. At this point he could hardly have stopped if he'd wanted to. He had to bend his knees up; he couldn't quite stretch out his legs. It didn't seem possible that there was room for Paula. But a minute later she piled in between his legs.

Up until this point the anticipation was mostly theoretical. Now suddenly she was here, her body pressed against his. The two of them were crammed into the little sled. Even with several layers of winter gear between them, he was about as intensely aware of her as it was possible to be.

"Race you, kid," Paula told Lissy, who was stretched out on her belly in the orange sled.

Lissy of course needed no encouragement to immediately kick off and glide down the hill with a squeal.

"That's cheating!" Paula called after her. She tipped her head back to grin at Dan, cheeks pink, eyes bright. "I think our honor is at stake."

"Honor," he said faintly. "Yeah."

If the plan here wasn't to fall instantly in love, he had made a tactical error.

"Hey guys!" Sandy yelled, tramping back up the hill at a dead run. "Are you sledding too?"

"Trying to," Dan said. "How do we—hmmm." It was hard to concentrate on the practical problem of getting the sled moving from the flat part of the hill when he had the even more distracting matter of Paula in his lap.

"Maybe we can—let's see." Paula squirmed a bit and got a leg out.

She pushed with her foot on one side, and Dan pushed with his good hand on the other side. After a little bit of wobbling, they got the sled moving. Gravity caught it, and they began to slide faster.

It actually was exhilarating, even if the sled was really too heavy with two adults in it to go terribly fast. But they moved down the hill at a brisk clip, the wind in their faces and snow flying up from under the sled.

Between living mostly in cities or bigger towns, and not having spent a whole lot of his childhood in parts of the country with severe winters, Dan had only been sledding a few times in his childhood. He had nearly forgotten the out-of-control feeling of the ground flying past, the sled virtually unsteerable, taking its passengers where it was going to go.

"There's a big pile of snow at the bottom of the hill," Paula yelled over her shoulder. "By now it's packed down like a ski jump. Lean to the side or we'll hit it."

Dan leaned, but Paula leaned too, and abruptly there was the feeling of gravity turning topsy-turvy as the overloaded sled lost its balance. Paula gave a short yelp, and they both tumbled into the loose snow at the bottom of the hill. Dan tried to curl around her to protect her, thrusting his arm awkwardly out to the side to make sure not to bruise anyone with the clamp end.

At least they weren't moving too fast. They ended up tangled together, half buried in snow, with the sled on top of them. Paula was laughing helplessly, and Dan realized that he was too.

"You folks okay?" a male voice called out to them.

"We're fine!" Dan yelled back when he got enough breath back from laughing. "Nothing bruised but my pride!"

"We didn't hit the ski jump," Paula pointed out between uncontrollable giggles.

"I think it hit us instead."

The sled wasn't covering them completely, but it was over their heads, trapping them in strangely violet-tinted light. Dan became aware that, in the position they were in, her face was only a few inches from his.

Her hat was askew, snow plastered on her hair and even her eyelashes. Her cheeks were flushed with more than cold, with a bright red spot on each one. The faintly purple-tinged light made her eyes look like pools, the deep blue of the sky just after sunset.

The same inevitability that had pulled him toward her from the first moment he saw her tugged on him now, drawing them together like opposite poles of a magnet until their lips clicked together.

It was a fast kiss, barely more than a quick peck, a brush of her cold lips on his. But there was nothing at all chaste about it. Her lips were half open, and he got just the slightest taste of her, a hint of searing warmth in brilliant contrast to her wind-chilled lips.

"Oh, my gosh," Paula murmured, staring into his eyes.

A weight hit their legs.

"Pull me up again!" Lissy cried from somewhere very close. Way too close.

Paula took a deep breath. "Rain check," she whispered, and rolled away from him.

Dan removed the sled from his face, and looked up to see Paula already on her feet, caked in snow, holding a hand down. She helped pull him up—providing opposite-side leverage, mostly, since she wasn't big enough or heavy enough to get him to his feet all on her own.

They had just a moment to stare at each other with a combination of breathless amazement at their own daring and anticipation. Their hands were still clasped together. He could taste her lips.

And then Lissy tugged at Paula's hand, and the Rugers arrived, en masse. They had picked up Ben and Tessa along the way. It was the first time Dan had seen the Keegans' daughter as a little girl instead of a baby dragon. She was absolutely adorable, a chubby toddler about Mina's age with her mother's light brown skin tone and a pair of huge dark eyes underneath a fluffy pink and white hat with a pompom on top. Combined with a matching pink and white snowsuit, it made her look like a peppermint candy.

"Well, that's just about the cutest thing I've ever seen," Paula said, tweaking the pompom on top of Skye's hat.

"Her Grandma Loretta sent it. And you two look soaked," Tessa said, grinning. "There's cocoa by the bonfire. We were just going to head over there and get some."

The kids ran on ahead, and Dan found himself hanging back with Ben and Tessa. Tessa was trying to pull down Skye's little hat to cover as much of her head as possible.

"We're hoping," Ben said under his breath, "that if she shifts, the snowsuit is puffy enough to hide her until we can get her to shift back."

"Is it likely?" Dan had never really appreciated the challenges of raising a shifter child in a human world. He hadn't been around other shifters much as a kid. Most of the other kids in his various group homes had been human.

"She's ... *sort* of learning that we don't want her doing it in public. I think." Tessa hoisted Skye against her shoulder. "Ben and Gaby are lucky that Mina isn't shifting yet. And Sandy isn't a shifter at all."

"Mina might not be either," Ben said. "Children of a shifter and a human parent don't always inherit the shifter side of their heritage."

Dan couldn't help himself: his mind went straight to the idea of having kids with Paula. Adorable little children with Paula's huge blue eyes. Whether they were bear cubs or normal human children, he knew that he and Paula would love them just the same. He loved her kids already—even Austin, with his prickly standoffishness. Austin reminded Dan of himself at that age, in a lot of ways.

"Dan!" came a high-pitched cry, and Lissy barreled into

his legs. She looked up at him from under her frog hat. "We're getting cocoa! Don't you want some?"

"Coming," he said with a grin. "Where's the sled?"

"I don't know." She pulled on his leg. "Come on!"

Dan looked around and saw that Paula was returning the sled. He took Lissy's mittened hand, and she settled in happily beside him.

It was weird how much they already felt like his kids, in a way. He could feel his bear's protective urges extending to cover Paula and her family, and the Ruger kids too, and Skye in her puffy little peppermint-drop snowsuit.

Anyone messes with these people, they're gonna have to mess with me first.

They joined the others at the bonfire. Dan's city childhood might have had a few sledding hills, but it had been notably lacking in outdoor bonfires, so this fascinated him: a big firepit full of giant crackling lumps of wood. He had vaguely pictured neatly arranged logs, but this was more like a big pile of stumps and other debris. He could feel the wash of heat even from a distance. It had melted the snow back to bare gravel around the firepit.

"Where do they get the wood for the fire?" he asked Derek and Gaby, while they waited in the cocoa line.

Derek shrugged and looked at Gaby, who also shrugged. Paula rejoined them just then. "What are we talking about?" she asked.

"Dan was just wondering where the wood for the bonfire comes from," Gaby said.

"It's not that important," Dan said, embarrassed. "I was just curious. I like knowing how things work."

Paula smiled and leaned her shoulder close to his. It seemed that he could feel the heat of her body even through their coats.

"I think it's farm trash, mostly," she said. "Farmers clearing land or ripping out stumps cut them up and bring the bigger, cleaner pieces out here for the town to use in the winter bonfires." She took a deep breath. "Mmm. Smell that woodsmoke. There's nothing else quite like it."

To Dan, it just smelled like smoke, but she was right that there was a sweet, campfirey quality to it.

They reached the front of the line and picked up cocoa parceled out into little paper cups. Each cup was topped with whipped cream and little colorful sprinkles, and the cocoa underneath was rich and chocolatey and piping hot, with just a hint of peppermint.

"Oh, that's nice." Paula half closed her eyes. "There's nothing like hot chocolate in the wintertime. Especially outside."

They wandered over toward the skate pond. Like the sledding hill, the skate pond had a hastily erected rental booth, and a short line of kids and parents standing in line to pick through the available sizes of skates.

"You have to get here early to get skates in your actual size," Paula explained. "A lot of people bring their own, but we just don't go skating enough to be worth buying them for the kids as they outgrow them. Do you skate?"

Dan shook his head. "Couple of times when I was a kid, a really long time ago. I don't really know how."

"Okay, we are definitely doing it." Paula dug in her pocket. "I just need a few bucks for the skate rental. Kids? You want to go skating?"

Dan was expecting Austin to grumble and wander off, but instead the teenager looked interested, the first time Dan had seen him interested in anything. Dan had been prepared to beg off and just watch from the side, but now he thought that this might be a good opportunity to bond with Paula's kids.

"Okay, I'll do it, but you'll have to show me how."

Since most of the skaters out on the pond were kids, they

actually had more trouble finding skates that fit Lissy from the remaining options than pairs for the adults.

"Here, she can borrow Sandy's," Gaby said, coming up beside them with a pair of skates dangling by their laces. "He's firmly stuck to the sledding hill right now. And I think their feet are probably close enough to the same size. They're about the same height."

Lissy plunked down and began lacing up the borrowed skates. Austin was already out on the skate pond with a pair of adult-sized skates. Out on the ice, the awkward teenager was abruptly graceful, spinning around and weaving in and out of the younger skaters. He neatly cornered at the edges of the small pond and whipped back around.

"He's really good at that," Dan said, as he crouched to change out of his boots. He wasn't looking forward to doing this with an audience. Although he could do it, tying laces was one of the trickier things to do with the metal clamps. He usually just left his boots laced up and pulled them off without untying them.

"I know. When he was younger, I actually would drive the kids over to the skate rink in Archerville, but ..." Paula frowned, jerking at her laces with her tongue sticking out of the corner of her mouth. It was adorable. "I don't know what happened, I guess I got busy and he stopped acting like he wanted to do it, and I was having to buy new skates every few months because his feet were growing so fast, and we just stopped. I ought to ask him if he'd appreciate starting up again."

"Mom!" Lissy called. She had stopped at the edge of the ice. "Hold my hands!"

"Oh come on, you haven't forgotten how to do this. It hasn't been *that* long since last winter." Paula turned to Dan, who was still struggling with his laces. "Can I give you a hand?"

His automatic urge was to say no. He knew he could get it; it would just take longer than it would have with two hands.

Right after losing his arm, he had been stubbornly and angrily determined to do everything on his own. And he had in fact learned how to do just about any everyday activity that way.

But he had mellowed a little since then. He knew he *could* do it. That was the important part.

He didn't have to prove himself to Paula.

"Yeah, sure," he said, and let go.

Paula didn't make a big deal about it, just crouched and matter-of-factly began pulling the laces tight.

"Mom!" Lissy wailed from the edge of the ice.

"I'm coming! Keep your shirt on!"

"I got it, Mom," Austin called, and glided up to the edge of the ice, stopping with a flourish. "Come on, nerdbus. Give me your hands."

"Noooo, you'll make me fall," Lissy complained, but she let her brother pull her out onto the ice. He was gentle with her, Dan noticed. Austin skated slowly backward with both his hands wrapped around hers while Lissy got her balance, then let go of one hand, and the brother and sister gradually picked up speed, skating side by side.

"There, you're done." Paula stood up and tottered on her skates. She held out a hand. "Ready to go?"

"Not really," Dan admitted, but he took her hand. They both set their skates on the ice.

"If you've done it before, I think it's sort of like riding a bicycle. You probably aren't going to lose the knack."

She was right. He wobbled slightly at first, but he could feel his innate shifter reflexes starting to pick up on the variations in his balance. Shifters were, in general, good at learning new physical tasks quickly, especially something like this, where it was mainly just a matter of leaning into the way the skates moved under his feet.

"Wow, I knew you'd be a natural." Paula let go of his hand and skated a slow circle around him. "Come on, last one to the other side of the pond is a rotten egg."

"I don't want to run over a toddler," Dan fretted, skating slowly, but with increased confidence, as he got the hang of it.

Paula, meanwhile, had reached the other side, turned around and skated back with greater speed as she, too, settled into her balance on skates. "Team skating event!" she said, and took his hand.

They skated together, finding their rhythm. It was astonishingly fun, working with her as a team like this. They anticipated changes of direction by reading the changes in each other's body language, settling into perfect teamwork.

It was like—*sex* was the first thing that came to mind, and it was, in a way; good sex was about understanding your partner's needs from their verbal and nonverbal signals. But it was something different too. It was like working with his squad in the field, the way that a good team seemed to connect with something almost like telepathy.

Except in this case it was charged with the intense, intoxicating awareness of Paula's presence: her scent, her sparkling eyes, her laughter.

He could have stayed out here forever, and he was so lost in Paula that he didn't notice, until she pulled him to a stop, that the sun was going down. The skating pond was emptying out; they were among the few skaters left on the pond. At the edge of the ice, Austin was helping Lissy take off her skates.

"This was amazing." Paula was laughing, her cheeks pink and her eyes bright. "I haven't had this much fun ice skating in years. You really are a natural."

Dan laughed too. "I had a good teacher."

Tired and a little sore, they skated hand in hand to the edge of the ice and stomped into their cold, half-frozen boots. They deposited their skates back at the rental booth and wandered over toward the bonfire, a warm spark of light in the gathering blue dusk.

"Oh, look!" Paula said, holding out a hand.

A snowflake spiraled down into the palm of her glove. It was followed by another, and another.ABruptly the cheerful chatter and laughter around the bonfire grew quiet as everyone noticed.

Dan knew he would remember that moment for the rest of his life. It was absolutely magical, the sudden hush and sense of shared wonder as everyone in the park, from small children to old people, were captivated together by the whirling snowflakes that had come on them out of the dark.

Then the gathering at the bonfire began to break up. Kids and teens, even some of the college-age adults, ran cheering into the snow, or spun around to catch snowflakes in their mouths.

Paula looked up at Dan. Her hat had slipped to one side at some point when they were skating, and now the flakes were settling in her curly, sweat-damp hair. They landed on her lashes. One settled on the full swell of her bottom lip and crumbled slowly to a bead of water.

Dan followed that snowflake down, mouth opening, and she stood on tiptoe to meet him halfway.

At the mini golf place, he'd had only the barest taste of her, enough to whet his appetite for more. Now he found that she tasted as wonderful as she smelled, a hint of cherry lip gloss and the cold sharp flavor of the snow—and the taste of *her*, spicy and warm and female, calling to something deep inside him.

Their lips parted, but they stood with their foreheads

together, his hand behind her head and her gloves clasped on either side of his face.

"I am officially considering this our first kiss," Paula said breathlessly. "Sir Putts-A-Lot is a terribly unromantic place for a first kiss."

This, on the other hand, was almost ridiculously picturesque. It was like something out of a Hallmark movie, with the gently falling snow and the crackling of the bonfire, the smells of woodsmoke and cinnamon. Christmas was almost a month behind them, but it appeared that Autumn Grove hadn't gotten the memo.

And the taste of his mate was on his lips. He wanted to savor it forever. He wanted more.

He sampled her full, warm lips again, and she pressed closer to him. The dusk provided a kind of privacy, the falling snow even more so.

And then a voice yelled, "I knew it!"

Paula and Dan broke apart, startled.

Austin came stomping out of the falling snow. "Get away from my mom!"

"Austin, no!" Paula exclaimed. "He's fine—*I'm* fine—"

But Austin was worked up into a fury that had tears standing in his eyes. "I don't want you here," he yelled at Dan. "We were fine without you. My mom doesn't need a boyfriend and we don't need *you*!"

Paula reached for Austin's arm, but he shook her off.

"Stop it," she told him.

Dan had no idea how to handle this. His bear's protective instincts were torn between defending Paula and defending her cubs, and he was caught in the middle. He moved casually forward, between Paula and her furious, raging son.

"I don't mean any harm to your mother," he told Austin. "Or to you or your sister. Trust me, I—"

"You're not my dad!" Austin yelled. He planted his hands

on Dan's chest and shoved him. "I already have a dad, and he's a jerk! I don't want another one!"

"Austin!" Paula snapped. She pushed past Dan and seized Austin's jacket in a firm grip. She gave him an abrupt shake. "You're completely out of line. Go to the car *now*. We're going home."

There was a moment when Austin stood there, feet planted, visibly defiant. He was taller than Paula now; he wasn't a small child anymore, and the bond of parent-child authority between them wavered.

And then his defiance crumbled. He really *was* just a kid, and he seemed to become abruptly aware of it. Not looking at either of them, he ducked his head and turned around, storming off toward the parking lot.

Paula drew a shuddering breath and wiped her gloved hand across her eyes.

"Are you okay?" Dan asked quietly. He hesitantly touched her arm, and when she didn't pull away, he put his arm around her shoulders.

"I'm fine," Paula said, and then raised her head and abruptly became aware—as Dan did, in that same instant—that they had attracted an audience. "I'm fine!" she snapped at everyone around them, while Dan moved wordlessly to block her from view.

Gaby came out of the crowd, carrying Mina. "What's wrong? We heard shouting."

"Austin got upset, that's all." Paula nudged Dan. "It's okay," she muttered. "I really *am* fine."

She didn't sound fine, or smell fine. But he had to take her word for it.

"Are you good to drive?" he asked her quietly. "Because I can—"

"No. I'm fine. I just need to find Lissy—is she with you?" she asked Gaby.

Gaby nodded. "Derek has both her and Sandy—oh, here they come."

Paula leaned in to Dan, and there was a moment when they were on the verge of another kiss, but instead, she gave him a tight one-armed hug.

"I had a very nice time," she said quietly. "It was great. I want to do this again."

"Me too," Dan said softly, and giving in to temptation, he kissed her forehead.

He felt as if he should say more, as if he should *do* more to stop her from walking away. Now she was going, walking into the dark and falling snow. And some desolate part of him hoped that she wasn't walking away forever.

But she turned back. There was just enough light left in the sky that he could see her face clearly, and her smile. That wasn't the smile of a woman who was walking out of his life. It was warm and inviting. It promised much more to come.

"Say goodbye to Dan, Lissy," Paula called, and Lissy waved vigorously, her little mitten flashing in the dark.

"Goodbye, Dan!" Lissy yelled.

"Goodbye," Dan called, and then, directed mostly at Paula, "See you later?"

Paula beamed. It was a smile that could melt solid ice, a smile that closed the distance between them and made him feel, for a moment, as if she was in his arms again.

"See you soon," she said. Her voice wasn't loud, but he heard it with more than just his ears: it went straight to his heart.

PAULA

Austin was quiet and sullen for the entire drive home. Paula had no idea what to say, and she didn't want to have that conversation in front of Lissy, even a Lissy who was half asleep in the backseat.

"You were very rude to Dan," she said at last, quietly, when she was pretty sure Lissy had drifted off. "You don't have to like everyone I like, Austin, but I have to draw the line at hitting people and shouting at adults."

Austin mumbled something under his breath.

"If you have something to say, please say it where I can hear it."

"You don't ever ask me what I want," Austin muttered. "Or Lissy either. I'm thinking of her too, even if you aren't."

There was a stabbing feeling under her ribs, as if a steel wire had constricted around her heart. "I'm thinking of both of you."

"Yeah? After everything with Dad, now you're just going to—"

"Just because things didn't work out with your father, Austin, doesn't mean I plan to be single forever." Her voice came out louder than she meant it to. Mindful of Lissy in the backseat, she moderated her tone. "I always put you two first. I hope you know that."

Austin muttered something that sounded like, "Can't prove it lately."

Paula blew out a breath through her teeth. *Don't have this conversation if you can't keep your temper,* she told herself sternly.

"We need to have a serious conversation about this," she said quietly. "And about your behavior lately in general."

There was a jerk; Austin stiffened all over in his seat, like she'd caught him doing something illegal. "What do you mean?" His voice cracked a little. He had always been an honest kid, and he was a terrible liar.

Her heart sank. What was he into?

"Are you doing drugs?" she asked, point blank. Might as well just get it out in the open.

Austin made a tiny weird sound. He relaxed a little and looked out the window. "No."

That sounded sincere.

"You've been cutting class and missing your shifts at the diner. I don't know what to think."

"I just want to have fun, Mom. Stop giving me the third degree."

Paula didn't know what else to say. She pulled through the alley and into the garage.

"You know you can come to me about anything, right?" she said a little bit desperately, as the garage door rolled down behind them.

"Yeah right," Austin said. He undid his seatbelt and opened the car door. Paula reached for him and found herself grasping at air.

"Austin, we have to talk. Don't you walk away from—"

The door slammed. In the backseat, Lissy made a startled squeak.

"Are we home, Mom?" she asked sleepily.

"Yeah, baby. Just a minute."

Paula clasped her hands on the steering wheel and rested her forehead on them for a minute.

She desperately missed the days when Austin was just a little boy Lissy's age, who would crawl into her lap and put his arms around her neck. She had read about divorced parents who ended up taking it out on their kids, especially once the kid got older and started to resemble their other parent, and she had sworn she would never be like that. It was true that she saw a little of Terry in Austin, but it was all the best parts of Terry, and none of the worst. She loved Austin desperately. He was a smart, kind kid with an interest in science, and she was so proud of him. Up until this year, he had never been in trouble, never even missed class except when he was sick.

She had wanted so badly, if and when she started to date again, for her kids to get along with her new boyfriend. It meant so much to her.

Now it seemed like the opposite was happening.

But she couldn't push aside everything that she felt in Dan's arms. There had to be some way to reconcile Austin's dislike of Dan with her need to have both of them in her life.

She felt like she was having to walk a tightrope between her budding relationship with Dan and her urge to protect and care for her kids, between her responsibility to Austin as his mother—to listen to him and support him—and the need to stop him from getting away with his recent behavior. She didn't know what to do.

"Mom?" Lissy said, with a yawn.

"Yeah, honey." Paula took a deep breath and opened the

car door. "Why don't you go change into your pajamas, and I'll be up in a minute to say goodnight."

At least Lissy's problems were still easy to fix. Whatever was going wrong with Austin, though, wasn't simple.

∼

IN THE MORNING she woke tired and restless and conflicted. She and Austin had walked on eggshells around each other for the rest of the evening, with Austin spending most of the time holed up in his room. Selfishly, she hadn't wanted to blow it up into another fight by pushing to have the conversation they really needed to have. Now she wished she'd just gotten it over with. But she didn't even know how to open a talk like that when she still hadn't figured out where things were with Dan. She had thought of texting him fifty times last night, but stopped herself every time.

The first thing she did, by habit, was check her phone. There was a text from Dan.

Just checking you got home okay last night. Hope you have a good day at the diner!

Paula had to blink back tears, and for a minute she just sat and held the phone. She hadn't actually thought Dan would walk away from her just because of Austin being rude to him, but ... well ... sometimes boyfriends left for smaller things that that.

Is he my boyfriend? Is it that serious?

It was, she knew. It was rapidly growing far more serious than that. She had felt a fire last night, driving out the winter night's chill, that could all too easily build from a small flame to a raging inferno that would put the Garber Park bonfire to shame.

But she had to take it slow for the sake of the kids. She

couldn't let this turn into another Terry situation, for their sake and for her own.

Before she could weaken, she texted, *Got home great, thanks! Hope you did too.*

She forced herself to send it before she could add more. Like, *I had a really wonderful time yesterday.* Like, *your kisses are amazing.* Like, *I can't stop thinking about you.*

Already there was a silly smile creeping onto her lips, just at the thought of him.

She forced herself out of bed and into the shower. Wrapped in a bathrobe, with her wet hair piled on her head, she moved quietly through the house, making sure that Lissy's lunch was in the fridge and her homework was in her frog backpack. The door to Austin's room was shut, and Paula stood outside it for a long minute and then went into her room to get dressed for work.

One of her increasingly serious problems with Austin's unreliability was that she could no longer trust him to get his sister ready for school in the morning. For the last couple of years, with the house right across the alley, she had felt comfortable enough leaving Austin to take care of getting himself and his sister off to school. Now she began to realize that this was a tremendous amount of unfair responsibility to put on a kid who was only in the 10th grade. No wonder he was starting to show the strain.

Maybe she could start having someone—a sitter, a neighbor, maybe even Dan—come in for a couple of hours in the morning while she opened the diner.

For today, I'll just duck back to the house for an hour or so after we get through the early rush, she thought as she let herself out into the predawn chill. The stars were sharp and clear overhead, making her think of long-distance star-watching with Dan the other night. Her partly dried hair instantly started to freeze. *I know it's busy around that time, but I'll call a couple of the part-time waitresses and see if any of them can start doing earlier shifts. I can't keep treating Austin like a miniature adult. He's only a kid. It's not fair.*

Wrapped up in these thoughts, she crossed the alley to the door leading into the kitchen. Mitch usually got there about the same time she did, and today was no exception; the door was already unlocked, and she let herself in, expecting the usual heat of the brightly lit kitchen with Mitch firing up the griddle and starting the coffee.

Instead, she stopped in her tracks, shocked to her core.

One thing Mitch always, always did was leave the kitchen immaculate before he clocked out. He gave the general impression that his personal life was a mess, possibly involving jail at some point in the past, but he was absolutely reliable about making sure that the pots were all scrubbed, the counters wiped down, every sack of trash taken out.

But even at its worst, after they had been slammed for hours with the entire high school basketball team or the aftermath of the Autumn Grove Garden Society Flower Show, it had never looked anything like this.

At first she couldn't even tell what she was looking at. The neat world of the kitchen—her parents' kitchen and now hers—was unrecognizable chaos. Slowly she began to pick out specific items: overturned mixing bowls, smashed eggs, bags of flour torn open, the top of the burger grill ripped off, torn-open packages of salad and buns littered everywhere ...

Mitch was in the middle of it with a broom. "Miz DeWitt," he said, and his face was a study in tragedy. "I was hoping to get some of this cleaned up before you came in."

"No, you shouldn't have to deal with it on your own," she said, dazed.

She couldn't seem to feel anything properly. It was too much to take in. Everything was going to need to be thoroughly cleaned and sanitized, most of the food thrown out.

She couldn't even walk through the kitchen to see if the dining area was like this too.

"Have you," she began shakily, and waved a hand toward the rest of the business. "Have you been out there?"

"It's not too bad," Mitch hurried to reassure her. "Some chairs tipped over, that's all. Nothing broken, not like in here."

Paula nodded and drew in a shuddering breath that hitched in the middle. "Who did this? Who would do this?"

Mitch swallowed and reached for a folded piece of paper on the bare range top. "This was taped to the door. I, uh, took it off before I knew what it was. I don't know if you want to save it for the police."

It was a piece of yellow lined paper. Paula took it with shaking hands and opened it.

Just a reminder, Mrs. Raines. We don't care about you, but we want your ex. Stop hiding him, or next time will be worse.

Very carefully, she refolded it. "Do you see any bags, or ..."

Mitch produced a clean Ziploc bag. She put it in, feeling a little stupid, like someone playing CSI. It wasn't like she didn't know who had left it. She just had absolutely no idea what to do about it.

"You live right across the way, don't you?" Mitch said. "Did you have any trouble?"

Her heart clutched. She had a sudden horrifying vision of her porch lights broken, her house vandalized. Her *children*—but no, she had gone through her normal morning routine without any disruptions. And the house was locked up.

"I don't think they came over to the house at all," she said. "I would have heard it. In fact, I don't know how I didn't hear them over here last night. The town is so quiet."

But even as she said it, she knew what must have happened. Of *course* they hadn't done it late at night. They must have come earlier in the evening, when everyone was at the carnival, and no one was around to hear or see.

She hadn't even thought to check that everything was okay at the diner when she got home. Why would she? There was no reason to think it wasn't.

In a way it was a relief, because it meant the vandals hadn't been anywhere near the place while she and the kids were there. But at the same time, she was reeling from the horrifying invasiveness of it. How could she ever feel safe here again? Let alone safe to have her kids here?

She didn't want to deal with this on her own. She *couldn't.*

And then she realized she didn't have to.

She had her phone out before she knew what she was doing, and was already texting Dan. It was like she had gone on pure autopilot.

There's a situation at the diner. Please come. I need you.

She regretted it as soon as she had pressed send. It sounded so desperate. So needy.

But it was true.

To her surprise, the reply came back immediately. The content of it was even more surprising.

I already know. I'm on my way.

How? she texted. *Did someone call you?*

There was a pause this time before he answered. *I just knew,* came the reply at last. *Gaby's headed in to work. I'm getting a ride with her.*

What did that mean, he just knew?

Paula pressed the heels of her hands to her eyes. Then she got herself together and took charge.

"We'll be closed today," she said decisively. "If anyone asks, I'll just say a family situation came up."

It was already sinking in that she couldn't let the town know about this. Autumn Grove was a close-knit place, with both the good and bad qualities of small towns. If she needed to, she could probably rely on a dozen neighbors for emotional support and food and help cleaning up. But at the same time, letting it get around that her ex's debts and misdeeds had brought a criminal element to town who might threaten *their* businesses, or even threaten them if they were seen eating at the diner ... she could easily imagine how that might bring about the collapse of the local business that the diner relied on.

"Meanwhile," she added, "I'm going to make us some coffee. We're going to need it. If you can find one of the coffeepots—oh." Her inward resolve collapsed a bit as Mitch wordlessly held up a coffeepot handle with a little glass clinging to it. "In that case, I'll—I'll go back to the house and make us some coffee and bring it back over here." And also, not incidentally, check on her kids.

The kids were fine. The house was fine. She peeked into both bedrooms and looked out at the porch, which looked exactly like it had last night. The loan sharks had confined their attack to the closed business.

Next time could be worse.

She swallowed hard and made a pot of coffee that she poured into two large thermoses. Austin came into the kitchen, yawning and rubbing his eyes, just as she was finishing up. He stopped at the sight of her.

"Whoa, Mom—why aren't you at work?"

"The diner is closed today, sweetheart," she told him, keeping herself brisk and businesslike. "There was some damage last night."

"What sort of—"

"Austin." She put her hands on his shoulders. "I really need you today, all right? You *cannot* leave your sister alone in the house this morning. Just get some breakfast ready for both of you. I'll be back over to check on you soon."

He looked at her in silence, and suddenly she could see

hints of the man he was going to be, serious and strong. "Something's really wrong, isn't it, Mom?"

Paula bit her lip. She couldn't lie to him. *Wouldn't* lie to him.

"We were vandalized last night," she said. "I think they were people who are angry at your father." She saw Austin's brows start to draw together into a thundercloud scowl. "I'm taking care of it," she said quickly. "They didn't come to the house. I think they did it while we were at the carnival. I'm going over to clean up, but as soon as I can, I'll be back over to help out, okay? I'm going to drive you two to school. I don't want either of you taking the bus today."

For once, Austin's air of teenage sarcasm gave way to sincerity. "I promise, Mom," he said solemnly, and to her surprise, he hugged her. "I'm *really* sorry about Dad," he said into her shoulder.

"Oh, baby." Her heart broke, and for yet another time that morning, she hovered on the edge of crumbling into tears. "You listen to me, Austin. It is *not* anything to do with you. Nothing your dad has ever done is your fault."

She disentangled herself and patted him on the shoulder, then, because that didn't seem like enough, kissed his forehead.

"You're a very good kid, Austin." She picked up the thermoses. "I'm taking these over to the diner. If you want coffee, you know I don't like you having it all that often, but I've already loaded up the pot again, so all you have to do is press the button. I'll see you very soon."

She juggled the thermoses while locking the door behind her. The back door let her out onto a narrow strip of snow-covered lawn and the wooden privacy fence with a gate in it that led to the alley and diner. In her entire life, she had never felt nervous walking through that gate. About the worst that could possibly happen, the worst that had ever happened was a delivery truck blocking the alley or a stray dog wandering by.

This time, she had to brace herself inwardly to open it. It was only by girding herself with fury that she was able to do it. *They have no right. They don't belong here. I won't let them make me afraid in my own yard, in my own business.*

They have no RIGHT!

The back door to the diner was standing open. Yellow light poured out into the alley—with the short January days, it wasn't even starting to get light yet this early—and framed in that light was a man's large, broad-shouldered figure. Adrenaline raced through her like cold water and then dissolved into an aching sense of relief when she recognized Dan.

"Paula," he said. His voice cracked.

He didn't even hesitate, just took her in his arms, coffee thermoses and all. She leaned into him as relief crashed through her like a tidal wave. She didn't have to bear this alone. Even if he didn't lift a finger to pick up a broom (and Dan really didn't strike her as a guy who stood by idly while other people worked), just being able to stand here with his arms around her, lifting some of the burden off her shoulders, was worth more than she could ever say.

He kissed the top of her head. As she pulled back, she saw that he was wearing sweat pants and a T-shirt underneath his coat. It looked like sleeping clothes.

"I really didn't mean for you to rush out of the house," she said, embarrassed.

Dan shook his head. "I told you. I was on my way anyway."

And from the look of things, he had rolled out of the house half-dressed. She was baffled.

"So are you psychic or what?" She tried to play it off as a

joke, but she really did wonder how he could possibly have known.

"I just had a feeling," Dan said, very seriously.

Before she could ask him any more questions, Mitch called out from inside the kitchen, "Miz DeWitt, what d'you want me to do with anything that's still good? We got a lot of flour and buns, that kind of thing, that wasn't spoiled, but there's nowhere to put it."

Paula dashed at her eyes with the backs of her coffee-occupied hands. She leaned a shoulder against Dan for a moment and then went past him, braced this time for the state of the kitchen. "Just put them out in the front," she said. "We won't be using it today for anything else, so we might as well move everything that's salvageable out there so we can clean up in here."

∼

By early afternoon, the kitchen was restored to a level of order that Paula wouldn't have believed possible. To her astonishment, Gaby had left the bakery in the hands of her kitchen assistant and come over to help. Paula hadn't wanted to get the Rugers involved, but there was really no way not to—they obviously knew that Dan had rushed out early for some reason.

"You know, we're literally bodyguards," Dan pointed out. "I mean, Derek and Ben are. We could protect you."

"I can't afford to hire anyone," she protested as she pushed a mop across the floor.

Dan looked aghast. "You don't have to *pay* for it."

"Dan, I can't expect your friends to do their work for free. It would be like someone coming into the diner expecting free sandwiches."

"You just got done giving free coffee and sandwiches to

everyone in here."

"Because they're helping me clean up!"

"Paula, listen." Dan moved into her space, arms going loosely around her waist. She was very aware of the warm weight of his broad hand at the small of her back, the light touch of the steel hooks on the other side. "It's not an imposition. If anything, they'll appreciate it. They're trying to get a security business off the ground. You'll give them practice and a good reference from a respected local business."

"Respected if I manage to keep from tipping off all my customers that I had to hire security guards to keep loan sharks off my back," she muttered.

Dan took his hand off her back so he could lightly curl his fingertips under her chin, tipping her head back to look into her eyes. His gaze was sincere, and so intent that it almost hurt her, like looking directly into the sun.

"For what it's worth," he said, "I think you're wrong about people judging you if they knew. I think they'd help if you needed it, like Gaby did. But you know what you want, and I won't second-guess you." The corner of his mouth tugged into a slight grin. "Look, it'll be good practice for Derek and Ben at working around the small-town gossip mill. They won't tip anyone off, I swear. You can trust them."

Her resistance crumbled like a house of cards. There was just no saying no to those eyes.

"All right," she sighed. "It would make me feel a lot better to have someone around, you're right."

The person she really wanted to stay with her was Dan. She hovered on the verge of just asking him.

But she couldn't quite bring herself to come right out and say it. He had a life. She had no right to pull him away from it and expect him to drop everything to protect her.

Even if he had literally dropped everything to come out here today.

"So I don't suppose you're going to tell me how you knew I was in trouble, are you?"

"I ..." Dan looked like he was groping for words. "It's like I told you. I just had a feeling. It woke me out of a dead sleep."

"That's really weird. Maybe you just happened to have a nightmare at the same time."

Dan gave his head a short, hard shake. "No. It was definitely about you. It ..."

He trailed off, and she got the weirdest feeling that he was right on the edge of telling her something, and had backed off. There was something *there*.

In her years of marriage to Terry, she had started to develop a finely honed sense for when he was lying to her. Terry had been good at lying without actually lying, just letting her assume things. She didn't get quite the same feeling off Dan. He wasn't deceptive; in as short a time as she'd known him, she had figured that out right away. Dan put everything out there. What you saw was what you got.

And yet, there was something he wasn't telling her. She was absolutely sure of it.

"Definitely about me?" she prompted.

Dan shook his head. He brushed his hand down her cheek and neck—it was all she could do not to lean into it—and took a step back. "So if you're okay with it, I'll call the guys to come out and have a look around, okay? I'll make it clear that it needs to be kept totally on the down low. They'll respect that."

"Yeah," she said. "That's a good idea. Let's do that."

She couldn't help feeling intensely disappointed. There was some kind of secret between them now, and after everything with Terry, she wished that she could trust that it was something that wouldn't hurt her. But she just couldn't.

What are you hiding? she wondered.

PAULA

Ben Keegan showed up later that day.

Paula sort of knew the Keegans, in the way you knew everyone in a small town, by sight at least. But despite hanging around them a bit at the winter carnival yesterday, she didn't really *know* them. She didn't think they had ever exactly been introduced. She just had a general impression that Ben had a cabin somewhere outside of town and his wife ran a cat rescue out of the old building up on the highway that used to house Karpet Kountry and an insurance office.

Ben Keegan wasn't what she expected of a bodyguard. He wasn't big like Derek, or even like Dan. He was unassuming and quiet, and from his general demeanor she would have expected him to be something like ... she wasn't even sure, a doctor or an engineer or something. He had black hair and gray eyes and an air of quiet, graceful competence.

After he had shaken her hand and offered condolences on the vandalism, he walked all around the diner, looking things over. Paula trailed him, curious. Dan was still around—he had been helping her bleach the fridge in the kitchen; she had decided to deep-sanitize everything before opening again—and he joined them after a little while.

"What are you doing?" Paula asked as Ben went down to one knee to look at her door.

"Thinking about security," he said, glancing up. His steady gray gaze went past her to Dan. "This place isn't very secure."

"It's a diner," Paula said, feeling embarrassed. "It's not supposed to be secure."

"C'mon, man, I didn't bring you in here to pick on her," Dan said, putting an arm around her shoulders.

Paula decided to relax against him. She had managed to get over her hurt, more or less. She was just being a little bit careful now. Whatever Dan wasn't telling her, she didn't think it was *bad*. It was just a reminder that she needed to be cautious before diving into anything.

Ben's mouth quirked. "What I mean is, you might want to think about getting an actual alarm system. That's my area. Derek handles the heavy lifting, so to speak—Derek and you, Dan, I should say; sorry, I'm used to just the two of us. I definitely can handle the physical side if I need to, but I'm really more of a security analyst. It's the engineer in me."

"You mean you *are* an engineer?" Paula said in disbelief. She blushed when both men looked at her. "I was just thinking earlier that you looked more like that than a bodyguard. Sorry, I didn't mean to be rude."

"You're not," Ben said easily. "Civil engineering, technically, before I was a cop and then a bodyguard. Back in the day, I used to design bridges. Actually, I met Derek and Dan while doing infrastructure analysis overseas. But I do actually have some electrical engineering background as well, and over the past couple of years I've been getting certified or re-certified in various aspects of security systems installation and maintenance. I was the one who put in the alarm system at Derek and Gaby's farm."

"I didn't even know they had one," Paula said, her voice faint.

"We've had to deal with situations like this before," Ben said. He glanced up at Dan. "Actually, while all of this is going on, we might consider moving your family out to the farm. We'd need to shuffle people around a bit to make room, that's all."

Paula shook her head firmly. She could only imagine from her own parenting experience how much of a hassle it would be for Derek and Gaby to uproot their established routines for their three kids to accommodate an entire family moving in with them, however temporarily. "No, I don't think that'll be necessary. After all, that's the whole reason you're here, isn't it? To keep us safe here."

"Well, that's the idea, anyway." Ben straightened up and dusted off his knees. "If you don't mind me staying here late, I can make a supply run this afternoon and install something quick and dirty this evening."

"Yeah, sure," Paula said, surprised by how fast this was moving. "Are you sure it's not an imposition?"

"Are you kidding?" Ben grinned. "I can't *wait* to do this."

"See?" Dan murmured. His arm tightened around her. "We've got this."

∼

DAN WAS RIGHT, they were discreet about it. For the next couple of days, though, they were almost always around. They set up a rotation watching the house and diner—which she only knew about because Dan told her about it; she never actually saw them. Not a single glimpse of a car on a stakeout or one of the guys walking past—nothing.

The only sighting of anything out of the ordinary was Lissy claiming she'd seen a bear in the alley behind the house, but there was no chance of getting a bear in town at this time of year. They did occasionally have wildlife wander down from the mountains, but all the bears were in hibernation in the winter. Lissy had obviously been having a particularly vivid dream.

"How are you guys this good at hiding, anyway?" she asked Dan.

The diner was back open again, more or less as before, although with a slightly stripped-down menu. Dan had come in to hang out with her during one of the slow times. He was on one of the bar stools at the counter with the Rugers' baby Lulu in a front carrier and Mina eating a dish of ice cream on the stool next to him.

It was all Paula could do not to die of delight when Dan had walked in wearing the baby carrier, the little baby cuddled against his broad chest with just a tuft of dark hair showing. She had never particularly liked the phrase "my ovaries exploded," but at least now she knew what it felt like.

"It's what they do," Dan pointed out. "They're professionals." He held out his coffee cup. "Could I get a refresher on this?"

Paula frowned as she poured the coffee. She had that evasive feeling again, for some reason. Like there was something he wasn't telling her. But she had no idea what it could possibly be, or even how to ask about it. There was no reason why he would try to conceal his coworkers' methods from her. It wasn't like she was going to reveal bodyguard trade secrets or something. Maybe he thought she wouldn't be interested, or had been sworn to secrecy.

"Well, they're good at it," she had to admit. "I don't think anyone has noticed anything. We certainly haven't."

The alarm system installed by Ben was also very discreet and easy to use. There was a hidden keypad by the back door, behind a loose bit of siding so that it looked like part of the wall. Paula had given the code to Mitch, so he could come in early to use the kitchen and lock up after hours, and to the kids, and no one else. If the alarm was tripped, an alert would go to the Ruger farm, to Ben's cabin, and to the whole group's phones.

Paula had reduced the diner hours yet again, opening a bit later than she used to so that there were more people around, and closing right after the lunch rush so she could go pick up Lissy and Austin from school. (To Austin's dismay. Having your mom pick you up at the door of the high school probably didn't do much for your adolescent social life.)

"And you haven't had any more trouble?" Dan asked. There was a darkly serious undertone. He was still furious on her behalf about the vandalism, in his quiet way. Having that kind of protectiveness directed at her was a new and strange experience.

"None. It's like they're gone." She added hopefully, "Maybe they are? Maybe they realize they went too far this time."

Dan shook his head. "If they're willing to do this, I don't think we can assume that. They might stay out of sight for a while, but they'll very likely be back."

Paula blew out her breath. "I was afraid you'd say that."

"What's your ex have to say about all of this?" Dan asked carefully.

Paula set down his warmed-up coffee a little harder than she meant to. "I'll only find out if he ever gets in touch with me. Right now I'd cheerfully point these goons in his direction if I had any idea where to send them."

"We could look for him."

"Is finding people what bodyguards do?" she asked, trying to keep it light.

"Not normally. But this is a special case."

"Wow, you guys really must not have much work."

She smiled, but this time Dan barely smiled back, just a

slight tug at his mouth. His eyes were serious and intense. "You're worth it, Paula."

Paula dropped her gaze, flushing. "I don't want trouble. Believe it or not, I don't even want to get Terry in hot water. I still don't know how things fell apart like they did. He wasn't a bad man, and I thought for a while after the divorce that we could still be friends. Now I don't even know how much of *that* was a lie. After all, he was lying to me about literally everything else."

"Whether he's good or bad or neither, he put you and the kids in danger," Dan said. His voice was icy, and hard enough to even make Mina—who didn't appear to be paying attention to the adults—glance up from the ice cream and coloring book spread out in front of her. "And he's not willing to man up and come back here and fix his problem."

"He might not even know about it." She couldn't believe she was defending Terry of all people. "I mean, I don't think he'd do anything to endanger the kids. Whatever else he is, I believe that he loves them."

Dan huffed out a sigh and looked like he wanted to argue further, but ground his teeth and backed down. "I'm not going to show up on his doorstep and hustle him, if that's what you're worried about. It's up to you. But it seems to me that none of this is going to be resolved, at least not easily, without involving him somehow. Or contacting the police."

Paula shook her head. "No police. Not yet. Look, I ... I can dig up some of my old correspondence with him tonight. The support checks and the kids' birthday cards, whatever I have around. How does that sound?"

"That would help a lot," Dan said earnestly. "And now, how about a topic that's not your ex?"

She had to laugh. "I really wouldn't mind, thanks."

He smiled too, but it dropped away, his gaze turning soft and serious. "How would you feel about a real date? I had a great time with your family—our families—" He said it unselfconsciously; he didn't even seem to notice that he had referred to the Rugers that way. "But I'd like to take you out to a nice restaurant. Show you a good time."

Paula's breath hitched in her throat. "Well," she said, "the options are the Char Pit bar and grill, or La Taquerita. Meat char-grilled, or meat with beans and cheese, that's what this town has for fine dining."

Dan broke into a brilliant smile. "Is that a yes?"

"Of course it's a yes." She felt ridiculously happy and light, as if she was half drunk on champagne. "We'll just have to work out childcare."

"That one's easy," Dan said. "Take the kids over to Derek and Gaby's. I'll have to ask, of course, but Lissy and Austin seem like sweet kids and not too much trouble. I don't think the Rugers would mind. They've been great about giving me time off in the evenings if I need it. In fact, if you're good with it, I can ask now."

"Yes." Her whole body seemed to be fizzing with that all-over happiness. "Yes, please."

The tinkling of the bell on the door was an unwelcome intrusion into her world of happiness. She went to give the newcomers menus and coffee, and when she came back, Dan had his phone out and was texting. "They're good with it anytime," he said, glancing up with a wide grin. "Are you free tonight?"

"Tonight," she said, dazed. "Yes, tonight. Tonight would be great."

A date. Wow. What was she going to wear? She wasn't sure if she even owned a dress anymore. Not that either the Char Pit or La Taquerita was the sort of place you wore a dress to.

"We're good to go," Dan declared after another round of texting. "Derek says you can bring the kids over this afternoon." He grinned at her. "So what's your pleasure, steak or beans?"

"Steak," she said promptly. "Steak and a beer to unwind at the end of the day sounds *amazing*."

"Do you need reservations?"

"It's a bar and grill, so no."

They went on chatting until the lunch rush got too busy for Paula to stay at the counter. Dan left with a cheerful wave. Paula whisked his and Mina's dishes into the back, feeling like her feet barely touched the ground.

"You look happy, boss," Mitch called.

Paula slammed the door of the dishwasher with a flourish and cranked it to the wash cycle. "I have a date tonight, Mitch."

"Yeah? With the big one-armed guy?" Mitch had perfected the art of having conversations while his hands went on with the fast-paced business of a short-order cook, whisking burgers off the grill onto their buns and slapping more burgers on to replace them. "He seems like a good guy."

"He's great," she said. "Really great. Wonderful. Amazing. And other nice adjectives."

She let Mitch off a little early, closing the kitchen except for sandwiches so that she could scrub things down and have the diner ready to close up as soon as she flipped the OPEN-CLOSED sign over in the window. She closed out the cash register and then drove to pick up the kids from school.

"This is so unnecessary, Mom," Austin complained, throwing his book bag in the backseat.

"Look, think of it as a favor that you're doing for your poor overprotective mom so she doesn't fret herself into an early grave waiting for you to get home from school."

She delegated Austin to fix a snack for Lissy in the kitchen while she went upstairs to take a shower and change into something nice. Well, nice-ish. It was the Char Pit, where the usual clientele's idea of dressing up was wearing your *less*-stained garage coveralls. She opted for a clean pair of jeans and a fluffy sweater that was nice enough to make her feel a little dressy while still practical enough that she could walk around the Char Pit without worrying about spilling a beer on it.

It was still too early to take the kids over to the Rugers'. The sound of the TV came up the stairs; it sounded like the kids were watching cartoons down there. It was rare for Austin to spend casual time with his little sister, and she didn't want to interrupt them. What else could she do with herself?

Oh right. She was supposed to dig out some of Terry's old stuff to help Dan and his friends try to find her ex.

She went down the stairs quietly, past the doorway to the living room with the TV blaring old Nickelodeon cartoons, and on into the little room that had been her parents' shared office back when her parents still lived here and ran the diner. Since they had retired to a Tampa condo, no one used the room much. Paula had gotten in the habit of doing most of her business paperwork at the kitchen table while the kids did their homework. It was easier to keep them on task that way, and answer questions if they needed help.

But it was still useful to have an actual office, with a desk and filing cabinets and everything. She just wasn't in here very much—so rarely, in fact, that in order to get to the desk, she had to edge around her (rarely-used) sewing machine and some crates of yarn that she'd moved in here over the holidays to clear space in the living room for the Christmas tree.

"Need to find a better place to put those," she muttered as she hunted through the drawers of the big, heavy wooden desk that had been her dad's. But she knew even as she said it that she probably wouldn't. That sewing machine would be living here until Austin moved out for college.

She wasn't completely sure that the papers from Terry would be here, but it seemed the most likely place. And actually they weren't that hard to find. There was a big bundle of check stubs from the child support checks in her tax records drawer, and a scattering of cards and torn envelopes in a loose pile, mixed in with other paperwork. It was all really a mess. She didn't remember leaving everything this messed up, but, well, it had been a busy year. Paperwork always seemed to take a backseat to more important work.

Looking at the envelopes only made her angry all over again. At first the checks had come regularly, as did birthday presents for the kids. Terry would drive down from the city to spend weekends with the kids, whenever he could get away.

And then he had just—what? Lost interest? Stopped caring?

"Mom, why are you looking at Dad's old stuff?"

Paula jumped. She hadn't even heard Austin come in.

Well, it wasn't like she had any reason to keep it from him. "Mr. Ruger and Dan are trying to find him for us."

She saw Austin's shoulders go up a bit, whether at the mention of Dan or his dad, she wasn't sure. But he looked intrigued. "Do you think they can?"

"I don't know. They're going to try." It occurred to her all of a sudden that the envelopes and things from Terry were all together, as if someone else had been looking at them too. That would also explain the mess. She wasn't ever going to be the world's greatest admin assistant, but she was usually better than this at keeping her important-paperwork drawers tidy. "Honey—have you been looking at these?"

Austin looked instantly guilty. Her heart broke a little.

"It's fine if you look at these, honey, he's your dad. Here."

She held out the bundle of envelopes. "You can have these for now. I'll show them to Dan and Mr. Ruger later."

Austin shook his head. "I don't—I mean—I hope they find him. I was just looking for a phone number or something. Like, for talking to him."

Fury at Terry rushed over her. He didn't deserve such a sweet, loyal kid.

"Well, if they find him, you can definitely talk to him. And maybe he'll call sooner." When was the last time Terry had called, anyway? Maybe for Lissy's last birthday.

"I don't *want* to talk to him," Austin said, not meeting her eyes. "I just wanted to ask him about—stuff."

"About what? About the—the diner situation?"

Austin shrugged, still not looking at her.

"Honey, it is *not* your responsibility to fix this. Not in any way. You know that, right?"

"I know," Austin said, a little too quickly. "I just want to—like, find out what he …" He started to raise his hands and then dropped them. "Never mind."

"You and me both, kid," Paula muttered.

She reached out an arm and wrapped it around Austin's shoulders. He held back for a moment before leaning against her and drooping his head on her shoulder, like he would have when he was a little kid.

Kids grew up, but they never stopped needing their moms.

"It's not your fault that your dad isn't in your life, kid," she said quietly. "And it's not your fault that he's kind of a … a deadbeat. But it's not your problem to fix. It's his—and mine. And I promise you I'm going to do what I can about that."

She had to. It was starting to look like finding Terry's sorry butt, wherever he was, and dragging him back to deal with his own mess was the only way she was ever going to get everything back to normal.

She kissed Austin on top of his head.

"Now come help me get your sister's stuff together. Do you want to take your homework over to Derek and Gaby's tonight?"

"I'd rather stay here."

Paula shook her head. "Not an option, sorry. Not right now."

"Can I could go over to Bobby Hogan's house, then?" Austin asked hopefully. "He just got Nukemaster III for his birthday and I haven't played it yet."

"Nukemaster? That doesn't sound very wholesome."

Austin rolled his eyes. "Mom, it's a shooter game. It's not supposed to be."

While she mulled over the counteroffer, her phone buzzed in her hip pocket. It was Dan.

Paula patted Austin's shoulder and answered it.

"Hey," she said, with a rush of heat flushing through her.

Damn. She had it bad.

Austin rolled his eyes, squirmed out from under her arm, and slunk out.

"Hey, there," Dan's warm voice said, and then grew apologetic. "So we might need a rain check on that date."

"Why?" Paula asked anxiously. "Did something bad happen?"

"No, not that. Gaby has an event tonight. They're catering some kind of thing at the high school, it's pretty big, and Derek promised to help her. He just forgot about it earlier with the security job on his mind."

"Oh," she said, disappointed. "So you have to stay in and watch the kids."

"Yeah. I'm really sorry."

"I'm not," Paula said. To her own surprise, she didn't even hesitate. "I can come over anyway, if it's okay. I'll bring my kids and we can watch movies. At the very least I can give you some adult company."

"You don't have to. I know you were looking forward to a night out."

"I was," she said. "But look, one thing about families is that you have to bend your plans sometimes. It looks like our dates just keep having the kids in them, but you know what? That's not a bad thing. I think it would be fun to hang out with you and the Ruger kids, and I'm sure Lissy would enjoy a play date. She's awfully jealous of Sandy having his own horse, you know."

Dan laughed softly. "In that case, why don't you come over a little early while it's still daylight and she can ride the horse?"

"Oh my gosh, she'll die of joy."

"And I can cook dinner for you," he said, sounding like he was starting to warm up to the idea.

"For me *and* the kids, I hope."

"Oh, okay, fine, I guess they can eat too." There was warm humor in his voice. Her stomach swooped pleasantly.

"I guess I'll leave the dress and the dangly earrings at home this time, then."

There was a slight intake of breath. "You don't have to. If you want to. I mean, it's not the Char Pit ..."

"But what is," she said, laughing.

"Really, I gotta go to this place to see if it's really *that* much of a hole."

"It's actually not. They do a really great medium-rare ribeye, and the beer is good. I just haven't been there in forever."

Dan turned serious again. "I'm definitely taking you out as soon as we can both get away."

"And I'm holding you to that." She smiled into the phone, even though he couldn't see it. She just felt so *good*. "And I just might put some makeup on. You know. Just because there aren't many opportunities to wear my nice lipstick around here."

"I can't wait."

"Me too," she said, and meant it down to the tips of her toes.

DAN

༄

"It smells like cookies in here!" Sandy yelled, bursting through the door with his school backpack dangling from one arm and his skates from the other.

"Boots off," Dan called. He was balancing a hot cookie sheet carefully with one oven-mitted hand and the other end resting on the tips of the metal clamps.

Exactly as much time later as it took to kick off two snow boots on the run, Sandy pounded into the kitchen. "Can I have a cookie? Can I have two?"

"There's a word missing from that sentence."

"Please," Sandy said, and underscored the point by curling his fists under his chin and looking as adorable as possible. With his brown curls and huge eyes, the results were both adorable and hilarious. Dan laughed and pointed him toward the tray on the counter, a plastic one with Santa on it that the family either used year-round or hadn't put away after Christmas; either way it had turned out to be a good cookie storage depot.

"Careful, the chips are still hot."

Sandy scooped up two. "Why did you make cookies?"

"Because I wanted cookies. And because we have guests coming over, Lissy and her brother." He laid the baking sheet in the sink and scruffed the kid's hair. "Do you want to show Lissy how to ride your pony when she gets here?"

"Lissy's a girl," Sandy declared through a mouthful. "Ow. Hot."

"Yes, and? Girls can ride horses too. Also, I told you it was hot."

"You smell weird," Sandy declared.

"Thanks, kid, that's what I needed to hear."

"Like ... perfumey," Sandy said, wrinkling his nose.

"It's called cologne, buddy. When you're old enough to date, you'll figure out why." Dan pointed to the book bag with his clamps. "Put that away and pick up your boots, would you? There's another cookie waiting if you get it done in the next five minutes."

Sandy pounded off, sounding just as loud in his sock feet as if he was still wearing boots.

"And don't wake up your sister!" Dan called after him.

A moment later, sock-clad footsteps that were carefully placed, and yet somehow loud, beat a tattoo up the stairs.

Dan busied himself scrubbing the cookie sheet and told himself that he was not at all stressing over Paula coming over. It wasn't going to be a terribly romantic date with several small children running in and out. He wasn't even entirely sure what had spurred him to bake cookies—

Feed mate. Mate might stay.

—right, okay, not that much of a mystery after all.

He had wanted to dress up for it, but had managed to stop himself from doing anything beyond putting on a clean black T-shirt that was also incidentally one of his tighter ones—he hoped she'd like that without making her feel like *she* should have dressed up—and shaving with extra attention to detail before dabbing a little cologne behind his ears.

What if she did dress up, though, and now she feels underdressed? he wondered. Maybe he should have a dress shirt handy just in case ...

This was ridiculous. What was it about Paula that turned him into a nervous teenager again?

Mate. Mate. Mate. It wasn't words from his bear exactly, just a sense of anticipation.

Right. That would be it.

The doorbell rang.

He ran a hand over his hair, second-guessed himself in twelve different ways in half a second, swooped to put away a dish towel, opened the oven to quickly check the pot roast, and then went to open the door.

Paula was standing on the front porch in her red-purple-green quilted coat, looking bright-eyed and pink-cheeked and impossibly beautiful. She was hand in hand with Lissy, who was wearing the googly-eyed frog hat.

"Hi," Paula began to say, just as Lissy chimed in over the top of her, "Where are the horses?"

Paula laughed. "One-track mind," she explained. "It was all she could talk about on the ride here."

"Hi," Dan said, slightly breathless. "Uh, come in. There are cookies."

Lissy was temporarily distracted from horses by the offer of cookies. "Boots!" Paula said, and Lissy kicked them off and ran into the kitchen with all her winter gear still on.

"Well, then," Paula said, laughing. "Lissy, honey! Two is your limit, okay?"

"Kay!" trailed back from the kitchen.

"Can I, uh—take your coat?" Dan asked.

She turned around and let him slip it off her shoulders. Under the coat she was wearing a white sweater with pink snowflakes. He couldn't help noticing how the hair curled on the nape of her neck, looking very touchable. It was pinned up loosely, exposing a stretch of neck that looked incredibly kissable, and before he could second-guess himself, he brushed his lips across that soft-looking skin. It was just as soft and nice as he thought it would be. She smelled amazing.

"Oh," Paula said, shivering all over.

"Should I not have? I—"

He was silenced by Paula turning around with the coat still half on. She put a hand around the back of his head and pulled him in for a solid kiss.

After a nearly endless moment of exploring each other's mouths, they broke apart. Her eyelashes had fluttered half shut. "Wow," she murmured, opening her eyes. "I could get used to that."

Dan took a breath. "So," he said. "Coat."

"Right. Coat." Laughing quietly, she relinquished it. "Though I'll just need to put it back on if we go out to the barn."

"Come in and have a cookie first, before your daughter eats them all." Belatedly it occurred to him that there was no one else with her. "No Austin?"

Paula smiled ruefully. "He's over at a friend's house. He tried to talk me into letting him stay home alone, and normally I think he'd be old enough just for the evening, but ..." She shrugged, her mouth twisting. "Not with everything going on."

Dan lowered his voice. "Do you feel safe there?" *Because I could stay over,* he wanted to say. Just the idea of her being in danger made his bear half crazy with the urge to protect her.

"I do, that's the weird part. I mean, when it's just me and the kids at home, I don't think we're in any danger, especially with all the security measures your friends have taken. But that's with me there. Austin's a good kid but he's only fifteen, you know?"

"Yeah, I get it." Cautiously he settled a hand in the small of her back. Her sweater was soft and fuzzy.

They went into the kitchen, where Lissy froze guiltily with a cookie in one hand and half of another one in her mouth.

"What number is that?" Paula asked. "Ooh, chocolate chip."

"Two," Lissy said, wide-eyed.

"Uh-huh."

"Horses now?" Lissy asked indistinctly.

"Horses it is," Dan said. "Just let me get the girls."

Just let me get the girls turned out to be an operation roughly equivalent in complexity to storming Normandy. Mina had to be rousted from watching her gazillionth episode of *Blues Clues*, while a drowsy Lulu was tucked into a front carrier. Boots were found, mittens located and lost again. In the five minutes since Dan had last seen him, Sandy had gotten into a video game and was unenthusiastic about being pried out of it to go visit a horse he could visit anytime.

Eventually they managed to get the entire herd roused, be-coated, de-gamed, and headed out to the barn with varying degrees of enthusiasm.

"Derek and Gaby's place is huge," Paula said, looking around at the wide sweep of snow-covered yard. In addition to the barn, there were a variety of outbuildings and a mother-in-law cabin that was Gaby's mom's domain when she was in town; the rest of the family treated it with reverence and left it alone.

"Yeah, it takes some getting used to."

There was a covered chicken run beside the barn, with chickens that set up a clamor at the arrival of people who might have chicken feed. Dan dispatched the older kids to scatter some grain in the chicken pen while he opened the horse's stall and led her out into the trampled snow of the corral, maneuvering carefully with Lulu in the front carrier and trying to look like he knew what he was doing.

The Rugers' horse was a black-and-white spotted pony, too small for an adult to comfortably ride, but sized just right for a child who wasn't too intimidated by large animals. Dan had no idea how to saddle her, but Sandy did, and went through the process under adult supervision, with Dan to do the one part Sandy was still too small to do—lifting the saddle onto the horse's back.

"What a pretty horse," Paula said, petting the pony's velvety nose. The pony lipped at Paula's hands, clearly expecting treats. "What's his name?"

"Her. Apparently the previous owners named her Merlot for some reason," Dan said. "Derek and Gaby and the kids call her Silver."

"Straightforward. A classic. I like it."

"When I have a pony," Lissy declared, "I'm going to name her Princess Ariel Margaret Butterball, but she will be called Bill for short, like the pony in *Lord of the Rings*."

"Notice the 'when' and not if," Paula said.

It was decreed that the pony was not to leave the corral, so the kids took turns riding her around the trampled yard inside the fence.

"Where's Mina?" Paula asked abruptly.

"She's right—" Dan began.

She wasn't.

"Damn it," he muttered. The kids were used to the barn and it was unlikely she could get into too much trouble here, but there were still a lot of things he wouldn't want a three-year-old investigating on their own. Heavy equipment. Pitchforks. His stomach tightened into a ball of nervous tension. "Mina!"

He went into the barn, with Paula behind him. It was an

old horse barn, semi-restored by Derek and Gaby, but there was still junk in the corners, and a million places for a small girl to hide.

The question resolved itself almost instantly, though, when he heard rustling from up in the hayloft.

"Is she up there?" Paula asked, looking up. "Is she allowed in there?"

"No," Dan said grimly. He bent down and picked up a small coat from the bottom of the ladder. There was a little pink dress draped a couple of rungs up. It looked like it had been torn down the back. He swiped it up before Paula could see it.

Oh, he thought, and then *Oh no.*

Mina had shifted for the first time.

Derek and Gaby were going to be upset they'd missed it. A cub's first shift was a big milestone, like their first step or their first word.

More worryingly, he did not want Paula finding out about shifters by seeing the Rugers' daughter as a bear cub.

Paula had seen the dress wadded up in his hand. She gave a little laugh.

"So she's naked up there? Lissy had a phase like that too. It's cold out here for it." She reached for the ladder.

"I'll get her," Dan said quickly. "Here." He began unstrapping the baby carrier, working awkwardly. Halfway through he realized he had to take his coat off; he ended up tangled in straps and the coat. "Take the baby for a minute."

"There's no need," Paula said, but she held his coat while he finished undoing the straps.

"I don't want her to spook and run off and maybe fall," he came up with. Falling out of the loft probably wouldn't hurt her at all if she was still a bear cub, but that was the one thing Paula couldn't see—not yet. Not until he managed to explain properly.

Paula took the baby carrier and passed him his coat back. "Okay, but let me know if you need help."

"Will do," he promised, and set foot on the ladder. "Mina, honey? It's Dan. I'm coming up."

There was a little noise from above, a sort of yapping grunt.

"Is she coughing?" Paula asked from below.

"Maybe she's allergic to hay." Dan poked his head over the top of the ladder. "Mina? C'mon out, kid. It's just Dan."

It was dim in the loft, and very chilly, colder than the relatively warm barn below. The end of the loft was open and light came in, illuminating scattered piles of hay in the cold gray winter daylight.

Dan hoisted himself over the edge onto the loft floor.

"Did you find her?" Paula called from below, and then there was a creak. He looked down. She was on the ladder.

"Stay down there!" Dan called hastily. "It might—uh—I don't know if it's safe for two adults up here. The barn is kind of old."

"Oh," Paula said. "Yes, of course."

Now that he'd said it, he wondered how true it was. He hadn't actually been up here himself yet. When he took a step forward, the floor creaked. It was no problem at all for a kid; he knew Sandy went up here sometimes. But Dan was a big guy.

He got down on his knees to spread out the weight a little more, and also bring himself closer to Mina's level.

"Hey, Mina? Honey? Come on out. It's Dan. Nobody's mad at you."

There was more rustling in the hay, and then suddenly a small ball of fluff, about the size of a beagle, shot out of the hay and ran straight into his arms.

"Hi, honey," Dan murmured. She was a medium-brown grizzly cub with blonde tips on her fur, and just about the cutest thing he'd ever seen, like a teddy bear come to life. She snuggled down in his arms, making happy little grunting noises.

"Did you find her?" Paula called up the ladder.

"Yeah, I'm just—uh—getting her calmed down. Stay downstairs!" he added.

A first shift could be very disorienting. Mina seemed content now, nestled in his arms. She also showed no signs of shifting back.

"Come on, honey," he murmured into her fur. She had a sweet smell, somewhere between baby and puppy. "Time to be a little girl again. Can you do that?"

Mina licked his face.

"Think about your sparkle ponies. You want Sparkle Magic, right? You can't pick up Sparkle Magic with paws instead of hands." Come to think of it, where *was* Sparkle Magic? She had been carrying the toy around the barn in her fist, the same way she carried it everywhere.

Mina made a little woofing sound and wriggled out of his arms. She scrambled into the hay.

"Mina—no—now is not a good time for hide and seek, sweetheart," he whispered as loudly as he dared.

Mina popped up out of the hay with bits of hay and straw in her fur, and Sparkle Magic Pony clenched between her teeth.

"Ah," he murmured. She'd lost all her clothes, but kept the pony. Of course she had. "Want to show me the pony? Here, let's take a look."

Mina growled softly and pulled back when he put a cautious hand on the toy.

"Right. Now you want to play tug of war."

"Dan?" Paula called up the ladder. "Do you need help?"

"Everything's fine!" he yelled back down. Dropping his voice, he went back to trying to coax Mina back to her little-girl shape. "Come on, sweetie. Let's go home and have a cookie."

Mina's round, furry ears pricked up.

"Yeah, that's right. Cookie. But bears can't have cookies. Only little girls can have cookies."

Mina made a grunting noise, and abruptly there was a small, naked girl with a toy pony in her mouth.

"Aha. There you are." He took off his coat and wrapped her in it.

Turning back to the ladder, he realized he had a problem. He wasn't confident of his ability to climb back down with Mina in his good arm and only the clamps to hold onto the ladder.

Ideally, he'd love to get Mina back to the house without involving Paula at all. He was not at all sure that she wasn't going to shift back to a bear cub. But trying to climb down the ladder with her was too risky. Anyway, he couldn't just abandon Paula.

He leaned over and saw Paula's face looking up at him, a pale oval, her eyes anxious.

"It's okay," he said. "I got her. I could use a hand getting her down, though."

"Is that a joke? Because it's a terrible joke."

She was already climbing up, though, navigating carefully with the sleeping baby on her chest.

"It wasn't supposed to be. On the other hand, if you want hand jokes, I have *so* many. All taste levels. Okay, mostly bad taste."

"Like what?" Paula asked. She reached the top of the ladder and held out an arm.

"That's hard to say, actually. I'm stumped."

It took her a minute, then her eyes grew round. "Okay, you're right, that's terrible. That's the *worst*."

"Told you," Dan said, grinning. He gently handed off Mina, with a slight twinge of worry as she left his arms.

She didn't look like she was about to shift back to a bear cub, though. In fact, she seemed to be falling asleep. Shifting could really take it out of you, especially for someone who wasn't used to it. She was going to be starving later.

"Hi, honey," Paula said, settling Mina against her shoulder. Dan watched her carefully—she was on a ladder with a baby on her front and a toddler in her arm, not the most stable condition, but she seemed to be handling it well enough.

Seeing his expression, she grinned.

"I know," she said. "I don't blame you, but don't forget, I'm used to carrying giant stacks of plates around the diner without dropping one. I have mad waitress skills."

With that, she began to carefully descend the ladder. She was right, she didn't even wobble, and stepped off onto the barn floor with a little flourish.

Dan cheered and climbed down the ladder after her.

"I would say that I can't believe she got her clothes off and climbed all the way up there in just the little time we weren't watching her," Paula said. She handed Mina back to him once he was on the ground. "But then I remember one time that I left Austin alone in the bathroom for *I swear* less than half a minute while I went to answer the door, and he emptied an entire can of baby powder all over himself. I came back to find something that looked like a powdered donut with two eyes looking at me."

Mina started to fuss and flail. She was slippery, tucked up against his shoulder naked in his coat. "Parkle," she complained indistinctly.

"Where'd her toy go?" Dan said. "She had it when we got on the ladder. It's a toy pony with wings, she carries it everywhere—"

"Here." Paula held up Sparkle Magic Pony by one foot.

"Has she been teething on this thing? It looks like it was mauled by a bear."

Dan decided not to answer that. He retrieved the pony and tucked it into the coat with Mina, who grabbed onto it with both hands.

"Let's go collect the cowboys out there and get back to the house. I have a pot roast in the oven."

"I didn't expect you to cook dinner," Paula protested. "Takeout pizza would be fine."

"Takeout pizza when I could feed you my world-famous pot roast?"

"Well, now you've raised my expectations." She settled in comfortably at his side as they went back out into the cold. "Weren't you going to tell me more bad jokes?"

"What, you expect me to come up with them single-handedly?" Dan said.

"I take it back. Please stop."

But she was laughing. And he knew right then that he would do anything to make her laugh like that again.

PAULA

DAN'S POT roast was amazing, meltingly tender and flavorful, nestled in heaps of potatoes and carrots. They all stuffed themselves, although Mina's ability to pack it away was particularly amazing. Kids that age could really eat sometimes, but Paula had never seen a child Mina's size stuff in that much food at one sitting. With Lissy at that age, she recalled, the problem had been getting her to eat anything other than her three favorite foods: fish sticks, olives, and Kraft boxed mac-and-cheese.

"She must be going through a growth spurt," Paula said, laughing, as Dan refilled her plate for a third time.

"You don't know the half of it," Dan muttered.

"Seriously, this is amazing." Paula grinned. "You cook, you clean, you're great with kids—I bet you do dishes too."

"It's one of my jobs, yeah."

"I didn't think the perfect man existed, but I've changed my mind. Pretty sure I've found him."

Dan gave her a look like he wasn't sure if she was teasing or not.

In all honesty Paula wasn't sure either. He *seemed* absolutely perfect, like her ideal man come to life. But then, she'd thought Terry seemed perfect at one point too.

Did you, though? a small voice in the back of her head asked. She had been in love with Terry, swept away by the rush of new infatuation and the excitement of college life after her small-town childhood. And look how that had turned out.

Maybe she just couldn't trust her own instincts with men.

"Here," she said, getting up from the table. "You cooked, so I'll clear away."

Dan hesitated, but nodded as she started picking up plates. "I'll go put this one down for a nap," he said, gathering Mina out of her high chair. She was nodding over the table.

"If you put her down now, she'll be up half the night," Paula warned. "Voice of experience here."

"That's all right." He smiled at her. "Small price to pay for a little alone time."

"Ewww," Sandy and Lissy said in perfect sync, and then looked at each other across the table.

"Come on, kids," Paula said. "Give me a hand with the dishes."

The kids washed dishes with her, and then ran off to the living room to play video games. When Dan came back downstairs, it was just Paula in the kitchen.

"Where'd the rest of the herd go?" he asked.

"They're playing something called Super Star Speeder, or at least I think that's what he said. I didn't think it would be a problem." She held out a Tupperware container of leftovers. "Where should this go? There's not much room in the fridge."

"I'll find a space." He went down to one knee and started rearranging things.

It was quiet and pleasant, Paula wiping down the counters with a sponge and dish towel, Dan putting things away. They worked together perfectly in sync, Paula handing him items, Dan stowing them in the Rugers' overloaded cabinets and stuffed fridge. From the living room came the kids' yells of glee as they scored points in the game, punctuated occasionally by Dan telling them to keep it down so they didn't wake the babies.

It just all felt so *domestic*.

She hadn't felt this way in a long time.

"You okay?" Dan asked quietly.

She hadn't realized it showed on her face. "Yeah, I was just thinking about ..."

She was thinking about the last time she'd felt like this, in her little apartment in the city with Terry and baby Austin, back before it all fell apart. But it seemed terribly rude to talk about her ex on what was basically a date.

"Thinking about?" Dan prompted after a moment. "You don't have to talk about it, but you can if you want to."

Paula grimaced. "If you really want to know, I was thinking about my ex. But not like *that*," she added hastily. "It's just that it's been a really long time since I was in a kitchen with a man—I mean, other than my cook at the diner, but that's obviously different. Sorry. I didn't mean to bring it up."

Dan laid a hand on her arm, very gently. She realized she was twisting the dish towel and made herself put it down.

"Paula," he said, his voice just as gentle as the touch. "You don't have to pretend that you were never in a relationship before. He was part of your life. He gave you two beautiful children." He took a breath. "I'm not going to hide that I wish I could bash his face in for hurting you, but I don't want you to feel like you have to walk on eggshells around me. I'm not jealous of a man who left you years ago." He smiled a little. "Well, not *that* jealous. I mostly just wish I'd had that time with you instead."

Paula was able to muster a smile herself. "Me too. But it

was more that I left him. He—do you really want to talk about this?"

"Only if you do. But there's no part of your life that I want you to have to hide," he said sincerely. "If you want to talk, I'll listen, and I won't judge you. What happened?"

Paula blew out a breath and turned away. It was easier if she wasn't looking at him. Outside the windows it was getting dark. She used the window like a mirror and started twisting up her hair, which was starting to slip out of the messy bun she'd put it up in before leaving the house.

"We started dating in college," she said. "I was fresh from Autumn Grove, off to see the world. I didn't know what I wanted to do with myself yet, so I was just getting a general arts degree—that I never finished, by the way. I quit when Austin came along."

She pulled out some pins and held them in her mouth while she pinned up the rest of it, talking around them. Dan was a blur behind her in the window's reflection, but she could feel his body heat. He was like a wall at her back, offering warm and nonjudgmental support.

"Terry was a business major. He was going into sales. Everything was so ... *bright*," she said bitterly, around the pins. "So hopeful. So exciting. We didn't have any money, but we shared a one-room apartment and lived on ramen and big dreams. When he graduated, he went to work for a major firm, and then went into business for himself. I worked with him, took night classes in accounting and did the office books. We still had to scrape to make ends meet, but it was idyllic. We didn't have much, but we had each other, and then baby Austin, and then Lissy. And yet ..."

She frowned, looking at herself in the window's crude mirror as she held her twisted-together ponytail with one hand and slipped in the pins with the other.

"There was always *something*," she said slowly. "Things

between us that I didn't understand. We had fights. I always got the impression he was keeping things from me. Holding something back, even when things were good."

"What was it?" Dan asked quietly.

Paula shook her head. She spat a pin into her hand and stabbed it into her bun.

"I don't *know*. I never did find out. That's the worst part, you know? I kept doubting myself and wondering if I was making it all up. But I wasn't wrong. He was weirdly evasive about his past, never took me to meet his parents. He said he was an orphan, but then sometimes he'd slip up and say something that made me think his parents might still be alive. There were late nights he couldn't account for, strange debits on our books. I went through all the possibilities from the likely to the completely insane, everything from a gambling addiction or mob debt, to witness protection, to Terry having a whole family hidden away somewhere, like you read about sometimes."

"What happened?"

Paula looked away from her face in the window, unable even to meet her own gaze, and instead looked down at her hands, clutched on the counter with a stray pin gripped in one of them.

"I finally confronted him, after he disappeared for two days on what he told me was a business trip. Except it wasn't. None of it checked out. I begged him to tell me where he'd been and what he was hiding from me. And he—he finally broke a little. He stopped denying it and just told me he couldn't. And when I pushed him to at least tell me why, he changed it to telling me he *wouldn't*." Her mouth twisted. "And that was it. We separated a week later. I couldn't keep working with him at the business, not even knowing what he was using it for when it could be a mob front for all I knew.

"I didn't have any work references besides Terry and my

parents. I was working two minimum-wage jobs to try to pay rent on an apartment for me and the kids. Lissy was just a baby and Austin was only a few years older. There was no way I could give them a good life on what I could afford, even with child support from Terry. I did the only thing I could do, and moved back home to work at the diner."

She sniffed, wiping her hand across her eyes, and then was startled by the feeling of Dan's arms closing around her. One was fully flesh and blood, the other plastic from halfway above the elbow, but they already felt like a comfortable haven that she never wanted to leave.

"Paula," Dan said into her hair. "You *have* to know—not a single part of that is your fault, right?"

"But there were so many signs," she said helplessly into his chest. "I should have seen it. I can't believe I didn't. It was like a whole checklist of warning signs that I never noticed because I—because I—"

"Because you believed that your husband, the man you loved, the man you promised to honor and cherish, would never lie to you about anything important? Paula, that doesn't make you weak or gullible. It makes you a good person who was keeping up your end of the bargain that *he* broke."

She gave a shuddering sob. No one had ever put it like that before. Her family had welcomed her back, but there had still been an implied sense of judgment that she had made mistakes.

But they weren't MY mistakes, she thought, pressing her face into Dan's chest. Somehow it was just easy to believe him; all her attempts to beat up on herself fell apart against the rock of his belief in her. Because he was right, wasn't he? She had treated Terry as if he was as responsible and loving and dependable as a good husband should be. She didn't want to nag him or question the places he went or the things he spent money on. It had all come back to bite her in the end, but—

But if I had it to do all over again, would I do it differently?

Would she be suspicious of her husband's every purchase, check up on him, treat him like a pathological liar?

No, she thought, and the realization was like a huge weight lifting off her. *No, I'd do it all just the same. Well, maybe I'd tell college-age me not to marry the jerk—*

But no, even that would have meant Austin and Lissy would never have been born, and she wouldn't want that for anything in the world.

I didn't do anything wrong. I'm not the one who fucked up. He did. And I'm not going to spend the rest of my life paying for his mistakes.

She became aware that Dan was slowly and gently petting her hair. Her recently redone messy bun was probably getting wrecked again, but right now, that felt like the least important thing in the world.

Finally she drew back and wiped her eyes. "Thank you," she said in a small voice.

"Everybody needs a shoulder to cry on now and then." He leaned down a little, so that he could look her directly in the eyes; he really was tall. "Are you okay?"

Paula nodded. Then, steadier, she said, "I haven't had a decent shoulder to cry on in a long time. You have a good one."

She patted his shoulder, meaning it in a playful way, but somehow her thumb lingered around his collarbone, brushing across the soft skin of his neck. And it wasn't at all playful.

His gaze into her eyes turned heated. When he leaned forward, she was already stretching up eagerly to meet his lips with hers.

She had never experienced kisses like Dan's. It wasn't that

he was somehow fantastically skilled at it; it was that his kisses lit her up like a bonfire. Every time their lips closed together, the world went away. There was nothing else on earth but Dan's soft lips moving on hers, his tongue teasing against her lips, his hand in her hair and her arms around his waist.

When they finally broke apart, he said breathlessly, "Is it just me or is that really nice?"

"I'm not sure if *nice* is the word I'd use," she said, running her hands lightly over his well-muscled back. God, he felt good.

"What word would you use?" he murmured, looking down into her eyes.

"Fantastic. Wonderful. Amazing. Toe-curling."

"Are they curled?" he asked teasingly, looking down at her sock feet. Since they'd all left their boots by the door, the whole family was sock-footed, her pink and black socks next to Dan's gray ones.

"Yep, see?" She curled her toes.

Dan laughed, and her whole body thrilled to the sound of it. When they were pressed this close, she could feel it vibrating through him.

"You know," he said, "unless you want to stand in the kitchen all evening, we could go somewhere a little less ..."

"Kitcheny?"

"Yeah. That." He looked over his shoulder at a burst of childish laughter from the living room. "Unfortunately it looks like the living room couch is claimed, and I don't know how easy it's going to be to peel them off the game so we can watch a movie."

"It's a big house." She hooked her fingers through his belt loops. "There must be somewhere else we could go."

Dan grinned. "Ms. DeWitt, do you want to come back and see my room?"

Paula giggled. "I don't know, are you allowed to have girls in your room?"

Dan winked at her. "I won't tell if you won't."

They peeked in on the kids in the living room, who seemed thoroughly engrossed in their game, and then went quietly behind the stairs to the guest bedroom.

"It's not very big," Dan said, sounding embarrassed, as he opened the door.

It wasn't, but it was also somehow very him, even if it was obviously a room in someone else's house, full of someone else's things. It was very tidy, the bed made with military precision—which made sense, she supposed—and covered in a bright quilt. The walls were lined with bookshelves full of fat, tempting-looking paperbacks and discount-bin hardcovers, books that wanted to be taken down and read. There was a small chest-of-drawers and a cedar chest, which took up enough of the floor space that they had to make their way carefully around the furniture to the bed, which was the only place to sit.

"This is cozy," Paula said. She planted her hands on the quilt, leaned her shoulder against Dan's, and tried not to think about how much *more* cozy it would be if they were both underneath the quilt ... naked ... but no, not with the kids right out in the living room. They had left the door open, as if to complete the illusion of innocent teenage dating.

"Did you ever bring boys back to your room?" Dan asked. He was clearly on the exact same wavelength; it was getting to be a habit.

"Of course I did. Door open and a three-foot distance at all times, at least according to my dad's rules." She grinned. "We broke *that* all the time, of course. But I never went past first base like that."

"I never understood all of that anyway. First, second, third base, what's all of that mean anyway?"

Paula feigned shock. "A sports metaphor you don't understand? Aren't they going to take your guy license away?"

Dan laughed. "I understand baseball just fine. Mixing baseball with sex is just weird."

He rolled his shoulder, grimacing. Paula, who had been slowly oozing back on the bed, sat up again.

"Do you need to take it off?" she asked, looking at the straps over his shoulder. It did look uncomfortable to wear all day.

Dan hesitated. "I usually take it off at the end of the day."

"You can take it off around me. I don't mind. In fact ..." She gave him a warm smile, as encouraging as she knew how. "If you wouldn't mind me seeing, I would be interested in knowing how it goes on and off. But only if you don't mind."

"I don't mind," he said quietly.

He was only wearing a T-shirt, so the straps were exposed. Taking it off was simple and fast. He raised his arm and, with his other hand, pulled the entire thing off over his head, straps and arm and all, just like taking off a T-shirt. It slipped easily off the end of his stump, leaving the stump covered in a white cotton tube that resembled a sock.

"Whoa," Paula said, impressed. "I thought it would be a lot more complicated."

"Nah. Like I said, this is a really simple device. It's what I like about it." He hesitated again, but then she saw his face grow firmly resolved. He rolled down the socklike thing and slipped it off, exposing the soft, scar-laced end of the stump.

"What's that for?" Paula asked. "Oh, it's to cushion it."

"Yeah. Keeps it from chafing." He showed it to her, a plain white cotton tube. "They're called socks."

"I was just thinking that it looked like one."

"It's not exactly a sock like you'd put on your foot. But if you needed to, you could probably use one. It's pretty similar."

"And that's it?"

"That's it."

He leaned over to lay the arm on top of the cedar chest, and draped the sock over the side.

Paula lifted a hand. "Do you mind if I ..."

She didn't finish, but he clearly knew what she was asking, and held out the stump.

It wasn't unpleasant or even strange. His arm ended halfway between the elbow and shoulder. There was some scarring around the end, but when Paula laid a hand on the skin just above it, she found that it was smooth and normal. His shoulder on that side wasn't any less muscular than the other, although his biceps was a little less impressive.

She ran her hand up his arm, slipping it under the sleeve of his T-shirt, reveling in the feeling of his skin against hers. Then she slid her hand down the arm, hesitating as she approached the scarred area. "Does it hurt?"

"Not really." He was watching her hand, his head turned to the side to follow it with his gaze. "I rub lotion on it all the time. It's a little sensitive, but that's not a bad thing."

She carefully ran her hand over the end. It was actually very soft. The skin puckered slightly when the muscles of his arm flexed.

"Do you mind ..." She hesitated, feeling her way around the question she wanted to ask. "I was wondering—"

"What happened to me?"

Paula nodded. "Only if you don't mind talking about it. I don't want to push you into anything."

"You told me about your ex. I could tell that was hard for you." He turned to meet her eyes, his gaze steady and serious. "And honestly, this isn't actually *that* bad for me to talk about. I kinda got used to it, talking to shrinks at the VA."

"It happened in the military?"

He nodded. "On deployment. It's really not that much of a story. I mean, it's not a huge exciting thing, nothing like you might be thinking. It wasn't in combat. It was more of a dumb accident."

"You really don't need to tell me unless you want to."

"I don't mind," he said gently. He reached around and brushed a curl out of her eyes. "It was a vehicle crash. Just an ordinary thing, like might have happened on a wet road here in the States. The vehicle in front of me in the convoy had to stop suddenly, and I rammed a Humvee up his ass—er, rear-ended him, that is. It shouldn't have done more than shake me up, but the road was really bad, and when the guy behind me hit me too, the Humvee ran its two side tires up on a pile of rubble and flipped. I was trapped in the wreckage."

His voice had gone tight. She smoothed a hand over his shoulder and chest, ran it up the back of his neck.

"Was anyone else hurt?" she asked quietly.

"Nah, just me. Some bruises for the other guys, that's all. But my arm was crushed. It took them hours to cut me out, and then it was straight to the hospital, and ..." He drew a shaky breath. "Yeah. So there's my big damn hero combat story."

Paula kissed the corner of his mouth lightly. She could tell he was underplaying it, that the story was more painful for him than he wanted to talk about. But she was honored that he felt comfortable enough to tell her.

"You could tell people that you were hurt saving a bunch of kids," she said. "No, orphans. And kittens. Orphans with kittens."

Dan laughed quietly. There was a hitch in the middle of it, but it sounded sincere.

She snuggled closer to him. "No, seriously, I think you were brave. Knowing you, I bet you did everything you could to avoid that accident and make sure no one else got hurt. Sometimes things like that just happen to people."

Dan didn't answer immediately, but she could feel him playing with her hair, stroking his hand through the curls. After a moment he said, "You know, a lot more vets are wounded like that than in actual combat. Just dumb accidents. The kind of thing that you get when you have a whole lot of people running around on no sleep, especially when half of them are 19-year-old kids."

"How old were you then?" she asked.

"Early thirties. Practically a geezer by military standards. I was a supply specialist."

"That sounds important."

"Well, if you ask anyone in my department, it's obviously the most important job you can have. After all, how far is anyone going to get without food, boots, or functional vehicles?"

"Right?"

Dan laughed, and for a while they just lay on the bed, cuddled and kissed, and swapped stories. He told her tall tales about the military that she genuinely couldn't tell if he was making up or at least exaggerating for effect, although he swore up and down they were true, like the guy who used to go out every time he could get off post to prospect for precious gemstones, and ended up filling his entire shipping allowance back to the States with what basically amounted to worthless gravel. ("Though he claimed it was uncut diamonds," Dan said.)

She talked about the diner, about serially nonpaying customers and the old guys who came in every Saturday morning and played checkers for hours at a corner table.

His presence was intoxicating, but the open door acted as a restraining influence. (*Damn it,* she thought, *Dad was right.*) They could keep track of the kids just by listening to the noise from the living room. She would have loved to rip his clothes off; just inhaling the scent of his skin made her dizzy. But there was also something special about taking it slow, learning about each other's lives as they learned each other's bodies. Between stories, they kissed, slow languid necking that sent her right back to those heady teenage days, when the world of dating was brand new and every gentle touch felt like a revelation.

It was a startling interruption when her phone buzzed. She sat up and checked it, and was astonished to see what time it was. Hours had passed as if they were nothing.

"Important?" Dan asked.

"It's Mrs. Hogan—Austin's friend's mom. She just texted to let me know that she dropped him off at my house." She took a deep breath and mustered a smile as she typed out a quick reply, then looked up. "I guess that this is my signal to head out for the evening. I'd be more comfortable if I don't leave him there alone too long."

Dan nodded. "I get it. Believe me. I could put the kids in the car and come along, if you want me to do a sweep of the neighborhood. I'm pretty sure Ben's on patrol out there later tonight."

"I don't think it'll be necessary. We'll be okay."

"Well, call then," he said. "To let me know you got home okay."

"I will," she said, deeply touched.

They kissed again, slow and lingering, until she knew she had to get on the road or she was never going to leave. She was going to be drawn down into his narrow bed, and she'd undo his jeans and he'd undo her bra and ... yeah. Right. On task, brain.

"I'd better get going," she murmured against his lips.

"Yeah," he said.

Neither of them moved. Then Paula grinned against his

mouth, kissed him one more time, and rolled off the bed. She took a minute to make sure her sweater was straight and her hair was pulled back.

"What do I look like?" she asked.

"Amazing."

"I *mean*, do I look like I just spent hours necking with a guy?"

Dan laughed. He got up and carefully tweaked a curl behind her ear. "There. Perfectly respectable." He kissed the tip of her nose.

She looked up at him, at his laughing eyes and the quick flash of teeth as he grinned, and it hit her all at once with a force that made her knees wobble: *I am falling in love with this man.*

"You okay?" he asked, catching her elbow.

"Yes," she said faintly, and then a little more strongly, "Yeah, just ... a head rush." Though not from standing up. "Come on, let's go roll my rugrat into her winter gear."

Prying Lissy off the couch and away from the video game was difficult. Paula managed to get her up and moving by bribing her with a cookie, and the promise of another one once they were in the car. As soon as she was bundled into her winter gear, Lissy started yawning, so Paula suspected that they had timed it well.

"I'm glad they get along," she said, wrapped up in Dan's arms for a lingering goodbye while the car warmed up and Lissy sprawled on the floor in her unzipped coat and complained about being too hot. "They're acting almost like siblings, aren't they?"

"We had a little awkwardness in the beginning about sharing his horse with a *girl*, but he seemed to get over it as soon as they actually got on the same page."

"Oh no," Paula said, between kisses. "Not a girl. How awful."

"Mommmm," Lissy moaned from the floor.

"I guess we need to get on the road," she said reluctantly, and hauled up her tragic, drooping bundle of videogame-deprived daughter.

"Call me," Dan said. He pecked her cheek and then, to her surprise and delight, kissed the top of Lissy's head.

"Say thank you to Dan for a nice evening," Paula told Lissy. "And for the cookies."

"Thank you," Lissy mumbled, dangling out of Paula's arms as if all her bones had turned to Jello.

"Do you really want to be carried to the car?"

"Yes," Lissy said, and spoiled the effect by giggling. She had oozed down until her knees were on the floor.

"You're much too heavy. Come on, honey, this isn't funny. You need to walk."

"I'll carry her," Dan said, and Lissy squealed in delight as he picked her up and slung her over his shoulder.

"Put me down, no, I'm too big!"

"Not for me," Dan said cheerfully. He winked at Paula. "Open the door, would you?"

Paula laughed and opened it.

It wasn't exactly the romantic walk to the car that she might have liked, not with a giggling, shrieking little girl slung across Dan's shoulder. But somehow it seemed appropriate to end the evening like this. Her life couldn't be separated from her children's lives, and one of the things she loved in Dan was that he didn't want to try. He accepted the complete package, kids and divorce and all.

Lissy shrieked louder and clung as Dan threatened to drop her in the snow, but when he set her down, she buckled herself into the backseat with a surprising amount of agreeableness.

Dan leaned over to give Paula one last goodnight kiss. It

felt like they were banking kisses to be saved for the next few hours.

"See you," she whispered against his cheek as he hugged her.

"See you too," he whispered into her hair.

And then she was pulling out of the driveway in the snow, looking back to see him standing in the cold, bare-armed with just his T-shirt on, waving. She rolled down the window to wave back, ignoring Lissy's squawk from the backseat.

"Okay, okay, don't be a fragile flower. I'm rolling it up now."

"Can I have my cookie now?" Lissy asked, and Paula passed it into the back.

"So did you have fun playing with Sandy?"

"He has *so many games*," Lissy said rapturously. "He has Ponymaker 12 with all the special patches and things. We made a pony with sixteen legs. And he has Truck Racer Evolution and we made a giant centipede truck that was actually a lot of little trucks all jammed together and it turns out that you can actually run them up the side of a building if they're long enough—"

Paula went on making listening noises as she was regaled with the greatest hits of the night's gaming session all the way back to town. The house was mostly dark, with a light in the living room and another in the window of Austin's room.

We're back, she texted Austin from the garage as she rousted Lissy out of the car, along with the Tupperware container of cookies that Dan had given her for the road. She was pleased to see that Austin had remembered to make sure all the doors were locked, and let herself into the house quietly.

"Austin?" she called.

No answer. He was probably upstairs. Still, while Lissy fussily peeled out of her outside gear in the entryway, Paula took a quick walk through the downstairs, turning on lights. Everything was fine, of course, and she turned them all off again and texted Dan to let him know she was home. *Call you after Lissy's in bed,* she texted. It was ridiculous, they'd just talked for hours, but already she couldn't wait to hear his voice again.

Mina just woke up, so I'll be distracted for a while anyway, he texted back. *Call anytime.*

Lissy had reached the cranky stage of tiredness and adrenaline crash after the games. Paula herded her upstairs and deposited her in the bathroom for teeth-brushing.

"You go change into your pajamas when you're done, and I'll tuck you in soon, okay? I'm going to check on your brother."

The door of Austin's room was firmly closed, with a stripe of light showing underneath. So he was still up. Paula tapped on the door, at first quietly, then more firmly.

"Austin?" she called through the door. "Honey, it's Mom. I just want to say good night."

There was no answer. He must have his headphones in, or maybe he'd fallen asleep with the light on. She knocked again.

She really didn't like invading his privacy. And Austin, of course, being a teenager, had become increasingly defensive of his mother entering his personal space. She totally got it.

But this was important.

"Austin? Hon? I'm coming in."

She cracked the door open and took a quick peek. There was no yell of "Mom, *please!*" In fact, there was no visible sign of Austin at all. Relieved that she wasn't about to walk in on him doing anything that would cause a teenager terminal embarrassment, she opened the door the rest of the way.

Austin wasn't in the room.

"Austin?" she said, startled.

The room was bathed in warm light from the bedside lamp. There were some clothes scattered on the bed and the typical explosion of books and papers on his desk. And not a single sign of Austin at all.

She had a moment's startled thought that he was hiding in the closet for some reason, and even knowing it was stupid, she crossed the room in two quick steps to yank it open. No Austin. Not that she had actually thought he'd be there.

"Austin?" she said again, foolishly, turning in place. There was nowhere else he could be.

Maybe she'd missed seeing him downstairs?

Maybe she had misunderstood the text from Mrs. Hogan, and he was staying with his friend overnight?

She scrambled for plausible explanations, even as she felt panic clawing its way through her chest.

Stumbling to the bed, she sank down while taking out her phone to send a text. Something in the mess crinkled under her.

Paula twisted around and pulled it out. It was a sheet of paper from one of his school notebooks.

Dear Mom,
I'm sorry. I have to find Dad. It's important.
Please don't worry about me.
Love, Austin.

DAN

Dan was halfway down the stairs from giving Mina a late-night drink of water when the urgency of Paula's fear hit him like a hammer blow. He staggered and clutched at the railing.

It was the second time he had felt this; the other time, of course, was when she had found the destroyed kitchen, waking him out of a sound sleep.

Mate needs us!

Mate needed them, but he couldn't leave the kids alone. His phone was downstairs on the table. He made it in a series of giant strides, taking three steps at a time, and was picking it up to call her when the phone vibrated and Paula's name came up on the screen.

She was already talking when he answered.

"Dan." Her voice was breathless. "Austin's gone."

"Gone how?" He kept his voice steady. He needed to be a wall of strength for her now. "What happened?"

"He's run away," she said, with a hitch in the middle of the sentence.

Dan felt a little inward rush of relief. It wasn't *good*, but it wasn't a kidnapping or a home invasion or any of the other dire scenarios that had run through his head when her emotional turmoil had hit him through the mate bond.

"When did he leave? How long has he been gone?"

"I don't know." She swallowed. "No, wait. It can't be that long, because he was at his friend's house most of the evening. It's got to be sometime after Mrs. Hogan dropped him off. But I don't know where he went from there. I found a note on his bed saying he'd left to find his father. I've tried his phone a hundred times, but either he's not answering or it's turned off or—"

"Okay, this is actually good," Dan told her. Dimly he was aware of the door opening, of quiet talk and giggling as Derek and Gaby trooped in, trying to be stealthy to avoid waking the kids. "We might not know where he is now, but we know where he's going, and we know he hasn't had time to get far."

"Except we *don't*," she burst out miserably. "Because I don't know where his father is either!"

"So where does he think his father is? Where would he go?"

Paula swallowed. "The bus station," she said. "He might go there first. Oh my gosh, he might still be there. It's up on the highway—"

"I know where it is." It seemed like a hundred years ago when he had stepped off the bus there, not knowing what the town held for him, knowing only that there was no future in what he left behind. "Derek and Gaby just got home. I can drive up and look."

"Would you?" She sounded near tears. "I could get Lissy into the car, but she's in bed and I don't want to wake her up and panic her."

"Don't worry about it," Dan told her. "I've got this. If he's not there, I'll get Derek and Ben on it. We'll find him."

Between the three of them, following the boy's scent trail should be pretty easy if he hadn't hitchhiked.

He hung up and bounded the rest of the way downstairs. Derek and Gaby were just taking off their coats as Dan snatched his off the hook.

"You going out?" Derek asked in surprise. "You don't need to get anything out of the car. Gaby and I took care of it."

Dan shook his head. "It's Paula. Her son is missing."

Instantly Derek switched to business mode. "*Damn* it. We didn't have anyone on her house this evening. Ben is monitoring with his gadgets, but—"

"No, it's not what you're thinking. Paula says he ran away." Dan zipped his coat one-handed, shoved a hand in his pocket to check for his wallet. "I'm going to check the bus station. If he's not there, though ..."

"All hands on deck for a search," Derek agreed. "Man, it's not a good night to be a runaway out there. It's cold."

"I'm hoping it won't come to that. If all goes well, in twenty minutes I'll fish him out of a nice, heated bus station lobby and take him back to his mom."

As he reached for the door, Derek stopped him with a hand on his arm. "Tell me something," he said quietly, regarding Dan with his dark brown eyes. "About this woman. Paula. You're serious about her, aren't you?"

"Very," Dan agreed, just as softly.

"Is she your mate?"

He didn't want to say it out loud, even to his best friend. He closed his eyes briefly instead.

"Damn it," Derek muttered under his breath. "We were starting to suspect, Gaby and me. Does *she* know?"

"No," Dan said shortly. "She doesn't know about shifters either. And that's something she has to hear from me."

"I know. Trust me, I went through the whole 'by the way I turn into a bear' thing with Gaby." Derek smiled lopsidedly.

"I'd offer pointers, but in our case Gaby was being stalked by another shifter, and she'd already seen him turn into a bear, so it wasn't a huge shock when I did it."

"Okay, yeah, that's not gonna work here, unless it turns out that Terry's loan sharks are shifters, and I think Paula would have mentioned it."

"Loan sharks who actually turn into sharks?"

"Best case scenario. Sharks on dry land aren't much of a threat." Dan lifted his chin in a sharp nod. "And now I'm going to go get her kid back. I hope."

"Take the Subaru," Derek said. "It's already warmed up."

Derek was right, it was fiercely cold out in the country night, but his bear appreciated the bracing chill. Hot air blasted out of the Subaru's vents as he drove toward town.

There was no sign of a teenager on the quiet streets of Autumn Grove. Dan drove through town slowly, keeping an eye out, and parked in the bus station's small parking lot. It had a big glass window facing the lot, with two short rows of plastic seats; it wasn't a big place.

And Austin was clearly visible through the window, stretched out on one of the seats with his backpack tucked under his head.

Dan huffed out a breath of tremendous relief. He killed the headlights so Austin didn't notice him, and called Paula.

She picked up on the first ring. "Dan!"

"Found him," Dan said. "We were right. He's at the bus station."

Paula gave a shuddering exhalation that was close to a sob. "Are you with him? Can I talk to him?"

"I'm still out in the parking lot. I haven't gone in. Don't want to spook him."

"I don't think he'd run away from you."

Dan wasn't so sure. Paula didn't know what it was like to be a teenage boy, mad at the world. But he did.

"Do you want me to come?" Paula asked. "I can get a neighbor to stay with Lissy, or bring her along."

"Not yet," Dan said. He was trying to think through what *he* would have wanted at that age. What would have convinced him to stay. "We don't want to make him feel crowded."

"I'm just so worried about him. He's going through things, Dan. He won't talk to me."

"He might talk to me. One guy to another. I can try. If it doesn't work, I'll call you."

There was a pause and then she said softly, fervently, "I trust you."

His heart clutched. "Thank you," he said quietly. "I won't let you down."

"I know," she said. "You're not my ex." She managed to laugh a little. "But keep me informed. And let me know if you need me there. It's not like I'm going to bed until all of this is resolved."

"I promise."

He teetered on the edge of adding "I love you" at the end. It was true. But humans didn't fall in love as fast as shifters did. It might only spook her, especially since she'd had so many reminders lately of how the last man in her life had broken her heart and disappointed her.

Instead, they said their goodbyes, and he shot off a quick text to Derek, then put away the phone and went into the bus station.

The place hadn't changed at all—but of course it wouldn't have. He still couldn't get over how much his life had changed in that short time. He hesitated at the door, inhaling the smell of cleaning chemicals and mildew, and then Austin noticed him and sat up abruptly. Dan hadn't been sure if he was asleep or not.

"Hey, kid." Dan held out his hand, trying to appear as nonthreatening as possible.

"What are you doing here?" Austin demanded, clutching his backpack.

"Your mom sent me to look for you."

Austin let out a shuddering sigh and drooped over the backpack. He stiffened a little when Dan sat down beside him, but didn't try to get up or run. He seemed to realize that the jig was up.

"Is Mom really mad?" he whispered.

"Of course not. No one's mad. She's just really worried about you. Everyone's worried."

"I know," Austin said faintly. He rubbed at his eyes, and Dan was reminded that even though Austin had shot up to almost his adult height, he was still a kid. "I never wanted to worry or scare anyone. I just needed to find my dad. I have to talk to him about something."

Dan still had to squash a surge of protective anger at the thought of Paula's ex. "Look, just because your mom's upset with your dad doesn't mean she'd hate the idea of you getting in touch with him. She wants you and Lissy to get to know him if you can."

"I know!" Austin sounded desperate now. He sniffled, on the verge of tears.

"It's not your responsibility to try to resolve your mom's problems with your dad, you know that, right? The adults can handle it."

"That's not what I need to talk to him about." Austin mumbled it, staring down at his backpack.

Dan worked on keeping his voice level and calm. He remembered what it was like to be that age, when everything seemed vitally important and every problem was the biggest problem in the world. He'd run away a couple of times too ...

though of course he was running away from group homes and not from a loving mother and sister. "Look, the, uh—problem that you needed to talk to your dad about—could you talk to me about it instead? I know it can be hard for teenage guys to talk to their moms about things, but *I'm* a guy. And I promise that I won't judge you, and I won't tell anyone."

Austin shook his head vigorously, but he didn't move toward the door. Dan felt that they were getting onto more solid ground now.

"Hey," he said gently, resting his good elbow on his knees. "Whatever it is, I bet I've been there. Drugs or trouble at school, I've been there and got past it. Shoplifting? Girl problems?"

Austin was shaking his head at every suggestion. He drew a hitching breath. "I don't think anybody ever had a problem like this one before."

Yeah, that was a fifteen-year-old talking, all right. "Austin, I can assure you," Dan said in that same gentle voice, like he was trying to calm down Derek's horse or coax Mina out of hiding under the bed when she was having a temper tantrum. "Every problem you've had is probably something a lot of guys your age have gone through. Like I said, I'm not going to tell your mom." Though he hoped that was a promise he could keep. What if Austin was in really serious trouble—with the law, say? Maybe he could take it to Derek and Ben, and they could find some way to help.

More vigorous headshaking. "No, you're wrong, you—listen, there's no way you can help me. Nobody can help me except maybe my dad, but I don't even know how to find him!"

His voice cracked with desperation.

"Try me," Dan said. "I swear to you, no matter how embarrassing or—or *bad* it is, we'll find a way to—"

"I turn into a monster!" Austin blurted out.

As soon as the words were out of his mouth, he clapped his hand over his mouth and looked wildly around the bus station. This late at night, no one was around to pay attention. Even the woman behind the bulletproof glass in the ticket station had earbuds in and seemed to be watching a movie on her phone.

And Dan had to fight with all he had to suppress a grin of pure relief. Out of all the problems he'd expected, this wasn't one of them, but at least it was vastly easier to deal with than just about anything else he had thought of. And he was the perfect person to do it.

"What kind of a monster?" he asked quietly. "Dragon? Giant bear?"

Austin jumped up off the plastic seat. "You're making fun of me," he snapped, his voice shaking.

"No!" Dan said quickly. He got up too, picturing the kid running out into the winter night. "I swear I'm not. I've ... dealt with problems like that before. Kid, I turn into one too."

Austin stared at him. A range of expressions passed over his face, desperate hope warring with suspicion and anger. "You're just saying that. There is no one else like me, except maybe my dad, but I don't know and I can't find out. Maybe our family is just cursed."

"There's nothing wrong with you. You aren't cursed. It's called being a shifter," Dan said. "I turn into a bear."

Austin's eyes went briefly wide, then narrowed in teenage suspicion. "You're lying."

"No, I swear I'm not. I can prove it, but not—" He glanced around. "Not here. Get in the car with me and I'll take you somewhere that I can show you. And you can show me too."

"This is stupid," Austin muttered, but he shoved his hands in his pockets and slouched toward the door with Dan. A fragile hint of hope quivered in his voice, cracking it. "You're lying. You're just going to take me to my mom's house."

"I'm not. I'm going to find the nearest patch of woods and show you what a grizzly bear looks like."

He tried to push down the nervousness rising in his chest. He just hoped that when it came down to shifting for the first time in years, he would be able to actually do it.

∽

HE TEXTED Paula from the car. *He's in the car with me. I'm gonna take him to get something to eat & talk about things before we head home.*

"What are you doing?" Austin demanded.

Dan showed him the text before he sent it. "I promised to tell your mom what's happening, and I'm keeping that promise. But I'm also keeping my promise to you. Not a word about monsters. I always keep my promises."

"You're a regular Captain America," Austin muttered, slouching down in the passenger seat. But he didn't jump out of the car.

Not knowing the area well, Dan decided to just randomly drive until he found a side road that looked like it headed into an uninhabited stretch of woods where they could shift unobserved. It helped that it was the middle of the night, so there was almost no traffic. He drove slowly, the heating vents beating back the chill.

And he tried not to think about the fact that the last time he'd shifted, he'd had two good arms, and four good legs as a bear. He knew he hadn't lost touch with his animal entirely, which was a risk for shifters who hadn't shifted in a long time, but would it come out for him after all this time? He was trying very hard not to worry about that.

"So you're not gonna tell me what you turn into?" he asked.

"I don't believe you turn into a bear," was Austin's reply.

"It's pretty easy to prove, and I'm about to prove it as soon as I find a—aha, this looks good."

He turned onto what looked like an old logging or hunting road. Vehicles had driven over it earlier in the winter, flattening down the snow, but the road surface was loose and sloppy even with the car's all-wheel drive. He stopped just a few yards in. All he needed to do was get off the road where he couldn't be seen. He didn't want to get stuck.

"This is so stupid," Austin said, but when Dan got out, he got out too.

It was very quiet in the woods, and very cold. The snow had the soft luminescence of a north-country winter night.

Dan inhaled deeply. The sharp, cold air seared his sinuses. This was going to be chilly, although he knew that he would stop feeling the cold as soon as he shifted. He took off his coat and then stripped out of his shirt.

Looking up, he saw Austin staring at him.

"Uh, whoa, what's going on?" Austin asked. "Did you just go crazy or something?"

"Gotta take off my clothes so I don't wreck 'em. You can look away. Watch for cars for me."

"Oh, so you can do your magic trick without me watching," Austin said, but he turned his head to look at the road.

"Yeah, kid," Dan grunted, stripping off his jeans. Goosebumps prickled his skin. "Because a grizzly bear is so easy to hide in a Subaru Outback."

All he had on now was his T-shirt and prosthesis. He stripped that off too, and put it inside the car carefully.

As he'd feared, his bear was being worryingly reluctant to come out. He stood naked in the snow, standing with his bare feet on top of his folded jeans to avoid flash-freezing his feet. He was already starting to shiver.

Come on, bear, don't be like this. It's gonna be pretty embar-

rassing if I have to tell the kid that I WOULD have turned into a bear, except my bear wouldn't cooperate. That's really going to help get him to cooperate and listen.

He focused on his bear in a way he hadn't had to do since he was a very young kid, still struggling to control his shifts. He had spent most of his early life terrified that someone would find out that he was a bear and put him in a zoo. He hadn't been able to understand much about himself, but he had known that most people didn't turn into zoo animals.

Come on, bear. Let's go.

"So is this going to take much longer?" Austin asked in the classic tones of a bored teenager. "Because—"

"I'm trying to focus here," Dan said. "Give me a minute."

He became aware of his bear, a dim ursine presence deep inside him. It was reluctant. Well, he had figured that part out already.

What are you doing in there, you furry menace? You've been pushing at me to give you this for years. Now here we are, we're in the woods and you can shift and run, just like you want to.

I ... His bear's mental voice was unusually hesitant.

Normally it was the instinctive animal part of himself, the part that didn't suffer from doubts and fears. His animal self knew exactly what it wanted and went for it. It wasn't supposed to be hesitant, needing to be coaxed out like a shy barn cat.

They couldn't both be uncertain. If his bear wasn't sure, then he had to beat back his own doubts and have enough certainty for two of them, the same way he'd had to keep up a front of strength for Paula earlier.

You can, Dan told it. *Come on, I'm freezing here. I didn't take off all my clothes in freaking JANUARY just so you can get shy on me. Man up, or bear up, or whatever, and get yourself out here!*

He wasn't sure if it was the encouragement or the goading or if his bear had simply needed that long to work itself up to it, but suddenly it rushed up out of the back of his mind.

He fell into the shift, as easy and effortless as it had always been. Instinctively he dropped forward, trying to catch himself on his front paws—but there was only one front paw, and he wobbled before he managed to stabilize.

He was right, the forest felt much warmer now that he was covered in a bear's pelt. He breathed deeply of the night air. Its winter bite in his lungs was more of a pleasant tang, and it was full of the rich scents of the wilderness. He'd almost forgotten how much he could smell in his shifted form. He could smell mice under the snow, and the tingle of pine needles, and the hot feathered bodies of owls hunting in the woods.

"Whoa," Austin whispered.

Dan swung his shaggy head to look toward the kid. The one sense that wasn't sharper as a bear was his vision. Bears weren't as nearsighted as some people thought, but he couldn't see colors and he didn't have particularly acute night vision. Austin looked like a dim blob in the moonlight, just the same as he had to Dan's human eyes.

"You really do turn into a bear," Austin said. His voice cracked.

Told you, Dan wanted to say, but of course in this form he couldn't.

Instead he took a step forward—or tried to. He had forgotten, again, about the missing leg. His forequarters dipped alarmingly and he caught himself by swaying backward, centering his weight over his one foreleg.

This was what he had been afraid of. He could feel panic beginning to set in. All his instincts were closer to the surface in this shape. He forced his rational mind to remain in control.

There had to be a way to walk like this. There were three-legged dogs and cats and even deer. He knew it could be done. It was probably going to look a little silly as he figured it out, and he would have preferred to do it without an audience, but ... hell. If this made Austin feel better about his own transformations, wasn't it worth looking a little silly?

He took a cautious, hopping step. That worked okay. *That's the key,* he thought; he just had to get used to hopping a little when he moved. It would probably have worked better, or at least looked more graceful, on a fifty-pound dog than a thousand-pound bear, but he could do it. In fact, he found that it was much easier when he just kept moving and didn't try to stop between steps. His back legs could do most of the work, his front leg worked mostly to prop up his front end, and he took a few hopping steps over to Austin.

Austin smelled fascinated rather than afraid. He reached out cautiously to touch Dan's coarse, shaggy fur. "You know," he said, "I guess I never wondered how a three-legged bear would work."

Dan gave a coughing grunt. It was meant to be agreement and rueful laughter, but Austin jumped a little. *Okay,* he thought, *let's keep down the sudden noises and movements when I'm bear-shaped.*

Anyway, it was about time to shift back, since he couldn't talk when he was bear-shaped either, and they were starting to need to have a conversation. He turned and shuffle-hopped back to the car. This wouldn't be fun, but it wasn't the first time that he had shifted and gotten dressed in the cold. He braced himself as if for a dive into an icy pond, shifted, and snatched up his jeans as he stamped his feet into his cold boots. He had to take out one foot at a time to get his underwear and jeans on. Skin prickling, he reached for the coat and swung it around his shoulders, and then turned to look at Austin.

"Proof enough for ya?" he asked.

Austin shook his head and grinned. "Okay, yeah, that proved it. You're right. There's no way to fake that."

"Nope," Dan agreed. He pulled the coat closed over his bare chest, one-handed. "Your turn now."

Austin tensed, his body language reflecting anxiety. "Do I have to? I mean, I believe that you believe me now, and we can just go back to Mom's—"

"Kid, you just saw me turn into a bear. How much worse can it be?"

"You'd be surprised," Austin said. His voice was grim and old for his years. "You're a bear, which is at least pretty normal. I'm not. I'm something *weird*."

"*How* weird? I know people who turn into dragons."

"Really?" Instantly Austin dropped the jaded-old-man persona and reverted back to a kid. "Dragons are real too? Whoa. Cool. Can I meet one?"

"Not yet," Dan said, backpedaling hastily. "I'll need to ask them first. It's a big secret, you know. Like me being a bear. We don't tell it to just anyone."

"I know. I mean, I can guess." Austin fidgeted with the zipper of his coat. "But seriously, I'm not a dragon, and I'm not a bear, and maybe it's coming out like this because I don't know what I'm doing, okay? Maybe if I, like ... practice a little more, I'll be able to turn into something nice, like a glorious eagle or something."

What the heck did he turn into? All the shifters Dan knew personally were pretty normal types, like Derek's bear and Ben's panther. He knew that there were shifters who turned into most kinds of mammals, a few reptiles and birds. And dragons, of course. Ben had once said something offhand about gargoyles, so apparently those were a thing too.

How unusual could Austin's shift form be? It was probably a platypus or something. Unusual to him, but not *that* weird.

But now Dan's curiosity was churning in earnest. What *else* was out there? He decided to offer some more painful honesty as an enticement.

"Hey, you got to see me learning to walk as a three-legged bear. That's the first time I've turned into a bear since I lost my arm."

"Really?" Austin asked softly.

"Yeah. Really. It hurts shifters a little bit not to be able to shift, once we grow into our animal form. You might have noticed it too. You probably have to struggle not to shift sometimes."

Austin gave a reluctant nod.

"I've been fighting it," Dan went on. Now that he'd warmed up a bit, he slipped the coat off his shoulders and reached inside the car for his prosthesis and shirt. It gave him something to do rather than focusing on the words that were coming out of his mouth—the brutally honest words, the words he'd spoken to no one. "I didn't know what would happen when I turned back into a bear. I didn't know what it would feel like, or what I'd look like. I was—scared," he admitted. "I was scared, and I didn't want to face it, until tonight. I know it's not the same thing, but believe me, kid, I know what it's like to be afraid of a shift and have to face up to your fears and get it over with."

He turned to look at Austin square on.

"You don't have to," he said quietly. "If you decide not to, that's your choice. I'll take you back to your mom's, no questions asked. But the longer you put it off, the harder it's going to be to make yourself do it at all. And right now, tonight, is about as good an opportunity as you're going to get. We're in the middle of nowhere with no one around, and you just watched me push past my fears and turn into a three-legged bear. Whatever you turn into, I won't laugh and I won't judge you. You don't have to show me, but I'd be honored if you'd trust me that much. And then," he added, "we'll find an all-night burger joint and get something to eat, because I am *starved*."

Austin hesitated. Then he gave a strange, twisted little smile, barely visible in the moonlight.

"Okay," he said softly.

He turned around, turning away from Dan. At first Dan thought that he meant to strip off his clothes and was prepared to look away to preserve the boy's modesty, but Austin didn't do that. He arched and rolled his shoulders, stretched out his arms, and hunched over a bit.

He's not expecting his clothes to tear up, Dan thought. *Only mythic shifters take their clothes with them. What the heck IS he?*

Austin arched his back and gave a soft, pained cry, and in the moonlight, a great feathered mass of wings burst from his shoulders.

Dan had been expecting something to happen, but not that. He took a step back, and another as Austin's body contorted and seethed.

He had absolutely no idea what to prepare himself for. Austin's head bent forward, his back humped up, and he hit the snow with all four legs. His head had extended into sleek feathers and a beak. A long tail with a tufted tip lashed at his flanks. He turned to look at Dan, cocking his head to the side since an eagle's eyes were not well suited for looking at something right down the center of its beak.

"Oh, hey!" Dan said as he finally figured out what he was looking at. "You're a griffin. *Cool.*"

Austin snapped his beak. He stretched and half-spread his wings in the moonlight. Like all adolescent animals, he was gawky and awkward, with gangly legs out of proportion to his lion body and oversized paws. His wings weren't fully fledged yet, with downy tufts of baby fluff sticking out between the half-grown flight feathers.

"Yeah, you're a griffin," Dan said. "Do you know what that is?" Austin slowly shook his feathered head. "I've read about them in storybooks, just didn't know they were real. Then again, I didn't know dragons were real either, until recently. Griffins are part eagle, part lion. You look amazing, kid. Two really cool animals in one. Do you mind if I touch you?"

Austin shook his head again. The effect was very strange on his lion-eagle body. He held still while Dan cautiously stroked his neck and shoulder, feeling the transition where eagle feathers changed to soft, tawny fur.

"So yeah. You're no monster, you're a mythic shifter. Your dad must be a griffin too, since Paula sure isn't. No wonder you wanted to find him. Can you change back?"

Austin concentrated. The return shift was faster and smoother; his griffin body collapsed back into the lanky body of a teenage boy, clothes and all.

"Yeah, I think he must be," Austin said, the words spilling out in a rush. "That's why I had to find him, to ask him—but, are you sure? I've heard of griffins, I just didn't know what they were. Is that really what I am?"

He was so excited that he was nearly babbling. Dan grinned and clasped Austin's shoulder with his good hand.

"You're fine," Dan said. "I've never seen a griffin before either, but there's a first time for everything, right? Tomorrow I can see about trying to help you find your dad, if that's possible. Right now, though—"

"Home," Austin said. "Yeah."

"And food. I wasn't kidding about that part." Dan's stomach was cramping with hunger. "Shifting takes it out of you, especially when you aren't quite used to it yet. If you're not hungry yet, you're going to be starving soon."

Austin flashed a quick grin. "I'm *always* hungry. Mom says as soon as I hit my teens, I developed a hollow leg." As they got back in the car, he grew pensive. "What are we gonna tell Mom? I hate lying to her."

"Me too, kid. We'll have to figure out a way to tell her."

"She doesn't know you're a bear either, does she?" Austin asked, looking over at Dan as he buckled his seatbelt.

"No," Dan admitted.

"Are you going to tell her?"

"Of course I am," he said, putting the car into reverse. "It's not something I feel right keeping from her. It's just ..."

"You don't know how."

"Right."

"Can't you just do like we did tonight, and take her out in the woods, and turn into a bear?"

"And what do you think she'll do at that point?"

"Uh ... probably scream," Austin admitted.

"Yeah."

"But I didn't scream."

"But you had already turned into a griffin at least once," Dan pointed out. He carefully backed onto the deserted country highway. "So you knew it was a thing. It didn't come completely out of the blue for you."

"Yeah," Austin said. He looked down at his hands. "How *are* you gonna tell her?"

"I have absolutely no idea. But I promise you one thing, kid," Dan added, looking over at the teenage boy hunched in the seat next to him. "Your secret is safe with me. I'll tell your mom about shifters first, and then you can break it to her if you want, or I can do it for you, or we can just wait for a while. But either way, I'm not spilling the beans unless you tell me it's okay."

"Thanks," Austin whispered.

Dan wished he had a hand free to reach over and scruff Austin's hair, but his good arm was on the wrong side. He settled for grinning at him, and reluctantly, a little shyly,

Austin smiled back. It was the smile of a shared secret, a burden halved, the two of them sharing a strange wild magic that neither had to deal with alone.

"No problem," Dan said. "Now let's get some burgers and go home."

PAULA

Paula was waiting up when Dan and Austin pulled into the driveway. One look at her son's drawn, pale face, tears standing in his eyes, told her that running away had been almost as traumatic for him as it had been for her. She gave him a tight hug and sent him up to bed, and then threw her arms around Dan.

"Thank you," she sobbed into his shoulder, muffled. "Thank you, thank you."

She had managed to keep it together in front of Austin, but feeling Dan's arms come up gently around her, one strong and muscled and one made of metal and plastic, broke some wall inside her. She didn't have to deal with this kind of thing alone anymore. She had someone to lean on. She had *help*.

"It's okay," Dan said. He patted her back awkwardly, and then just held her. "I, uh ... I brought you back a burger if you want it. Except I realized you probably don't, because you serve hundreds of them a day."

She choked on a wet laugh. "Hundreds? I *wish*." But that helped pull her together, enough to realize that she was standing in the open doorway with all the heat escaping. She took the greasy paper bag. "Come on in. You must be exhausted. Do you have to go back to the Rugers' tonight?"

Dan shook his head. "I texted them from the car. They know what's going on."

He stamped snow off his boots on the entryway mat and then slipped his feet out of them. Somehow he'd gotten snow on his socks too, and there were damp patches on the legs of his jeans. It looked like he'd been rolling around in a snowbank.

"You look wet," she said with a laugh, wiping her eyes with the back of her hand. "What'd you have to do, chase the kid down and wrestle him back to the car?"

"No, he was totally cooperative. He's a *really* good kid, Paula."

Dan's tone was sincere and earnest, almost pointedly so. Paula got the feeling, strangely, that he was trying to convey something that he couldn't quite put into words.

"I know," she said. "I probably don't tell him that often enough. I mean, obviously I don't, since he ran away."

"It's not you," Dan said, again with that strange tense sincerity. "He's just working through some things."

"Did he talk to you about it? Is—" She dropped her voice and glanced toward the stairs. "Don't *ever* tell him I asked you this, but is it ... drugs?"

"What?" Dan said. "No! I mean, if there's something like that, he didn't tell me. Look, Paula, we did talk about some things in the car, man to man. I'm going to try to get him to talk to you too, but for now, I promised him it would stay between us. He just needed a male adult to confide in, I think."

He looked down and away as he said it, but Paula hadn't been the mother of a teenage boy for all this time without figuring out that there were some things boys didn't want to tell their mothers, and she also recognized that teenage boys, like everyone else, were entitled to their privacy.

"Okay," she said. Taking a deep breath, she went on, "I told you I trusted you. And I do. But I also trust you to tell me if anything he told you affects the rest of us. Like ... say ... if he's gotten involved with his father's loan sharks or something."

"No," Dan said quickly. "No, nothing like that."

"In that case, I won't pressure you to break your promise." She took him by the arm and led him toward the kitchen. "Come on in here and have a cup of coffee or cocoa or something. But just, since you now know more of what's going on with him than I do, I'm going to trust you to tell me if it ever turns into something the rest of us need to know about."

"I will," Dan said. He gently detached her grip. "I'd love a cup of coffee some other time, but right now, I can't stay."

"You said you don't have to go back to the Rugers' tonight."

"I know," he said with a rueful smile. "But I've just realized that's where all my dry clothes are."

Paula leaned in, close enough to feel the heat of his body through the damp fabric. "You could dry them here," she said quietly, looking up at him.

She heard his breath catch in his throat. He touched the side of her face lightly. "Are you sure?"

All she could do was nod.

He leaned down and his lips met hers. They were chilled from being outside, but warmed quickly, igniting a heat in the pit of her stomach.

This is happening. We're doing this.

Dan's hand rested on her waist and a thumb slipped under the loose edge of her blouse. She gasped against his mouth as his thumb stroked across the bare skin above her jeans waistband. Then she broke the kiss.

"Okay, we need to not do this here," she whispered. "I'll show you where the laundry room is."

She put the burgers in the fridge for later, and they tiptoed through the house, giggling and clinging to each other. It was amazing how he made her feel like a teenager in the best possible way. Except instead of sneaking around to avoid her parents, she was sneaking around avoiding her own kids. The thought made her laugh out loud.

"What?" Dan whispered.

"I'm just ... happy." And she was. Happier than she'd been since she left Terry. Happier than when she was with Terry. Maybe happier than she'd been *ever*.

She let him into the laundry room and turned on the light. It was a cramped space off the living room, halfway between utility room and closet. There were no windows in the small space, just walls of bare white-painted drywall and a clutter of typical utility-room items: washer and dryer, mops and brooms, folded linens and towels, plastic crates of cleaning supplies. Paula shoved a basket heaped with clean, unsorted laundry out of the way with her foot so that she could get inside and close the door behind her.

There was very little room with just the two of them in here, as cluttered as the place was. She couldn't move without brushing against Dan, not that it was a problem; every touch heightened her awareness of him, tingling through her body.

She leaned past him to open the dryer, and sighed when she found that it was full of socks. "Lissy was supposed to sort these, but I guess the last week has been hectic for everyone." She raked out an armful and dropped it into the nearest hamper, on top of a bunch of towels that she was pretty sure were clean. "Here, put your things in. If they're muddy, we can run them through the washer first."

"Probably best. I don't want to get your dryer dirty or anything."

Dan rolled his shoulders and slipped out of the prosthetic, which he laid carefully on top of a crate of floor-cleaning supplies. His T-shirt followed, and Paula sucked in her breath. She hadn't been ready for the glorious sculpted pecs, the smooth flat belly with a trail of dark hair vanishing under the waistband of his jeans.

Dan grinned at her. "Like what you see?" He gave a little pelvic thrust in her direction. "Here, give me a hand with this."

"Give me a—oh, funny," she muttered, but she didn't hesitate. The button of his jeans and the zipper were warm from his body heat, and when the jeans fell away from his narrow hips, she discovered that he was a briefs man and there was a pointed bulge.

Paula swallowed.

She looked up at Dan, and saw him looking down at her, eyes dark with wanting. And suddenly the electric charge that had been growing between them grew to a lightning bolt, a flood of current pouring heat through her body.

She pulled down Dan's jeans with hands that trembled with the intensity of what she was feeling. He stepped out of them. It was like a slow-motion strip tease. Even fully clothed, she was already wet.

"I think you might need help with these too." Her voice came out in a whisper as she hooked a finger under the waistband of his briefs. She heard his intake of breath, the only sound he made as she pulled his briefs down to his knees.

His cock sprang free, erect and already beaded with moisture at the tip.

Paula swallowed and pulled down the briefs to the floor. Every move made her thighs tingle. Dan's hand came to rest lightly on her head, stroking her hair. He wasn't pushing her in any direction. She breathed in the smell of him, kissed his inner thigh, and then gathered the clothes together.

"Washing machine," she said hoarsely. She was almost shaking with the effort of keeping herself together and not flinging herself all over that. She stuffed the clothes down into the machine, closed it, and had already pushed the button to start it before remembering that she hadn't added soap. *Oh well, who cares.*

Dan rested his hand in the middle of her back. Without saying anything, Paula leaned over the machine as it began to vibrate. She spread her legs under the skirt, tingling with need.

Dan lifted her skirt, moving it out of the way. As she had done for him, he hooked two fingers into the waistband of her panties and slid them down. The cool touch of air on her wet heat drew a shuddering breath from her.

She couldn't see him, but she could feel him, bending down behind her as he pulled down her damp underwear. She lifted one sock-clad foot, then the other, stepping out of her panties.

The washing machine was going now, agitating its contents and shuddering its vibrations through her body. She could feel the vibration in her clit.

Dan was still kneeling behind her. His hand came to rest on her thigh, sliding her legs a little farther apart.

She leaned forward, her overheated forehead resting against the back of the machine.

Dan's breath stirred the curls between her legs. She shivered again.

The touch of his tongue was an electric jolt that snapped through her spine.

She clenched her hands into fists underneath her chest on the vibrating machine and squeezed her eyes shut, focusing on the sensations.

Dan ran his tongue up her folds, exploring her. He flicked his tongue lightly across the top of her clit, and she jerked. The heat of arousal pooled in her hips. She felt molten.

The light, teasing movement of Dan's tongue flickered lower down, skirting the edges of her opening. She was dimly aware that his hand was no longer touching her thigh. From the small sounds behind her, she realized that he was touching himself while he licked her.

She spread her legs wider as his tongue flicked in and out. She was so aroused she could barely breathe. Then abruptly he withdrew, leaving her gasping.

Before she could voice her wordless complaints, his hand settled firmly on her buttock, pressing her against the machine. The vibration shivered through her clit. His fingertips were wet. She groaned.

Dan leaned over her, and she groaned again as he pressed into her from behind. She was wet and open, and he slid into her, filling her.

She had never experienced anything like this. He filled her and covered her from behind, moving his hips with small thrusts that moved him inside her without ever letting up on the pressure. She tried to match those small movements. When she pushed forward, the vibration of the machine against her clit was so intense she had to struggle to control the molten heat rising in her; when she pushed back, her buttocks pressed into his groin and he filled her so deeply that the hot ache turned her bones to jelly.

She was rising toward climax faster than she would have thought possible. Every tiny movement, as they shifted back and forth in sync, pushed her higher. The washing machine covered any sounds they made. Paula rolled her hips against Dan's groin and was rewarded with a throaty gasp. She realized he was as close as she was, struggling just as hard to ride the edge without going over.

His movements paused, and Paula moaned, teetering on the edge. Dan leaned forward. His lips brushed the back of her neck, which right now seemed to be connected straight to the hot core of her.

She spread her arms, gripping both sides of the machine as Dan began to move again while he licked and nipped at the back of her neck. "I can't ..." she gasped out, her voice all but covered in the noise of the machine as it hit the spin part of the cycle. The vibration was almost more than she could bear.

With Dan's lips pressed to her neck, she felt more than heard the answer.

"Then don't," he whispered. "Go for it."

That sent her over the edge. Waves of pleasure rose in her and crashed over her, blotting out the world for an instant as she lost herself in the pure sensation of it. As she began coming back down, she felt Dan shudder into his own climax, and the heat of his release, to her own shock, sent her into a second, less intense wave, a mini-orgasm following the big one.

For a little while she lay draped over the machine with Dan on top of her, sweat sticking his bare chest to her back, both of them breathing deeply as their heart rates slowed. Eventually the discomfort of being on tiptoe with her chest pressed to the lid of a running Maytag started to penetrate.

"I think I need up now," she got out, and Dan's weight immediately eased.

He pulled back and she let her skirt down. Her knees were wobbly. She turned around and leaned against the machine and took some slow breaths. Dan was still gloriously naked, and the machine vibrated against her backside, making her aware that she was completely bare-assed under the skirt.

She wondered how many times a woman pushing forty could come in a row.

"Wow," she whispered. "You know, I've always fantasized about doing that."

Dan grinned. He leaned forward to kiss her. His lips were slightly salty.

"I hope I can make all your fantasies come true," he whispered.

"Gotta say, you're doing *great* so far." She drew in a ragged breath. "Okay, as amazing as that was, I'd rather sleep in a bed than a pile of laundry, so let's get upstairs and—oh. Hmm. Problem."

"My clothes are in there," Dan said, pointing to the washing machine.

"Yeah."

"Maybe there's something in here I could wear."

"I really doubt it. Even my skirts probably aren't going to fit you."

But there were lots of linens. They ended up wrapping him securely in a sheet. Paula dropped her panties in the dirty-laundry hamper, and Dan picked up his prosthetic arm.

Feeling terribly exposed, Paula opened the door and looked around the dark living room as if there were onlookers lurking in the corners. But there was no one around. The kids were deeply asleep. Dan and Paula tiptoed upstairs to her bedroom without incident.

Paula closed the bedroom door firmly and breathed a sigh of relief. She turned on a lamp.

"So here it is," she said.

It was a different experience to look around her bedroom and see it through a stranger's eyes. At least it wasn't a total mess, and she'd just changed her sheets that weekend, though the bed was rumpled; she hadn't bothered to fix it that morning, and there were some items of clothing thrown on the bedspread. Paula raked them off and dumped them on a chair, and then looked over to see how Dan was taking it.

Dan was holding his prosthetic arm, looking slightly embarrassed about it. He looked around.

"Where do you want me to put this?"

"Anywhere. It doesn't matter. The chair there, I guess?"

Dan set it down on top of her discarded clothes, and dropped the sheet. Paula sucked in a breath. She still couldn't get over this amazing naked man being *here*, for her.

Dan smiled, his uncomfortable look softening into something warm and loving and meant only for her. "That was amazing," he said quietly, "but I feel like you might still have too many clothes on."

"I think you're right."

Paula began unbuttoning her blouse, but Dan stepped closer and brushed his fingertips across hers. "Let me," he murmured.

She took her hands away and looked down as he carefully, one-handed, popped each button out of its hole. "That's really impressive."

"They taught me how in physical therapy."

"It's still impressive."

Dan grinned. "Wait'll you see me undo a bra."

"They taught you how to undo bras in physical therapy?"

Now he laughed softly. "No, but I bet I can get this."

"You're on." She slipped the blouse off her arms, one at a time, and saw Dan's eyes grow heated as her full breasts were exposed in the lacy cups of her bra.

She turned around and held her hair out of the way. Dan was right about being able to undo her bra. It only took a moment, and a little bit of fumbling that she could feel from the movement of his fingers against her back, and then it separated and fell loose around the shoulders.

"Some guys can't do that two-handed, you know."

"It's all technique," Dan said.

He kissed the back of her neck and slid the bra strap down her shoulder. She reached up to get the other one as she turned and peeled it off her breasts.

"Holy shit," Dan said.

"Always how I want a man to react to my rack."

"You have an *amazing* rack."

It was the soft, awestruck tone that got to her. He gently guided her to sit on the bed, and one at a time, caressed and kissed her breasts, lightly tonguing her nipples.

He was half-hard, and she felt a light surge of arousal as he caressed her, but it was slow and easy, without the urgency of earlier. She lifted her hips to slide her skirt off, and they were finally naked with each other, fully and completely.

"Things were a little rushed downstairs," Dan said. He ran his hand down her leg. "I don't think I have another go in me tonight, but I'd be happy to do anything you want me to do."

"Honestly?" She held out an arm. "Turn off the light, and hold me."

She hadn't thought it was possible for his face to soften any more. She was wrong.

"Anything you want," he whispered, and reached over to turn off the lamp.

The bed was soft and yielding, and big enough for two, though she had never had another person in it with her. Not here, in this house. She was suddenly, deeply glad of that. There was no ghost of an ex-husband in this bed with her. Just the two of them, his body warm against hers as he got settled. They had to roll around a little until they found a good position, with Paula spooned up against him and Dan's arm wrapped around her waist.

"Hey, I just thought of a big advantage here," she murmured.

"Mmmm?"

"You don't have the 'what do I do with the other arm' problem in spooning."

Dan laughed.

She felt guilty immediately. "Sorry."

His thumb chafed gently at the soft curve of her stomach. "You don't ever have to apologize. Remember, black humor is the amputee's friend. You're getting the hang of it."

She laughed too, and nestled back against him.

After a moment, he said, "Should we be using protection?"

Paula shook her head against the pillow, for all the good it did in the dark. "I have an implant. I got it about a year ago, thinking I might start dating again, now that the kids are getting older." She shrugged, feeling her shoulder move against his chest. "Between the diner and the kids and the extremely small Autumn Grove dating pool, it didn't really work out for me ... until now."

Dan kissed her neck. "Sometimes you just gotta wait for the right one to come along."

"Sometimes you do," she whispered sleepily, and sank into his embrace, letting the tide of the night carry her away.

DAN

Dan woke in midnight darkness, lit only by dim street light coming in through the window. Paula's smooth, gorgeous body was sliding out of bed. It must be time for her to go open the diner.

He lay in a state of lazy bliss, slowly working himself up to moving as he listened to Paula talking quietly on the phone, not too far away. He wanted to get up and make breakfast for her before she went to work. Eventually he mobilized himself to sit up, but Paula was already sliding back into bed.

"Go back to sleep," she murmured, planting a hand on his chest.

"Mmmm." He kissed her sleepily. "Want to get up, send you off to work right."

"I'm not going to work. I just called Mitch to tell him he has a day off with pay. The diner can stay closed today. It won't be the end of the world."

He woke up a little more. "Are you sure?"

"There's no place I'd rather be than here with you," she murmured, and rolled over on top of him.

As it turned out, neither of them was actually that sleepy after all, and it was some time later, after the quiet moving in the dark and the gasps that both of them tried to stifle, that they fell asleep again, sweaty and relaxed and wrapped up in each other.

This time, when he woke again, jerking out of dreams, there was dawn-gray daylight filtering through the window. Someone was moving around in the hall. A door shut. Water ran in the bathroom.

"I think that's Austin," Paula whispered, stirring against Dan. "I'm surprised he's up after the late night everyone had, but that's teenagers for you." She sat up and yawned. "Guess I'd better get the kids ready for school."

"I volunteer to cook breakfast," Dan said with his face buried in the pillow.

She placed a hand on his shoulder. "You don't have to. You can stay in bed."

Dan yawned and pushed himself up on his elbow. "It's my pleasure. Or at least it will be, as soon as I find my pants and make some coffee."

"Your pants are downstairs."

Dan pressed his face into the pillow. "Right."

"I swapped them over into the dryer when I was up for a drink of water last night. I'll go get your clothes if you want to nap a bit."

He drifted until Paula came back with an armload of clothing. While she went to rouse Lissy and take a shower, Dan got dressed and went downstairs.

"Jeez!" Austin said, spinning around with a box of Pop-Tarts in his hands. "I didn't know you were still here." He made a horrified face. "Okay, you know what? I'm gonna pretend you just got here."

"Thanks, dude," Dan said. He scratched his stump—he hadn't bothered putting the arm on; he noticed Austin trying to look without staring—and located Paula's coffeemaker. "Is that what you're having for breakfast?"

"It's got fruit in it," Austin said defensively. "Says so right here on the box." He wrapped his arm around the box of Pop-Tarts.

"Sounds good. Give me one, and I'll make you guys some omelets in trade. We can have the Pop-Tarts for the fruit course."

Austin eyed him with something more baffled and open than his usual hostility, and held out a Pop-Tart. Dan accepted it and took a large bite, then filled the coffeepot with water. He couldn't hold both at once.

"You weren't kidding," Austin said. He opened another of the foil-wrapped packages and put the box back in the cabinet. "Mom won't touch these."

"I was in the Army," Dan said. "Pop-Tarts were high cuisine. Do you know where your mom keeps the coffee?"

Austin shrugged and shook his head. Dan started opening cabinets.

"But seriously," Austin said. He dropped his voice, with a nervous glance at the kitchen doorway, and whispered, "Did you tell her?"

"I promised I wouldn't. Man to man. I'm not going to break that promise."

Austin was quiet. There was nothing but foil rustling and munching as he worked his way through a Pop-Tart two-pack, while Dan scooped coffee into the top basket of the coffeemaker.

Finally Austin said, "Are you gonna tell her? About you?"

"I think I have to," Dan said.

After everything she had told him about her ex, about Terry's secrets and lies—and especially now that he knew what at least one of Terry's secrets had been—he understood that he could no longer keep his own secret from her. Austin's happiness was riding on it as well.

Austin nodded without speaking.

"Once she knows about me, it'll be easier to tell her about you. I'm serious, I won't violate your confidence. It's up to you. But I think you'll feel better once she knows."

Austin shrugged.

"Dan!" came a squeal from the doorway. Lissy barreled into the kitchen in her pajamas and threw her arms around his legs.

"Uh, hi," he said, startled. He patted the top of her head.

"You came to visit again!" she declared, looking up at him.

"Right, kid," Dan said, steadfastly not looking at Austin, although he could hear faint snickering sounds from the teenager. "I came to visit. And to make breakfast. I'm cooking omelets. What do you want in yours?"

"Olives and gummi worms," Lissy said promptly.

"Uh ... I think I can do olives, if there are any."

"There are," Austin said, breaking off a piece of Pop-Tart. "There's a jar in the fridge. There always is. She loves them for some reason. I think they're like eating eyeballs."

"Ewww, no!" Lissy protested. "They're *nice*." She let out a sudden shriek. Dan almost dropped the coffee. "What happened to your *arm*?"

"Whew. Jeez, kid. Don't do that to me. I just don't have the prosthesis on."

"You literally never noticed he has hooks for hands?" Austin asked. He had moved on from Pop-Tarts to eating peanuts directly out of a jar on the counter.

"I know *that*!" Lissy said. "I just didn't know you could take it *off*!"

"Yeah, it's not actually attached to me," Dan said. He crouched down and held out the stump of his arm to Lissy. "This is what it looks like underneath. Want to feel it?"

"No," Lissy said, but she reached out obediently. Her small hands tickled. "Wow, it's soft. Does it hurt?"

"Not at all." It wasn't entirely the truth. Little sparks still danced through his nerve endings, trying to tell him about the arm that was no longer there. But it also wasn't entirely a lie. He'd mostly stopped noticing, and he had adjusted to it to a degree he'd once believed impossible.

He had worried, once, that a woman might see him as less than a man with both arms. But nothing in the way that Paula responded to him, or to his arm, had ever made him feel that way.

We are the entire person that we are. His bear seemed baffled. *We could not possibly be less.*

Dan tried to keep his wry smile on the inside. *You're right.*

Lissy lost interest in his arm and went to pester her brother for peanuts. Dan found a skillet and a mixing bowl, and started whisking eggs. By the time Paula came into the kitchen, wearing a fuzzy red sweater with her damp hair straggling in squiggly curls on her shoulders, Dan was already scooping the first omelet out of the skillet.

"Mine!" Lissy said. "It has olives!"

"We figured we'd go in order of age," Dan said. "Reverse order, that is." With a flourish, he deposited Lissy's omelet in front of her at the table. "Austin's up next. Put your order in —what do you want?"

"I'm not used to giving breakfast orders instead of taking them," Paula teased. "How about I grate some cheese?"

They moved in sync, perfect teamwork just like back at the Ruger house. He was intensely aware of her, especially when their hips brushed, or she reached for something just as he reached for it, and her warm skin slipped across his.

"There's something I need to talk to you about, after the kids go to school," Dan told her under his breath, during one of the lulls in the action. Lissy, with some reluctance, had gone upstairs to change out of her pajamas, and Austin was on his second omelet, which he had asked for politely while Paula looked on in amazement.

"Of course." She looked up at him with a little frown of worry. She was wearing no makeup, the first time he'd seen her without at least a hint of mascara on her lashes, and she was, as always, gorgeous. "Is it about Austin?"

"No," he said quietly. "It's about me."

"Oh," she murmured, and went wordlessly to put the milk away in the fridge.

Damn. He hadn't meant to worry her. Still, there was no way to lead gracefully into *So, by the way, I turn into a bear.*

He had no idea how to tell her. He was going to have to show her; there was no other way. He wished now that he'd asked Derek and Ben more questions about how they'd revealed their shifter status to their mates. Different circumstances were different, but still, it would have been nice to have a little more guidance than Derek's brief pep talk last night.

Oh well. He'd simply have to do what he always did, and wing it.

They finished breakfast, the plates scraped clean. "Go get your books and see what's keeping your sister," Paula told Austin. As Austin ran out, she got up and put her plate in the sink. "I can't believe how well you two are getting along."

"We bonded, I guess," Dan said.

"He said *please*! He doesn't even say it to me half the time."

"He's a really sweet kid. He's just going through some stuff."

"Thanks to Terry," Paula sighed, but it came out with surprisingly little heat. "So I'm gonna drive the kids to school; I think I'd be more comfortable doing that than having them take the bus."

"I'll get the kitchen cleaned up."

She looked, as always, mildly surprised, as if the idea of someone else cleaning up for her was a shock she couldn't get over. Dan was getting the distinct impression that Terry hadn't been much for household chores. Yet another reason to dislike the guy, as if breaking Paula's warm, soft heart wasn't enough.

"Okay," she said. "And then when I get back, we'll—um—talk?"

"Yeah." He wanted to reassure her that it wasn't a bad thing. But honestly, he had no idea how she was going to react to having a bombshell like *I'm a bear and you're my fated mate* dropped on her. He'd never tried to explain it to someone who wasn't a shifter before.

Paula went to corral the kids. Dan rinsed the dishes and loaded Paula's dishwasher. *The Rugers need to get one of these*, he thought.

"Dan! We're leaving!"

Paula came running in, with her coat on one arm and hanging off the other. She gave him what was apparently meant to be a quick kiss, but turned into something long and lingering and soft.

Dan ran his soapy thumb across her chin. "See you soon," he murmured.

"Mmmm," she hummed, and leaned into his chest briefly before she pulled away and darted out of the kitchen. Moments later, the door slammed.

Dan finished loading the dishwasher and started it running, then wandered into the living room.

It felt very strange to be in Paula's house without Paula here. Intrusive, almost. But, no. She had welcomed him here. He could almost feel his bear starting to settle into it, as if it was curling up in a new den.

Someone knocked on the door. Dan nearly stumbled over the coffee table, then went to answer it.

"Hi," Ben Keegan said. He slipped in with a light dusting of snow on his dark hair. "Derek told me about the kid disappearing last night. Why didn't you call us?"

"Because he ran away, he wasn't kidnapped," Dan said. "I handled it." He watched Ben go to a box on the wall. "What are you doing?"

"Checking Paula's security system." Ben touched some buttons, looked at his phone, swiped something. "Is there anyone at the diner?"

"She closed it today."

Ben nodded. "I normally have the system set to turn off during the day. If it's going to be unoccupied, it should probably be armed."

"So when does Paula get to stop living in a state of siege?" Dan demanded.

"When we find her husband," Ben said, attention focused on his phone.

Sudden inspiration hit Dan with the force of a thunderbolt. "Would it help if I tell you I'm pretty sure he's a mythic shifter?"

Ben froze. Very slowly, he turned around to stare at Dan. "You're just telling us this now?"

"I didn't know!" Dan protested. "Until recently. I've been asking around."

"Are the kids shifters?"

"I don't know," Dan lied blatantly. It was too big a confidence for him to even think about betraying Austin's trust in him. "I found a guy—look, it's complicated. I just need to know if mythic shifters have some kind of ... grapevine, or group chat, or something, some way of networking with each other, like if you wanted to find a specific one ..."

"I spent most of my life not talking to the dragon side of my family, so no," Ben said. "At least if there is, I'm not in on it. But I don't think so." He gave Dan a sharp, suspicious look. "Why is all of this coming up now? What happened?"

"I'm sworn to secrecy on this," Dan said. "I can't tell you who, what, or when, but—"

"So yes, something happened."

"Seriously, man, do not pump me for details. I can't give them."

"It's interesting that you said 'mythic shifter' and not 'dragon,'" Ben said. "Because even most people who *do* know about dragons think that's all there is." His sharp gaze sharpened further. Dan had a sudden sympathy for people Ben had grilled for information back in his police days. There was steel in those gray eyes. "Is he a gargoyle?"

"I can't tell you, how many times do I have to say this?"

"Because gargoyles and dragons are ancestral enemies."

"Oh, so you're carrying the family feud forward. Good to know."

"It's not a feud," Ben said. "They literally wiped out part of my family. They threatened my child and mate. So yeah, if there are gargoyles involved, I need to know."

Dan rolled his eyes. "No gargoyles. Slow your roll. There's no threat. He's not a gargoyle, he's not a dragon; it's something different, something I didn't even think existed, and seriously, that's as much as I can say and probably more than I should have. I just needed to know if you have some way to get me in touch with the mythic shifter underground, if there is any such thing."

"Like I said, not that I know of. I can ask my dad. Or lean on Tessa's old connections with the Corcoran clan. Between the two of them, someone's bound to know."

"Be discreet, would you? I don't want to get anyone riled up. And seriously, there's a promise at stake that it's important to me not to break."

"I'll be careful," Ben promised.

He had to trust that. Had to trust Ben. It wasn't such a big deal when he was trusting his own safety to his brothers in arms. But this was Paula's safety at stake, and the emotional health of Paula's children. It was a lot.

"Okay, the system's armed again," Ben said. He put his phone away. "If anything trips it, you'll get an alert and so will I."

"Thanks," Dan said, heartfelt. "For helping us. For helping *her*."

Ben clasped Dan's good arm. "Anytime, brother," he said, and let himself out into the snow.

Just to give himself something to do, Dan went upstairs, but he realized immediately that he couldn't put his arm back on without having to just take it off again when he showed Paula his bear. From her bedroom, he noticed that the window looked across the fence onto the back of the diner. Snow was falling softly outside, settling on the fence and covering the trampled slush in the alley.

He liked it here, he was starting to realize. He never could have seen himself living in a small town before. But as Derek had apparently found out also, once you found your mate and cubs, home was where they were.

The door slammed downstairs. "Honey, I'm home!" Paula's voice called. Then she giggled nervously. "Okay, that's just silly. Dan? Are you here?"

He came down the stairs. Paula was taking off her coat in the hallway, shaking snow off the shoulders.

"Kids all squared away?" Dan asked.

Paula spun around, and ran to slide her arms around him. "Hi," she said into his shoulder.

"Hi," he said, caught off guard. Her warm weight settled against him, feeling perfectly and exactly as if it belonged there. He leaned into her.

Mate.

"Ben came by to reset the security system," he said into her hair, realizing as soon as the words left his mouth that it was literally the least sexy thing he could have said in that particular moment.

"I'm so tired of that thing," Paula sighed. "I can't wait until we work out this Terry situation and I can just live my life." She looked up at him, a shy, quick glance. "Our lives."

His heart flipped over. Being invited into Paula's life—it was all he wanted. All he needed.

And at the same time, he refused to accept it under false pretenses. Or even the hint of false pretenses. Not after Terry.

No. There could never be anything but honesty between them.

"I need to show you something," he said.

Dan stepped away from her, giving himself room. Paula looked curious, and her eyes went wide when Dan started stripping off his T-shirt.

"If you're trying to distract me," she said breathlessly, "it's working."

"It's not a distraction," he said firmly, though now he was thinking of Paula, naked and writhing in pleasure last night, and he could feel himself developing an erection that she was going to get a good view of in a minute. "I want to share myself with you, Paula. All of me."

"I think I got most of you last night."

"Not quite." Dan slid his jeans and underwear down his hips.

"Seriously, if this is—look, if it's another scar or something, I don't care," Paula said fervently. She took a step toward him.

"It's not that." He stood before her, naked ... and mildly erect, half mast at least, just from her nearness. He saw her take that in and smile. "It's—Paula, I can't really explain this to you. I wish I could show you this somewhere more romantic."

He had thought about it. There was a part of him that wanted to take her out to the middle of the woods, bring a picnic, make it beautiful.

But shifting in the woods last night had reminded him how extremely unromantic it was to shift in a snowy forest in the middle of winter. Her living room would do just fine. It was, after all, the place that he wished and hoped could be their shared den someday. It was only appropriate that this house was where they had made love for the first time, and where he would now show her the other half of his soul.

She was the center of his heart, and her heart was here. So his was too.

"If you want to have sex on the couch, Dan, I have to warn you that I think there are a bunch of Cheetos ground into the cushions from the last time I had a movie night with the kids."

"It's not about sex," he said, and then plunged forward, going for it. Shifting without warning probably wasn't the way to go. "Paula—I turn into a bear."

Paula froze in the act of moving toward him.

"What?"

"You know, like a werewolf? It's sort of complicated. I don't go around telling people this."

"I can see why," she said, frowning at him. "Is this like ... a roleplaying thing? I think I've heard that bears are a thing in, um, in sex for ... some people. Is that what this is about?"

Possibly taking his clothes off before telling her hadn't been the best order of things.

"No, I mean I literally turn into a bear. A grizzly bear, specifically."

"Okay," she said cautiously.

"Is it all right if I show you?"

".... okay?"

Well, that was something like a yes.

Come on, bear. Showtime.

At least he didn't have to deal with his bear being a dick about it this time. It was probably a good thing that he'd gotten a test run last night. The shift was instant. The warm prickle of fur flushed over him, and he dropped to all fours—that is, all threes.

Paula stumbled backward. She smelled alarmed.

"Don't worry!" he tried to say, but it came out as a coughing grunt.

Paula stopped in the kitchen doorway. She clutched at the doorframe and stared at him.

Dan sat down on his back legs—bears at least were fairly well suited for this. Shifting in a living room was a little less familiar.

"Okay, wow," Paula said faintly. "That is—yes, there is *definitely* a bear there."

Well, she hadn't screamed. That was good? Probably?

"Can you change back?" she asked in that same small voice.

He shifted. Abruptly he was aware of his bare, human ass pressed into the carpet, his legs splayed out, one hand pressed against the carpet's rough nap.

Paula jumped.

"So I turn into a bear," Dan said, looking up at her.

There was a long, still moment.

Then the diner security alarm went off.

PAULA

❦

It took Paula a moment to realize that the ringing was external and not happening in her head.

A bear, she thought.

A bear.

He's a bear.

Huh.

"Damn it!" Dan snapped, scrambling to his feet. He was still gloriously naked. She could have stared at that all day, even if the circumstances were a bit weird.

—*he's a BEAR*—

And oh, okay, someone was breaking into the diner; that was a thing. That they should probably deal with.

Possibly she wasn't handling this as well as she thought.

Dan was charging for the back door leading to the yard and the fence. Paula caught him by his bare arm. She caught him without thinking about it, no hesitation. She had no fear of touching him. No fear of him, generally. Even though—bear. That was going to require some explanation later.

"Pants," she told him firmly. "My diner is a no shirt, no

shoes, no service establishment. I'll waive the shirt, but pants aren't optional."

Dan stared at her for an instant, gave a slightly strangled laugh that turned into a cough halfway through, and lunged back to get his jeans.

He didn't bother with anything else. She opened the back door and he ran out, barefoot and bare-chested, into the snow.

"You'll freeze!" Paula shouted.

"Shifters are tough!" he called back.

Right. Bear. He probably didn't even feel the cold. Still, she stopped to grab their coats before charging out after him.

"Here," she said, shoving his coat at him.

Dan pulled it on, barely slowing down. Paula lagged behind, struggling into hers. The snow was coming down more heavily now, fat wet flakes falling all around them.

Dan burst through the door in the fence, with Paula stumbling behind.

There was someone bent over the diner's back door, trying to open it, fumbling with the lock. It was a man, the collar of his wool topcoat turned up against his dark red-brown curly hair.

Paula had a moment to think that there was something weirdly familiar about him before Dan grabbed him by the coat and slammed him into the wall.

"Hey!" the intruder yelped. The thing that was in his hand, which turned out to be not lock picks but keys, slipped out of his hand and fell into the snow.

"Terry?" Paula gasped.

At the sight of her ex, she was frozen in shock. Of all the people she expected to see here—of all the places she expected to see him—

Then he saw her and gave her one of his old familiar smiles, the warm smile that had charmed her in college and then had somehow turned into a deflection, a mask, a cover for his secrets ... and her temper snapped.

"Paula," he began.

She lunged forward and punched him in the face, snapping his head back against the wall.

It wasn't hard enough to hurt him seriously—she just wasn't that strong—but Terry staggered, looking stunned.

"How *dare* you," she snarled.

Rage swelled inside her like a red-hot balloon, filling her to the brim.

"Ow!" Terry protested, covering his face with his hand. "Paula, okay, this is not how I wanted this to go down, I *swear*."

"Are you okay?" Dan asked her quietly.

"I'm fine." As much as she would enjoy watching Dan crush Terry against the wall of the diner, she put a hand on Dan's arm; he put up slight resistance but allowed her to guide him back.

"Is *she* okay," Terry muttered. He wiped a cautious hand under his nose and looked relieved when it wasn't bloody. "Did you change the locks?"

"Why the hell do you even have a key to my diner?" She almost said *My parents' diner*, because back when she was married to Terry, it had been. That was how thoroughly he'd rattled her.

"You gave it to me," he said. "Years ago, when we visited your parents."

"Oh." She didn't remember that. But then, when she married Terry, she had believed in an ethos of share and share alike—sharing everything with her husband. Heart of one heart, soul of one soul.

She still believed in it. She just didn't believe in it with Terry any longer.

Paula crossed her arms and stood shoulder to shoulder

with Dan—or more like shoulder to upper rib cage given their height difference—presenting a united front against Terry. With his back pressed against the wall, her ex-husband looked as if he was starting to realize the magnitude of the mistake he'd made.

"Yes," Paula said. "I *did* change the locks. Or I guess I should say that Dan and his friends did, because someone trying to find *you* trashed the place and has been coming around threatening me."

Terry's mouth fell open. He looked shocked, and although she didn't want to still be able to read Terry's expressions that well, it seemed genuine to her. He wasn't that good a liar. The only reason why he had gotten away with it so long with her was because she wanted to believe him so badly.

"Paula, I swear, I had no idea. I would never have wanted you and the kids to get in trouble because of me."

"Yeah, right." A decade of ruthlessly suppressed anger surged out of her again. "Because you cared a lot about me and the kids when you ran off to God knows where and didn't even bother to leave a forwarding address."

"Paula, I swear—" He started to move forward. Dan placed a big hand on Terry's chest, just high enough that it could slip up to the throat very easily. Terry was shoved back against the wall.

"Maybe you better think carefully about what you want to say to her," Dan growled.

"Who *are* you, anyway?" Terry asked. He made an attempt to squirm free, but Dan had way too much bouncer experience to let him. Dan shoved a knee against Terry's legs and pushed him into the wall again.

"I'm her mate, asshole," Dan snarled.

A warm, delighted feeling sank into Paula's chest. They hadn't even really talked about dating yet, and it was a slightly odd, old-fashioned way to say "boyfriend." But the way he said it was so matter-of-fact and *right* that she could almost feel the rightness of it click into place.

Terry's reaction was weird: his eyes bugged out, and all the fight went out of him. He sagged limply against the wall, propped up by Dan's hand.

"Oh," he said quietly.

"Yeah. Oh. Now here's a suggestion—how about we go somewhere a little warmer and have a chat."

"Your feet," Paula said. She had forgotten Dan was barefoot. Now she looked down, worried, at his cold-looking toes in the snow.

"I'm all right," Dan said, but between the bare feet and his bare chest under the open coat, he looked like he was finally starting to notice the cold. He was shivering slightly.

Paula unlocked the back door of the diner and reached into the hidden panel to reset the alarm keypad, angling her elbow so Terry couldn't see the combination she punched in. She opted for the diner rather than the house because she didn't want Terry in her house, though it was hard to put her finger on exactly why. It wasn't that she was afraid he'd steal her stuff or anything like that. It was more that she just didn't *want* him there. The house was *her* place.

The diner was her place too, but at least it didn't feel like she was letting her ex tramp all over her home place, her nest.

She turned on the lights and reached for a roll of paper towels. "Here," she said, handing it to Dan. "In case you need to dry off and warm up your feet. Are you sure you aren't frostbitten or anything?"

"Not in that short a time," Dan said. "Oh, hell, I better call Derek and Ben, and let them know to call off the cavalry before—"

A large black truck skidded to a halt in the alley, outside the half-open door. Derek and Ben piled out.

"Never mind, too late."

Derek was pulling off his jacket, revealing a massively jacked torso. Before today, Paula would have been puzzled. Now she had the sudden, shocking realization that he was preparing for a shift.

He's a bear too!

It was like the entire world rearranged itself around her. Maybe Lissy really *had* seen a bear in the alley.

"We got an alert on the system," Ben said.

"Who's this guy?" Derek demanded, jerking a thumb at Terry, who had backed all the way up against the wall and looked like he wished he could fade into it.

"My ex," Paula said. She crossed her arms again.

As one, all three of the other guys in the room turned to look at Terry. And Paula wondered why she had never noticed it before: there was a *wildness* to Dan and his friends, like she could almost see the animal beneath the surface.

"So this is the guy who's caused all this trouble," Derek said. A growl vibrated in his throat.

Paula sighed deeply.

"I can't believe I'm defending this deadbeat, but how about we don't rip him apart before we find out what he's doing here?"

"Thanks," Terry said.

"I'm not doing it for you, idiot. I'm doing it because my kids deserve a dad, even if it's you."

∼

TEN MINUTES LATER, everyone was sitting at a couple of diner tables, pulled together in the middle of the floor, while Paula brought out coffee. Terry was on one side; all three of the other men were grouped on the other side, boxing him in so that he would have to go past them to get to either the front or back exit. He looked almost pathetically grateful when Paula came out of the back with a coffeepot.

Paula filled their cups, pushed sugar and creamer to the middle of the table, and sat down beside Dan, leaning against his shoulder. He wrapped his arm around her. All his body language said *Mine*. She nestled into the unaccustomed feeling of being loved and wanted and protected, having all these big guys here just to make sure that her ex didn't bother her.

"So talk," Paula said. "Why are you showing up here, now?"

Terry's gaze darted around the room, back and forth between the men. He was a good-looking guy, tall and well-built with that curly hair she used to love to run her hands through. It was strange to notice how the desire to do so had faded completely.

"It would be easier if it was just us," he said.

"No," Dan said shortly.

Paula shook her head. "These guys are my bodyguards. They stay. Whatever you plan to say, you'll say in front of them, or you can walk out of here and don't bother coming back."

Terry blew out his breath. He caught Dan's eyes for a moment. "This is about—*people like us*. You get that, right?"

Paula felt Dan tense up.

"They're all like us," Dan said. "Paula knows. You can say whatever you need to say."

Terry picked up his coffee cup, like he needed something to do with his hands. "I swear, Paula, I never meant to lie to you—" he began.

"Oh, stuff it," Paula snapped. "If all you've come here to do is shovel up more apologies and self-justifications, don't bother."

She was expecting him to double down on how it wasn't

his fault. Instead, he squared his shoulders and looked her in the eyes.

"You're right," he said. "I hurt you, and I hurt the kids, and I can never make up for that. And I lied to you about things I should never have lied about."

"You got that right," Paula said flatly. "And you still haven't said where you went or why you came back."

Terry's gaze darted to the hostile wall of bodyguards staring at him across the table.

"There are parts of it I can't talk about," he said.

Paula's temper burst out of her. She slapped both hands on the table. As tightly wound as the tension was in the room, everyone jumped.

"You used to give me that line when we were married too! Forget it, buddy. You're telling me everything, and you're telling me now."

"I literally *can't*!" Terry said, his voice cracking. He pulled up his sleeve.

Paula remembered that tattoo very well. It was red ink, an elegant twisting glyph that curled around his forearm. It looked almost like a pair of wings. She used to tease him about it, because he was so straight-laced otherwise. He had always told her that he got it in high school on a dare.

"This stops me from talking about it," he said. "I want to, Paula, but I *can't*."

Paula stared at him, then looked at Dan to see how he was taking this. Dan and Derek were both looking at Ben.

"He's telling the truth," Ben said quietly. "How does it work?"

"I can't talk about it to anyone who doesn't already know," Terry said. He grimaced and pressed his other hand over the tattoo. "Ow. Even that much is getting pretty close to what it doesn't want me to talk about. The other person has to say it first, and then—"

"You're a griffin," Dan said.

His voice carried through the diner. There was a dead silence. Then Terry slowly, jerkily nodded, and rested both his palms flat on the table.

"You're a *what*?" Paula said, her voice rising up the scale to crack in falsetto.

"Oh, hey," Ben said. "This is why you were asking me about mythic shifters earlier, isn't it, Dan?"

Terry's gaze darted up from a coffee stain on the cracked plastic table. "That did it," he said. "I can feel the difference. For the first time in years, I can talk about it freely."

"I don't understand," Dan said. "The tattoo stops you?"

Terry brushed his thumb across the tattoo and then pulled his sleeve down. "This was given to me when I came of age, before I left the covert. Don't ask me how it works, because I don't know. It's some sort of magic and only a few people in the covert know how to make them. It prevents us from being able to talk about what we are to outsiders."

Paula swallowed. Her throat was very dry.

"It's the lair where a flock of griffins lives." Terry's gaze darted around, not quite meeting her eyes. "It's territory, home, nest—all of those things and more. We hardly ever leave."

"You must not," Ben said. "I grew up around dragons and other mythic shifters, and I've never even heard of you guys being real."

"I think we should get back to this griffin thing," Paula said. "What *is* it? What does that mean?"

"I can show you." Terry got up from the table, causing the men around Paula to tense. Then he glanced at the window. "Uh, if someone could shut the blinds. Shifting in front of a picture window looking out onto Main Street isn't great for the secrecy thing, you know?"

Ben jumped up and drew the big vertical blinds across the

diner's windows. The room grew dim. Ben flicked on the overhead lights and stayed there by the door, a silent, threatening presence.

"Okay," Terry said. He glanced nervously at his audience. "Uh ... it might take a minute. I don't shift much. My griffin's kind of shy."

"Just get on with it," Dan growled.

Terry shook out his hands like he was preparing to play the piano, and all of a sudden he melted and flowed and *changed*.

Paula had only the vaguest idea what a griffin was. She wasn't prepared for it to be this big. Terry's body was the size of the Rugers' horse, with powerful muscles rippling beneath tiger-striped reddish fur. His brown-barred wings filled that entire corner of the diner. His head was a hawk's head, bright golden eyes glittering under glowering brows.

"Oh, hey," Ben said from over by the door. "I thought griffins were a hybrid of eagle and lion, mythologically speaking, but you're some other sort of hybrid, aren't you? Tiger and some kind of hawk?"

He sounded almost academically curious. Paula was still trying to wrap her mind around the blank astonishment at seeing her ex-husband turn into a creature straight out of a storybook.

Terry shifted back, his griffin body collapsing into ordinary, everyday Terry, wool topcoat and all.

"Tiger and red-tailed hawk," he said, almost apologetically. "Yeah, griffins are different. We have people at the covert who are owls and eagles, jaguars and cougars, and a lot more. It doesn't seem to matter what type your parents are. I don't know why."

"You okay?" Dan murmured to Paula, who was still frozen in shock.

"Uh ... yeah. I'm fine." She couldn't take her eyes off Terry.

How could she have been married to him for all those years and didn't know?

Because he lied to me about it.

It was true that he had been stuck with the tattoo—and that was another thing she was currently having to wrap her mind around, the existence of magic tattoos as well as bear shifters and, apparently, other creatures as well.

But he could have found a way, if he had wanted to. They'd found a way around it already, in just a few minutes of talking to him in the diner.

It wasn't entirely his fault, but he had still deceived her for years.

And Dan hadn't. It was true that he hadn't told her about the bear thing right away, but would she even have believed him before getting to know him? He had told her as soon as he felt able to.

With that thought, she felt like tight bands around her chest and ribs had eased. She could draw a full breath again.

The *only* thing Dan and Terry had in common was that they were both shifters. Dan was honest and kind and true. Dan would never have vanished without a word. He would certainly never, ever have gotten them into a situation where thugs were breaking down her door.

"Okay, so you turn into a winged tiger. Big deal," she said. There was a huffed breath from Dan that sounded like a laugh turning into a cough. "Are your parents really dead?"

Terry gripped the back of his chair and bowed his head. "No, they aren't. I just didn't know what else to tell you. I couldn't think of a way to explain, otherwise, why I couldn't take you to see them."

"Was it all lies? What's your real name? It's not Terry, is it?"

Terry blew out a breath. "No. It's Tyr. Raines is a surname I chose for myself. We don't have last names in the covert."

"Great. So the last name on my children's birth certificates isn't even your actual name."

Dan squeezed Paula, a strong arm around her shoulders. She leaned into him, drawing a calming breath.

"So where have you *been* for the last year?" Dan asked. "Back in griffin-topia?"

"Some of it." Terry sat down again and twisted his hands around his cooling cup of coffee. "You know how I said that we're not supposed to leave? There's an exception to that, which is that we're allowed out into the human world for a few years when we're young adults. This way we can come back with skills and technology that's necessary for the covert. Sometimes we even come back with mates; it's not unheard of. We're just not supposed to *stay* gone."

"Griffin rumspringa?" Paula said, and there was a faint choking sound from Dan. "So your time ran out?"

"It ran out a long time ago. I didn't plan to go back. You were here, my kids are here, my *life* is here. And I like the human world. I don't want to go back to living on a remote island in the middle of nowhere where almost everyone is related to me and all anyone ever talks about all day long is hunting, the weather, hunting, and did I mention hunting?"

"And they eventually came looking for you," Dan said. His protective arm around Paula had loosened a bit, but it was still draped over her shoulders, offering support and staking a wordless claim all in one.

Terry nodded.

"I was basically living a double life, staying in touch with my griffin family, meeting with them sometimes, and trying to dodge the enforcers. That wasn't working out so well, so I thought I'd just go back for a little while and straighten it all out, but once I was there, they had no intention of letting me leave again. I would have said something, said goodbye to the kids at least, if I'd known it was going to be as hard to get off the island again as it turned out to be."

"What, they don't have phones there?" Paula said. Terry was shaking his head. "Mail?"

"No, it's very isolated. Most of the contact with the outside world is through young griffins who are at the traveling age, as well as between different griffin coverts in other parts of the world. They think of themselves as a world of their own. There's no place for outsiders ... or for people who have family outside. If I went back, I'd have to give up the kids, or take them with me, and I wasn't going to do that to them."

"So you ran," Derek said.

"I ran." Terry set the cup down carefully. His hand shook a little.

"They came here, Terry," Paula snapped. "They came to where our kids are!"

"I know! I *know*." He squeezed his eyes shut. "Paula, I would have done anything to keep the kids safe. Anything. I didn't know they'd come here. I didn't even think they knew about you. I came here as soon as I realized they'd been looking for me by harassing you."

"You could have *called* me!" she burst out. "Warned me!"

"I know," he said quietly. "I could have. I *should* have. But I didn't." He looked up at the hostile stares from across the table. "I want to make it right. Look, I came back mainly to say goodbye to the kids. The easiest thing would be if I just went back with them."

Dan gave a sudden, low chuckle. Paula looked up at him in surprise.

"Maybe you won't have to," he said. "There aren't very many griffins on this island, right? And most of them aren't allowed to leave? How are they sending people after you?"

"Enforcers," Terry said. "They're specially trained for it."

"But there can't be too many of them. Right?"

"What are you thinking?" Derek asked.

"I'm thinking we've got a bunch of big predator shifters right here in this room. And Ben knows some dragons."

Paula clutched at his hand. "You can't be suggesting fighting them!"

"I don't think we'll have to," Dan said. "I ran off one of their enforcers already. They don't want a big, public fight in a populated area any more than any other shifter does. We just need to make it clear that this town, and Paula and her family, are under our protection. We're not letting them take anyone who doesn't go with them willingly, and we aren't going to put up with them coming around hassling and threatening people in this town." His gaze flicked off Terry's. "*Anyone* in this town."

He glanced around the room at the others. "It's like a—what did you call it? A covert of our own. This town is our home, and the people who live here are our friends and neighbors, our family. We'll do whatever we have to do to protect them."

Paula's fingers laced through his, and he felt the conviction of his own words sink in. This *was* his home now. He was part of something larger than himself, a place to belong at last.

"I'm in," Derek said.

Ben laughed softly. "I'll talk to the dragons. This kind of thing is right in Dad's wheelhouse, and maybe Tessa can cash in some favors with Heikon's clan."

Astonished, Terry looked back and forth between them. "You'd do that for me?"

"We're not doing it for you," Dan said. He snugged Paula closer to his side. "I'm doing it for her."

DAN

All things being equal, Dan didn't think he'd have chosen to team up with his mate's ex-husband, let alone put his ass on the line to protect the guy. But Paula's kids deserved to have their father in their life. Even if Dan indulged in a few pleasant fantasies of kicking Terry's feathered ass down the street for causing them all this trouble.

Paula volunteered the diner as the location for their operation. Dan didn't like that, but she pointed out that their plan relied on having the meeting in a public place, where the other griffins wouldn't be able to fight back without revealing themselves. The diner was centrally located in town, and she owned it.

"I want you and the kids far away when the time comes," Dan told her quietly. They were loading the dishwasher in Paula's kitchen; she rinsed while he put things into the racks. "We can take you out to Gaby and Derek's farm for the day."

Paula shook her head. "I'm going to be there."

"Paula—"

She placed a wet fingertip against his lips.

"I know you want me safe. I want me safe, too. But this is

about me and my family. I need to be there, Dan. And ..." She smiled, and lifted her fingers away with a brush of her thumb across his lips. "*You'll* be there to protect me. I know you won't let anyone hurt me."

Dan took a shaky breath. The depth of her belief in him staggered him; he wasn't used to anyone looking at him like that, let alone with the connection of the mate bond to strengthen and heighten it.

"Okay," he managed at last. "But the kids—"

"The kids go to the farm," Paula agreed. "I don't want them around this either."

Dan nodded. She was still looking at him. "Is everything okay?" he asked.

"You mean besides the fact that we're about to take on a whole gang of griffin enforcers?"

He cracked a grin. "Yeah, other than that."

Paula smiled. But it was clear that she had something on her mind. He waited. After a moment, she spoke.

"Dan ... when you and Terry talk about mates, I got the feeling that it *means* something. That it's more than just a word for you. What does it mean?"

Dan hesitated. It was the final thing he hadn't told her yet. But this, of all things, she deserved to know.

"Every shifter has someone out there in the world for them," he told her, while she watched him with those deep, fascinated eyes, a cereal bowl forgotten in her hands. "Maybe humans do too, I'm not sure. But we *know*. When we first meet them, our animal tells us so."

"Your animal. Your ... bear?"

"Right."

"It talks to you?"

"It's not quite that, so much as—well, it's like the instinctive part of yourself. The part that knows things. The part that's sure."

"And that part knew that you and I were meant for each other."

Her voice was barely above a whisper.

"Yes," he said, gently but fervently. "Yes."

"So Terry ... I'm *not* that for Terry, am I?"

Dan was already shaking his head. "No."

"And he would have known that." Paula turned away, clutching a dish towel in a tight wad. "And he married me anyway."

"He must have loved you." It was hard to give Terry even that much benefit of the doubt. But if you didn't know what the mate bond felt like, if you'd never experienced it, you didn't know what you were missing out on. Dan wouldn't have known himself, before he met Paula.

Paula let out a long breath and then turned and stepped into his arms.

"Enough talking about my ex." She tipped her head back. "Mate, huh?"

"Mate," he murmured.

He ran his thumb up her long neck, tracing the fine line of her jaw. When he moved in to nuzzle at the side of her face, she had a light lemony scent of dish soap where she'd swept her hair back with wet hands. It was astonishingly hot.

"Mmm," she breathed, as he brushed his lips lightly across the soft skin along her hairline. "Ooh. Wow. You know, we still have dishes in the sink."

"And kids to pick up from school," he agreed, and moved on to nibble at the lobe of her ear.

Was this really his life? He couldn't shake a sense of unreality. Was this really him, talking about ordinary domestic chores with a woman he adored?

The family he'd always wanted, dreamed of, had landed in his lap fully formed. And not just Paula and the kids, but also the Rugers and the entire town, a ready-made home and family and community, just waiting to embrace him.

"What is it?" Paula asked, her lips a whisper against the side of his face, and he realized that he'd paused.

"Just thinking," he murmured, and moved down to nibble at her neck, while her hair tickled his nose. "We don't have to pick up the kids from school for a little while yet. And I'm thinking the dishes can wait."

Paula gasped as he hit an especially sensitive area at the nape of her neck. He made a note of that for later. "Dishes?" she got out. The dish towel hit the floor at her feet. "What dishes?"

"That's what I'm thinking."

A moment later, her blouse and his shirt joined the dish towel on the floor, followed by a trail of other clothing, all the way to the bedroom.

DAN

THE DINER WAS CLOSED, and as prepared for the confrontation as it could be, with the tables moved back to the sides of the room, the blinds closed to hide any shifting that might occur, and breakable items put away. None of them were sure how violent this was likely to get.

Terry had sent a message to the griffins, telling them he wanted to meet. Now he paced the room, rubbing his hands nervously together.

Dan hated having Paula this close to the action, but she had promised to stay at the back of the room, where she could easily duck out the back door if she had to.

While they were waiting, she passed cups of coffee around to the waiting shifters lounging in the dining area. Derek was sitting on the edge of the counter, while Dan leaned against the wall. Ben had just gone out to do a quick sweep of the alley and check on the electronic sensors he had set up to signal them if anyone tried to sneak in from behind.

"Thanks," Dan said, giving Paula a kiss. "Are you sure I can't talk you into heading over to the house while this goes down, at least?"

Paula shook her head, determined. "I feel safer with you."

A warm feeling rushed through him.

"Alley's clear," Ben reported, coming in through the kitchen doorway. "Has anyone else shown up yet?"

"How many people did you invite, exactly?" Dan asked.

"We've got a couple more coming." Derek checked his watch. "If they ever get here."

"Or if they come at all," Ben muttered.

But as if in response to his complaint, the bell on the door tinkled and then it opened to admit a man and a woman.

The woman wore a long coat with a fur ruff around the neck, and beneath it, a pair of bright yellow stretch pants, dotted with sunflowers, showing off her curvy legs. Her extremely curly red hair, shot through with silver, emerged in a floof from beneath a fur hat.

She was somewhat tall, but the man with her was much taller, and broad-shouldered, filling out his black overcoat in a way that suggested a kind of fierce strength. His hair was black, shot at the temples with silver. He surveyed the diner with a cool gaze.

"Hi, Dad," Ben said. "Hi, Loretta. You came."

"I believe it was made clear to me that I didn't have much of a choice." The tall, dark-haired man glanced at the woman, and Dan had a brief, sharp awareness of a mate bond between them. It wasn't a metaphysical sense; it was just the way that they seemed in perfect communion, as if each knew what the other was thinking.

Ben and the older man clasped forearms and traded a slightly awkward one-armed hug. Then Ben turned to the woman and they shared a friendlier greeting. She gave him a firm hug and kissed him on the cheek.

"You really shouldn't be here, you know," he said, gripping her hands. "It might not be safe."

"She wouldn't stay at home," the dark-haired man said, looking briefly exasperated.

Loretta stepped on his foot. "I'll be fine. It's not the first time I've dealt with a dangerous enemy, don't forget. Besides, I'll have an entire room full of big strong shifters to protect me. What could possibly go wrong?"

"You're shifters?" Paula asked cautiously.

"Oh, right," Ben said. "Yeah, this is my dad, Darius. He's a dragon. My stepmom Loretta is human."

Paula came over to greet Loretta. The two of them clearly hit it off immediately.

"Your sister and her mate are with us," Darius said. "In fact, there they are now."

The door opened again. This time it was a dark-haired woman accompanied by a huge blond man. The woman's resemblance to Ben was clear, even before she ran to him and hugged him.

"Melody," Ben sighed. "I'd feel better if you were out of this."

"Too bad," Melody said cheerfully. "The kids are with Mom. She seems to be enjoying the opportunity to play Grandma Esme."

"And what do *you* turn into?" Paula asked, not one to mince words.

"Dragon," Melody said brightly, pointing to herself. She pointed to her blond mate. "That's Gunnar. He turns into a bear."

Dan gave Gunnar a slight nod, and got an equally slight nod back.

This was starting to feel more like a family reunion than a trap for a dangerous enemy.

"They're coming!" Derek called from the door, and just like that, the mood in the room turned deadly serious.

Dan looked at Paula. She nodded and took Loretta by the hand. The two human women stepped back to the kitchen doorway, where they could keep themselves behind the shifters.

A moment later, the door opened, and the griffins walked in.

There were three of them, all dressed in long dark coats as if they were trying to be deliberately inconspicuous and had somehow ended up looking like TV secret agents instead. One was Sunglasses, with his sunglasses firmly in place. The others were a woman and a man. Both were redheads and bore a visible resemblance to Terry.

They all stopped at the sight of the group waiting for them.

It was, Dan had to admit, both intimidating and strange. Darius looked like a bodybuilder turned Fortune 500 CEO. Melody had stepped up next to him, slim and pale and pretty, dwarfed by her massive mate. Ben was on Gunnar's other side, with Dan beside him. They formed a line, roughly ranged in front of Paula and Loretta. Terry was in the middle.

Derek strolled over to close the door, and quietly flipped the lock.

There was a tense, waiting silence.

Then the red-haired man said calmly, "What kind of game are you playing, Tyr?"

"Uncle Adan." Terry's voice was tight as wire. "I go by Terry here."

"Is this some kind of attempt to intimidate us?" Sunglasses sneered.

"Oh, knock it off, cuz," Terry said. "You're a dick and you always were a dick, even back when we were kids. Being an enforcer doesn't make you special."

Adan sighed. "Just come with us, Tyr."

Terry shook his head. He folded his arms and straightened his back, and Dan felt a reluctant respect for him. It had to be hard to stand up to your family like that. "I'm not going back with you."

"You talk like you think have a choice about it," the woman said. "It's how things are done."

"Not for me," Terry said. "Not anymore."

Dan spoke up then. "You heard him give you his decision. Now it's time for you to leave this town and never come back."

His voice carried through the room. Terry fell silent, and Dan realized that everyone was looking at him now—not just the griffins, but everyone on Dan's side of the room as well.

He hadn't been prepared to speak for them.

But he was Paula's mate. Defending her was his responsibility and his joy.

"Look who's talking," Adan said calmly. "A one-armed man. Are we supposed to be afraid of you?"

"I don't care if you're afraid," Dan said. "I just want you gone. Time to have a look at what you're up against." He turned, with a slight smile, to the other shifters. "Derek?"

Derek Ruger growled low in his throat. He shed his shirt, and his bear erupted out of him, thudding down on massive grizzly paws.

This triggered an eruption of shifting all around the room. Terry shifted first, going from human to griffin with a gliding economy of motion. Ben shifted into a panther, lean and black. Gunnar followed a moment later. His bear was a huge white polar bear.

And then Darius shifted.

Dan knew that dragon shifters existed, but he had never

seen a full-grown one before. The only dragon he had met personally was cute little Skye.

Darius was huge. His great coiling body expanded to fill most of the floor space of the diner. He was polished silver, like hammered steel, covered in overlapping plates of metallic silver armor. His neck arched over the assembled group, and his head dipped until the tip of his muzzle was almost touching the human-form griffins. He opened his mouth slightly, displaying a gleaming row of teeth.

Melody shifted too. She was a much smaller dragon, about half Darius's size, and her metallic scales were a silver so pale that she was nearly white. If Darius was steel, Melody was platinum. Her silvery coils spilled over Darius's. There was barely room to stand.

For the first time, the griffins looked intimidated. There was a bear at their backs and dragon coils all around them. The griffins not only didn't have room to fight, they didn't even have room to shift. He hadn't quite realized how much of the space the dragons were going to take up.

"Now that we've got your attention ..." Darius said in a deep, rumbling voice that seemed to vibrate the tiles underfoot.

Surrounded by huge predators, backed up in every sense of the word, Dan stepped forward. He didn't shift, but he let his inner animal rise inside him, showing in his eyes.

"This is *our* town," he said. "You have your secret griffin islands. We have this town. It's off limits to you just as yours is almost certainly off limits to us. But this is *ours*. The people who live here are ours. If you stay on your island, we won't bother you, but if you come around looking for trouble, trouble is what you'll get."

Darius growled. It vibrated the counters and rattled dishes in the kitchen. Then he very lightly set his enormous teeth on Adan's shoulder.

Adan didn't twitch a hair. Sunglasses was frozen, and the woman seemed tensed on the edge of a shift.

This was when it would go wrong if it was going to, Dan thought. He had dealt with enough tense situations, in the military and as a bouncer, to know that people nearly always backed down if you got in their face with sufficient authority and backed it up with a show of strength. But there were always those few who had to prove a point, or the ones who didn't realize they couldn't win even if the odds were stacked impossibly against them.

The tension stretched. No one moved.

Then Adan said tightly, "Shift, Tyr, and give me your arm."

Terry ruffled his wings and, after a moment, he shifted back to human and stepped forward. He seemed to know what was happening, even if Dan didn't, because he pushed up his sleeve and wordlessly presented the arm with the tattoo.

Dan became aware of Paula nudging up to his side, glancing all around nervously at the big predator shifters. To Dan, she murmured, "Do we stop this?"

"I think he knows what he's doing," Dan murmured back.

Adan's fingers blurred and shifted into claws. Dan had never seen a shifter do that before, not without shifting their entire bodies. He wondered if it was something only griffins could do, or if all shifters could learn to do it.

Terry braced his wrist with his other hand.

Dan could see where this was going, where it must be going, but it was still a shock when Adan's claws slashed through the tattoo, leaving a line of gleaming blood behind. Terry barely flinched, but as the blood welled up rapidly and dripped off his fingers, he pressed his hand over the injury and took a step back.

"You are exiled from the covert," Adan said, his voice cool.

"Stay here with your humans and outsiders. If you return, we will kill you."

There was no expression on his face. Sunglasses looked smugly pleased, and the woman was visibly distressed, but neither of them said anything.

"And you'll leave," Dan said. "You'll never return, and you won't bother anyone here."

Adan gave his hand a brisk shake, restoring the normal human fingers. "First, it seems that we still have a slight problem. Tyr's tattoo prevents him from speaking of us, even in its current state."

Terry looked up, grimacing, from his blood-slick fingers wrapped around his wrist.

"But we have no such guarantee with the rest of you," Adan continued smoothly. "And you clearly know about us."

"Oh, who are we going to tell?" Paula burst out. "You people are so worried about secrecy, but we don't know where you are, we don't know how to find you, and if we tell anyone in the human world about you, they'll just think we're crazy."

"She's right," Terry said. "I can't reveal it—" He gestured with his bloody hand, and winced. "—and no one would ever believe it anyway. You're in no danger from anyone here."

"The children—" Adan began.

Dan tensed. He saw Terry go tense, too.

"Are not," Terry said shortly. "They're human, and none of your concern."

Dan kept his mouth shut.

Adan regarded them for a long moment. Then he gave a brief nod.

"I accept your terms," he said. "Keep our secret, and stay away from us, and we will do you the same courtesy."

Derek moved aside so they could leave. The three griffins filed out without a backward glance.

There was a brief silence in the diner. Then Paula flipped the lock on the door, and around the room, shifters began shifting back. The tense atmosphere changed to a low-key murmur of voices, saying things like, "Has anyone seen my shirt?" and "Oh, damn it, ripped up my jeans again."

Paula leaned against Dan.

"You didn't even shift," she murmured.

He laughed quietly under his breath. "You mind?"

"Hey, I'm never going to object to seeing you with your clothes off." She gave him a quick kiss. "You were amazing."

Loretta came bustling in from the kitchen carrying a dish towel. "Here, honey," she said to Terry. He was still clutching his wrist; blood welled up between his fingers. "Let me."

Terry allowed her to take his arm and bind the towel around it. He looked dazed, as if he was slightly in shock. "I can't believe that worked," he said faintly.

"Are they really gone?" Melody asked. She was helping her mate Gunnar back into his shirt. As a mythic shifter, her clothes had gone with her.

Dan took a peek between the blinds. The sun was dazzling outside on the remaining snowdrifts. The town went on about its business, completely oblivious to the shifter confrontation that had gone on inside the diner.

"Looks like it," he said. "You think they'll keep their word?"

"Honor is important to us," Terry said. He sagged against the counter, resting his hip against it while Loretta worked on his arm. "We're like dragons that way. We wouldn't break a contract."

"What did they do to your tattoo?" Paula asked Terry. She hadn't moved from Dan's side; he tightened his good arm around her.

"Mark of exile," Terry said. He flexed his hand with a

wince. "Any griffin looking at this will know that I'm banned."

"Did you know that was going to happen?" Dan asked.

"I thought it might. I've heard of exiles, although it's not very common. Usually it's criminals, people who broke the covert's rules." He gave Loretta a grateful nod when she passed him another towel, this one dampened, to wipe the blood off his hands. "But it goes both ways. As an exile, they have no authority over me. They won't come looking for me, and you and the kids are safe," he said to Paula.

Turning, he looked around the diner. "I don't know how to thank you. Any of you."

By staying away from my mate was Dan's instinctive response—but Terry was still Austin and Lissy's father, and Dan knew it wasn't fair to take that away from them.

Loretta laughed. "Now that all the action is over, I have to say that *I* didn't come all this way to leave without seeing my granddaughter. Where is she?"

Ben grinned. "Skye is out at the farm with Gaby and Tessa and the rest of the kids. Actually, we should head back out there now."

Paula's hand slipped down to squeeze Dan's. "Actually, I have a better idea," she said, pitching her voice to carry over the murmur of conversation among the others. "You're all invited to the diner to eat tonight. I haven't been open for dinner in a long time, and it's on the house. In fact, as far as I'm concerned you can all eat free forever."

In the brief silence, Dan heard Darius murmur, as he leaned over to Loretta, "Now that's a woman who knows how to thank people."

Loretta jammed an elbow into his ribs.

"Well?" Paula asked, looking around. "What do you all say? Dinner here, tonight? Get all the kids and bring them. This is a family business."

"And we'll get started cooking," Dan put in.

Paula looked up at him. "You don't have to. I can call Mitch and see if he'd like to pick up a late shift."

"I think it would be fun to do it together." He turned his hand around and laced his fingers through hers, palm to palm. "Teamwork."

"Teamwork," she murmured, and leaned her head against his shoulder.

PAULA

PAULA WOKE LAZILY, wrapped up in Dan's warm body. She could get used to this whole sleeping-in thing, she thought.

"Mmm, good morning, beautiful," Dan murmured. "Diner closed again today?"

"I haven't had a vacation since I moved back home. I think I've earned one. Especially after feeding all those people last night. Thanks for helping with that, by the way."

"Hmmm." He rolled over to prop himself up on his good elbow, looking down at her. "Any thoughts on how you might want to start your vacation?"

"I have some ideas," she said, and pulled him down to her.

A little later, lazy and sated, they took turns showering. He had an overnight bag this time, and Paula sat on the bed, combing her damp hair while she watched Dan putting his arm on.

"Any plans for today?" Dan asked.

"Not really. Well, it's a Saturday, so the kids are sleeping in. Then again, I guess we did too," she added, glancing out the window at the bright sunshine gleaming off the snow. "I'll need to get them up soon anyway. Terry's coming by to pick up them up in early afternoon."

"You're okay with that?"

"I want him to be part of their lives. He always was a pretty good dad until he disappeared."

"You know, that reminds me," Dan said, looking over from adjusting the straps around his shoulders. "There are some things about their dad, and about me, that the kids should probably know."

Paula paused with her hair parted at the side, comb in hand. "Tell them about the—the animal thing? Are you sure?"

"I think we should," Dan said. He hesitated and seemed to be struggling with some kind of dilemma. Finally he said, "If their dad is a shifter, one or both of them might be, too."

"But Terry said—"

Paula's mouth fell open. A sudden realization hit her like a thunderbolt, and she gave Dan a careful look.

"Is *that* what you and Austin talked about the other night? Is that his big secret?"

His face was a perfect picture of dismay, so much that she had to laugh.

"He swore me to secrecy," Dan said. "Please don't tell him I told you."

"You didn't tell me. I figured it out." Her son, a shifter. An abrupt coil of anger tightened in her chest. "Did Terry lie about that too?"

Dan shook his head. "I don't think he knows. I don't think anybody knows. Austin only found out recently. Anyway, wouldn't you rather have those griffin jerks think he's a normal human kid?"

"Jeez, you're right." She decided, even if it *was* a lie, that she was willing to forgive Terry for that one. "Is he a griffin? He'd have to be, wouldn't he? No, wait, don't tell me." She got up and went to give Dan a kiss. "You're right. We should have a family meeting about this, once the kids are up."

∼

Paula had always appreciated the privacy of having a large backyard with a high fence around it, especially living in a small town with nosy neighbors, but she had never appreciated it as much as she did now.

Lissy and Austin were assembled in the snow, wrapped in coats, hands in pockets, looking chilly and baffled. They'd had a leisurely breakfast with pancakes whipped up by Dan, and then Paula herded everyone into the backyard for a family conference before Terry showed up.

"Do we have to do this out here?" Lissy complained. "Why can't we talk about whatever it is in the living room?"

"Because there's more room out here." Paula looked around to be sure that no nearby neighbors' windows were aimed at the backyard. There was the Jamesons' place, but their second-floor curtains were drawn and they never used that bedroom anyway.

"What's all this about?" Austin asked. His gaze kept going to Dan.

He did actually have some idea of what this family conference was all about, Paula thought, and her stomach flipped with a strange feeling, excited and guilty all at once. Her son really *was* a shifter.

"If you want to tell us you're dating, we *know*," Lissy said. "Can I go in now?"

"No, it's not that. Well, not *just* that." Paula turned to Dan. "Show them."

Dan had left his arm inside. Now he turned away from them and stepped behind a bush.

Paula and Dan had discussed how to do this. Dan had told

her that shifter families were used to casual nudity around each other, like people in some cultures elsewhere on Earth. Paula had said that this may be true, but it definitely was *not* true in Autumn Grove. The bush worked as a reasonable privacy screen that allowed the kids to catch glimpses of what was happening without showing them a little *too* much.

"Is he taking off his clothes back there?" Lissy shrieked. "Isn't he *cold*?"

Austin didn't say anything. He shoved his hands in his pockets and looked down at the ground.

"Kids," Paula said, "there's something you need to know about Dan. Lissy, remember how you saw that bear in the alley the other day? And I said I thought you dreamed it? I was wrong, honey. I think you really did see a bear." Probably Derek on patrol, now that she thought about it.

"Told you," Lissy said, smug as only a vindicated nine-year-old could be.

"But it wasn't just a bear. It was a man who turns into a bear. There's real magic in the world, kids, and Dan has some of it too." She waved her hand at the bush, which was shaking a little, shedding snow off its branches. "Voila."

The bush gave a final shudder, and a grizzly bear stepped out from behind it.

He looked a little more natural out here than he had in her living room. With the backyard layered in snow, this was a more proper environment for a bear. She hadn't actually seen him walk before, and she was struck by how carefully he did it, with a lopsided, slightly hopping movement.

"Wow," Austin said. He sounded like he was aiming for surprise. It didn't sound very convincing.

Lissy shrieked and clung to Paula's leg.

"It's okay, kids," Paula said. She didn't look at Austin, trying to maintain the polite fiction that shifters were a total surprise to both of them. At least now she knew how Dan got snow all over him the other day. "It's just Dan. He's the same as he is when he's human. He won't hurt you."

She had thought that she would have to work harder at convincing herself. But one look at Dan was all it took. She didn't know exactly how, but she could still see Dan in him, even if he was as massive as her car and covered with shaggy brown fur. That was definitely Dan. And whether he was a bear or a man, she would never, ever worry about the kids around him.

Paula ruffled Lissy's hair and took a step forward.

Dan flopped down abruptly in the snow. A bear lying down wasn't that much shorter than a bear standing up; it appeared that most of their height was not in the legs. He settled his head down in the snow and watched her approach.

Paula felt a bit weird petting him (was it rude to scratch your boyfriend behind the ears?) but she needed to show the kids that he was harmless, and anyway, she wanted to touch him. How often did anyone get the chance to pet a real live bear in perfect safety?

She touched him hesitantly at first. His fur was coarse on the outside, but when she buried her hands in it, she found that his underfur was very soft, and very warm.

Dan gave a small grunt, which sounded pleased. Paula dug her hands deeper and then leaned against his side, and it occurred to her that she was getting completely lost in the experience; she had halfway forgotten the kids. She turned around and beckoned to them.

"Come on, kids. Come pet a bear."

The kids both hesitated, Lissy out of nervousness and Austin from embarrassment. Lissy broke first, and trotted across the snow in her little green boots and coat. She looked absolutely tiny next to Dan's great shaggy bulk. But Paula felt no nervousness, not even slightly, as Lissy reached out a hesitant hand and petted his muzzle.

They looked like an illustration out of a children's book, especially with Lissy's bright green coat, a splash of color in the snow.

"Come on, Austin," Paula said.

Austin sighed, but he came over and gave Dan a token pat.

"What else can he turn into?" Lissy asked. "A mole?"

"No, honey. Just a bear."

"An eagle?"

"No, Lissy."

"A horse?"

"No, he only turns into a bear, Lissy."

As Lissy grew more confident, she became visibly more excited. "This is amazing," she said, and gave Dan a hug, wrapping her arms around his giant head as far as they would go. "I have my own *bear*. This is *awesome*. I can ride him and play with him and—"

"Don't forget he's also Dan," Paula said, stifling her laughter.

"—and take him to *school* and—"

"No!" Paula and Austin said at the same time. Paula glanced at her son, who looked down at his boots.

"Wait 'til that stuck-up Kimberly Burke sees my *bear*! I'm gonna—"

"Honey." Paula planted her hand on Lissy's shoulder. She should have anticipated this problem. "You can't tell anyone about this, not ever, okay? It's a really big secret. Dan would be in trouble if anyone knew. But you can talk to me and Austin about it, and to Sandy and his parents, and to your dad."

Austin gave her a sharp look. Paula hesitated. This was the tricky part. Dan had told her that it was a huge breach of shifter etiquette to reveal a shifter to other people. But Terry being the kids' dad, and especially since Austin had inherited his shifting, put them in a gray area. They really needed to know. In fact, Terry should have told them years ago, and Paula still wished that he had tried harder to find a way to do that.

"Your dad turns into something too," she said.

"Whoa!" Lissy didn't seem at all surprised by this. At this point, Paula could probably tell her that her fourth-grade teacher was a vampire and she would cheerfully take it in stride. "Does *he* turn into a horse?"

"No—"

"A dolphin?"

"No, honey, he—"

"A rabbit? A zebra? An alien? A boxer dog?"

"Lissy, I'm trying to tell you, if you'd just let me finish." Paula was laughing so hard she could barely speak.

"He's a griffin," Austin said quietly. "Isn't he? Mom?"

"Yes, honey." Paula sobered. She had the feeling of trying to coax a wild creature to eat out of her hand. There were so many ways this could go wrong. "How do you know that?" she added, remembering that she wasn't supposed to know.

"You're the *worst* at fibbing, Mom," Austin said. He scowled. "Dan told you, didn't he?"

"No!" Paula said, and Dan backed it up by shaking his big, shaggy head, almost knocking Lissy into the snow. "I figured it out on my own after I found out about your dad."

"How long have you known about Dad?" Austin asked defensively. He sounded betrayed, and she reached out a hand, struck by the hurt in his voice.

"Only since yesterday. I promise. I had no idea when I was married to him. After I knew that, though, it wasn't hard to figure out what you were hiding from me." She swallowed. "Do you mind showing me?"

Austin took a step back. Dan raised his head, twitching his furry ears forward.

"You don't have to," Paula said. "But I bet your sister would love to see it."

"I do, I do!" Lissy said, clapping her hands, and then looked puzzled. "See what, Mom?"

Austin heaved a deeply put-upon teenage sigh, and shifted.

Even expecting it, Paula still jumped back. It was hard enough to get used to it with Dan, but seeing someone else do it, someone she knew so well—her little boy, the baby she had carried around, the toddler who had followed her everywhere, the stubborn teenager who had been both her pride and a pain in her ass for the last year—

It was shocking and also amazing.

He was a beautiful griffin. Now that she knew griffins were made of different kinds of cats and birds, she could see that his body half was something long and tawny—a cougar, maybe? His wings were fluffy enough that it was hard to tell exactly what they were going to look like when they finished fledging, but from the shape of his head, she thought he was probably some kind of hawk or falcon, like his dad.

Austin looked as embarrassed as anyone with a cat body and bird head could look.

"You're gorgeous, baby," Paula said, which didn't seem to help.

Lissy, meanwhile, was almost speechless with excitement. She jumped up and down, clapping her hands wildly.

"Austin is a *kittybird*!" she shrieked.

"Baby, keep it down, people can hear. It's called a griffin."

"Kittybird!" Lissy shrieked at the top of her lungs, still bouncing. "Kittybird, kittybird—*awk!*"

Her wild squeals turned into a squawk. Between one jump and the next, the little girl vanished, and what plopped into the snow was a fat, fluffy kitten with a very startled-looking, round-eyed bird head and little unfledged wings covered in downy baby fuzz.

"Oh no," Paula gasped.

Lissy looked around in bafflement. She started to get up, tottered and nearly fell over. Her head rotated all the way around backwards, causing Paula to yelp, so that she could look at her wings. She spread first one, then the other, and gave them a cautious little flap.

She was so round and fluffy that it was hard to tell exactly what kind of cat she was, but she seemed to have spots. Her bird head had a cute little pointy beak.

Austin came over to poke at her curiously with his beak. Dan nuzzled her reassuringly. And Paula stared at her family there in the snow—her boyfriend the bear, her two griffin cubs—and didn't know whether to laugh or cry.

This certainly wasn't the life she'd envisioned just a few weeks ago.

Then she was overcome with the adorableness of it. She pulled out her phone and took a picture.

∽

AFTER PLAYING in the snow for a while, Paula and Dan coaxed the kids back to kid-shape again—Lissy had lost a boot, which seemed to have vanished utterly; Paula dug out a slightly outgrown spare pair—and Terry showed up, exactly on time, with a promise to return them in the evening.

Lissy greeted him with enthusiastic delight, Austin with a bit more reserve, but all three of them were laughing and talking as they left the house. Paula was cautiously optimistic that this might work out okay after all.

When the kids and Terry were gone, a cheerful make-out

session ensued. After they finally broke apart, Dan asked her, "What do you want to do with our free afternoon?"

She could think of any number of things, but still floating with satiation from earlier, there was one thing that came to mind ahead of all else.

"How about that date we never got around to?"

A few minutes later they were strolling down the street, hand in hand, looking in shop windows. After weeks of miserably cold, snowy weather, the sun was out today and the piles of snow were melting on the sidewalk. It wasn't spring yet, but it almost felt like it, as if the world had begun to thaw.

They strolled casually, in no hurry. Paula waved occasionally to people that she knew.

"It feels so strange to be out like this in the middle of the day," she admitted. "Between the diner and the kids, I've almost forgotten what free time feels like."

"Have you thought about delegating more?" Dan asked. "I know that running a business is two or three full-time jobs stacked on top of each other, but you might be able to arrange things so that you only have to go into the diner four or five days a week instead of 24-7."

"I'm thinking about it. I gotta say, I could get used to this."

Actually, she *was* thinking about it now—thinking seriously about it. It wasn't that she hated running the diner, she realized. It was that she never seemed to have any time for herself. Maybe she could take more of a manager's role and find someone else to handle the day-to-day work.

Maybe if she sat down with Gaby Ruger and talked about some kind of partnership, she thought. Gaby was hellishly busy too, but Gaby's café was booming, and perhaps between the two of them they could hire a couple more people to work at both places and give both of them more time to spend with their families.

Her work-life balance had been tipped toward *work* for too long. It was time to get her life back, and fit the work part of it where it belonged: as a job that she could leave behind at the door to spend time with her family.

They had been strolling all this time, and they were starting to run out of downtown. A winding path led into Dodd Park at the downtown cul-de-sac. In the summer, there were benches and a stream. At this time of year it was mostly snow and dead-looking trees, but they wandered down the cleared paths anyway.

"What about you?" Paula asked. "I mean, as far as the future goes. Are you going to keep working for the Rugers?"

"I think so," Dan said. "I like it. In fact, I don't know if I want to go on to work as a bodyguard with Derek and Ben. I'm actually having a blast cooking for their kids and taking care of the babies. I might want more excitement eventually, but right now, I can't think of anything else I want to do more."

"And ... do you want to go on living at the Ruger farm?" she asked cautiously.

Dan looked down at her. In the bright sunshine, he looked like he was lightly glazed with gold. "Do you have another offer?"

"I might. There's a lot of room in that house, you know."

"I don't see any reason why I can't drive out to the Rugers' to work," Dan said. "Nothing about the job means I have to sleep there. Especially when there's such a tempting offer elsewhere."

Paula grinned. Her heart felt so full of joy that it was brimming over. She laced her arms around his neck and kissed him. The sun was warm on her shoulders.

"I still want to take it a little slow because of the kids," she said when they came up for air. "Are you okay with that?"

Dan brushed his thumb lightly over the corner of her mouth.

"I'm fine with whatever you want to do. We can go as slow or as fast as you want. There's no time limit, no deadline. We have forever."

"Forever," she echoed, and right now, with her heart impossibly full, she felt as if she could see ahead to it. All those tomorrows, filled with love and family and delight.

She couldn't wait for it.

EPILOGUE

VALENTINE'S DAY

THERE WERE several cars already parked in Derek and Gaby's yard when Paula and Dan pulled in. It was late afternoon, with sun glimmering on the snow. The warm weather had continued for the past couple of weeks, with just a single brief snowstorm in early February that hadn't really stuck. As they got out of the car, Paula noticed that the grass on the pasture was showing in a brown and gray patchwork through the snow. There were even crocuses starting to come up.

"Smells like spring," Dan said, scenting the air. He leaned into the backseat to get out their contribution to the Rugers' Valentine's Day potluck.

"Can you actually smell that?" Paula asked. She took the cherry pie he handed her, clasping it in her mittened hands.

Dan nodded.

"What does spring smell like?"

"Green growing things. Melting snow. Fresh buds on the trees." He breathed in deeply, and smiled down at her, making her dizzy with the intensity of it. "I'm looking forward to finding out what spring in the mountains is like."

"Yeah, well, you'll need a little patience for that," Paula said. "It can't possibly stick this early. In a week, we'll probably be in the middle of a major blizzard."

"Snowballs and sledding and bonfires? Sounds nice to me."

"I knew the winter carnival was a mistake," Paula murmured, but it was playful.

Terry's car was among the assembled vehicles, so the kids would be here already. It was surprising to her how easily she had adjusted to having her ex take the kids some of the time. They still lived full-time with her, for now, but they both seemed to be thriving with their father in their life again.

The Rugers' front walk was neatly shoveled and salted, and lined with rows of pink and red paper hearts on sticks stuck in what remained of the snow. The hearts had arrows and THIS WAY!! printed on them in a childish hand.

"Lissy helped make these," Paula confided in Dan as they walked up to the front door. "I think she and Sandy did most of them."

There were also pink and red paper hearts taped to Derek and Gaby's front door, an entire heart explosion. In neatly printed felt marker, they said things like BE MINE and ONLY YOURS and—

"This one says EWWW KISSING," Dan reported, leaning over to read the hearts lower down on the door.

"Yes, there's one here that says VALENTINES UGH." Paula freed up a hand from the pie to knock on the door.

While they waited, they found hearts reading NOPE and ARE WE THERE YET and POTATO. From inside, there was the sound of laughter and voices, and then footsteps rapidly approaching the door.

"Hi!" Gaby declared, swinging the door open. "Come on in!"

"You didn't tell us we were supposed to dress up," Paula said, laughing.

Gaby was wearing a pink and red dress with a puffy tulle skirt, and underneath it, pink tights with red hearts on them, and little red shoes. She also had put on a kid's headband with two springs on it, each one tipped with a sparkly heart.

"I don't know what you're talking about, these are my normal clothes," Gaby said loftily. She held the door for them. "Food's in the kitchen, so just find a place and grab a plate. There's no dinnertime. The shifters are in the backyard. The only rules are, don't track snow in the house, and pants are *not* optional for humans over the age of four."

"Well, that sounds—interesting," Paula said faintly. Adjusting to having her ex-husband back in her life was child's play compared to dealing with the world of magic and shifters that everyone else seemed to accept so casually.

But Dan's face had lit up at the prospect of other shifters to hang out with. Gaby gave Paula a commiserating smile that made her feel warm, reminding her that she wasn't the only human mate of a shifter around these parts.

The kitchen was absolutely groaning with food, from time-honored potluck standbys like macaroni salad and taco dip, to amazing-looking tamales, luscious chocolate-dipped strawberries, fancy layered pastries glazed with sugar and nuts, steaming dishes of cheese-covered potatoes sprinkled in bacon, and a pasta bake that looked like it had about 4000 well-earned calories per serving.

Paula shifted some dishes aside to make room for hers. Her pie seemed very plain next to the rest of it, but Gaby exclaimed over it and then went to take a muffin pan of mini quiche out of the oven.

"How are we going to eat all of this?" Paula asked, nibbling on a pastry.

Gaby laughed. "Have you seen how shifters eat?"

"The babies are down for their naps," came another voice, and Loretta entered the kitchen, her red hair spilling loose over a dark gold cashmere sweater. "Oh, hi, honey," she said, and hugged Paula. "It's so nice to see you again."

"Babies?" Paula asked, hugging her.

"My Lulu and Loretta's little Ryder," Gaby said. "There are kids all over the place. Skye is here, and Melody and Gunnar are in the backyard with Dash and Daria, their twins."

Paula looked out the window into the backyard. What she saw was a sight to behold. It was an entire *menagerie* out there. There were bears, there were dragons, there were griffins—of course her gaze went first and foremost to *her* griffins, Lissy with her little fluttering fuzzy wings and Austin wrestling playfully with a baby bear cub.

The only humans in sight were Tessa, sitting on a pile of snow with a couple of little dragons in her lap, and Sandy, who was riding on one of the dragons (Melody, Paula thought). He didn't seem bothered in the slightest to be the only non-shifter in the bunch.

"You want to be out there, don't you," Paula said to Dan.

He shrugged slightly, but he was grinning. "I can stay in here with you, if you'd rather."

"Get out there in the snow, you ridiculous man."

She kissed him and all but pushed him out the door. Dan left his clothes on the porch with all the other heaps of shifter clothes and lunged onto the snowy back lawn, brown and shaggy, to be met by Ben's panther and a grizzly bear that was presumably Derek.

"It's nice to have somewhere they can do this," Gaby said philosophically. She began stirring cocoa into hot milk. "Here, get down some mugs. Cabinet over the sink. While they tire themselves out, we can have hot cocoa and take advantage of the babysitting to put our feet up with a nice Hallmark movie."

"Also, we have all the food in here," Loretta said, picking up a plate. "We get our pick of the best of the buffet."

The Rugers' cabinets were full of the sort of mismatched variety of dishes, mugs, and glasses that families tended to accumulate of the years. Paula picked out a fat, round Santa mug for herself, a squat green mug shaped like a cactus with I <3 ARIZONA on it—presumably from some past family vacation—and a large mug with a unicorn on it, with a rainbow coming out its rear end and the words EAT MY ...

"Do you ever feel left out?" she asked quietly, setting out the mugs in a row so that Gaby could pour the rich, swirling hot chocolate. "With all of them out there doing—all of that."

It was Loretta who answered, as she collected mini quiche onto the edge of her heaped plate. "Sometimes. It's hard not to, sweetie. I'm married to a guy who can grow wings and fly. Pretty soon I'll probably have baby dragons flying circles around me too, once Ryder learns to shift. But you know, we all have things we're good at. I mean, Darius can't cook to save his life."

"Who wants a little Bailey's in their cocoa?" Gaby asked, waggling the bottle.

There were enthusiastic cheers for this, and they took their mugs into the living room, where Gaby moved some baby toys off the couch and shifted a sleepy and annoyed cat to one end. The coffee table was covered with a scatter of DVD cases.

"I should've asked people to bring their favorite movies, if anyone has movies anymore," Gaby said. "Oh, well, I bet we get through like half a movie before the guys come in and start demanding NASCAR or something."

Loretta pumped her fist in the air. "Sounds great. I love NASCAR."

"I am not watching NASCAR on Valentine's Day."

She wasn't wrong; they made it halfway through *When*

Harry Met Sally before a mob of cheerful, snow-covered, half-naked shifters swarmed into the house.

"Pants!" Gaby yelled over her shoulder.

"I'm wearing pants," Derek said, leaning over the back of the couch to put his arms around her. He was stripped to the waist. "Never said anything about shirts, though."

Dan had his shirt on, but he hadn't put his arm back on. If he felt self-conscious about it, he showed no sign of it. He leaned on the arm of the couch and rubbed Paula's neck with his good hand.

"What are you watching?"

"Romantic movies," she said, leaning into his touch. "We're having girl time."

Glancing up, she noticed that Terry, after saying goodbye to the kids, had gone straight to the door. She squeezed Dan's hand and gestured with her eyes. Dan gave a little nod and a supportive smile.

It was so weird to her, the way they seemed to know what each other were thinking, with no words needing to be said. It wasn't telepathy exactly—but it was something like it.

Mate bond.

She got up and went over to where Terry was putting his coat on.

"Thanks for coming," she said quietly. "It meant a lot to the kids. You aren't staying?"

Terry gave a little headshake. "Figured I'd bug out early. It's Valentine's, and ..." He shrugged. "I'm kind of a fifth wheel here."

It was true, she noticed, glancing around. Terry was the only adult in the room not paired off.

"I'm sure Gaby and Derek wouldn't mind if you stayed," she offered, feeling slightly insincere as she did so. Personally, she preferred the idea of being able to cuddle with Dan without knowing her ex was in the room. Still, it was the mature thing to do.

Terry shook his head again. "Nah. Gotta head back to the hotel. I'm going back to the city tomorrow."

Paula raised her eyebrows. "For good? I know it's none of my business what you do with your life," she added. "Not anymore. But there are the kids. It's been really good for them having you around. Austin's calmed down a lot."

Terry hesitated, fingers tapping on the door.

"To be honest, the business is on really shaky ground right now. Turns out you can't just disappear and leave a sales and marketing firm to run itself in your absence. I'm thinking about selling it and moving here, to be closer to the kids. Would you be okay with that?"

"I don't have the right to run you out of town, Terry. I'm not the boss of you."

"I know," he said, and quirked a small smile. "But I don't want to step on your life here."

It was a wistful smile, and the feeling that it evoked in her was strange—she remembered what it was like when that smile did things to her insides, but now that feeling was entirely gone. It was only an echo, like a fragment of a song from the past.

"It's okay," she said. "I want the kids to have you in their life. I mean, you and I have moved on, we both know it, but we'll always share the kids. And Dan understands that."

Dan was watching them from across the room. Not jealous, not really. Just very serious, his gaze locked on Terry in a way that clearly stated *Don't mess with what's mine*.

Terry nodded. He pulled a knit cap down over his ears. "Gaby was telling me that there's a business in town that's for sale and can't seem to get a taker. I might look into it."

"What business?"

He smiled again, looking a little more cheerful this time. "It's a garden center."

"Oh—what—the Tender Sprout is up for sale *again*? They can't seem to hold onto the same owner for more than a couple of years." She frowned at him. "Do you know anything about gardening at all?"

"No. But I can learn, right? Spring is coming, and it seems like that's a good time to start a garden business."

"Good luck," she said, and meant it.

There was an awkward moment when they jockeyed for something between handshake and hug; she settled for clapping his shoulder like she was sending him off to play a sports game or something. Then he left, and Paula turned around to find that Dan had come up behind her. She clasped her arms around his waist.

"Thanks for being okay with me having Terry in my life."

"Kids deserve their dads," he said seriously, and kissed the top of her head. "Assuming their dads aren't total wastes of space. But I don't think Terry is. I'm still not okay with everything he did. But he does love those kids."

"He does," she agreed, and leaned her head on his chest. "But so do you. You know, some lucky kids get to have *two* dads."

She felt him tense a little. "I'd be honored," he said at last, his voice rumbling through his chest, a pleasant vibration against her, "if they want to call me Dad someday. But I'll be happy just being part of their lives, and yours."

Paula leaned into him, listening to the cheerful babble of laughter and voices from the living room and kitchen, drowning out the sound of the TV. Despite all the people in the house, over here by the door it felt almost private, as if they existed in their own little bubble.

"What if you had someone else to call you Dad, too?" she asked quietly.

The words were pitched so low that she wasn't sure if he would hear them, but she felt him going still in her arms. "What are you saying?' he asked under his breath.

"I'm wondering how you'd feel about us having a baby."

He stayed still for a very long time, then brought up his hand to run it through her hair. "I'd love to, but how do *you* feel about it? You're the one who'd be doing the hard labor, so to speak."

Oh, she loved this man. "I don't want to rush into anything right away. There's a lot going on right now, with Terry back in the kids' lives, and the absolute last thing I'd want is for Austin and Lissy to worry about being replaced."

"Never," Dan said fervently.

"I know that and you know that, and I think they do too, but do they really *believe* it? Let's wait for things to settle down, until we all get used to the new normal. But after that ..." She hesitated, tilting her head back to look up in his face, the familiar, beloved features that she had already come to know almost as well as her own. "Spending all this time around the other little ones, Gaby and Tessa's babies, is reminding me how much I do actually miss the kids being that small. I never even *thought* about having more kids, with Terry out of my life and everything so busy at the diner. But now that I have time to stop and relax for a while, and think about what I want ... I *do* want that. A baby with your amazing brown eyes."

Dan's brown eyes looked somewhat misty at the moment. "I'm not gonna lie, ever since I met you, I've been thinking about a baby with your beautiful blue eyes."

"You know, I think that part might be out of our hands."

"You mean you can't special order them?"

Paula laughed, and Dan joined in with his deep, warm laugh. He had been doing that a lot more lately. She loved the sound of it.

"We'll just have to have twins, then," Dan said. "One of each. Blue eyes and brown."

"Okay, don't get ahead of yourself, buddy. Like you pointed out, remember who's going to be doing most of the work here."

There was a sudden crash from the kitchen, and the babble of cheerful conversation hushed. This was followed by a yelp of "Catch her! Oh no, not you too—"

A fat bear cub bolted from the kitchen, a pastry clamped firmly in her stubby jaws. Flying above her was a little purple dragon, wings beating so rapidly they were a hummingbird-like blur, absolutely covered from nose to tailtip in cherry pie filling and shedding bits of crust.

The two little shifters vanished upstairs, with several adults and a couple of excited kids pounding along behind them.

After the entire procession had vanished from sight, and everyone downstairs had stopped laughing, Dan said, "Still want one of those?"

"More than ever," Paula sighed.

Because this was her life, wasn't it? This wonderful chaos, these people who welcomed her into their lives. Her kids, and the Ruger kids, and all the glorious madness that came from knowing shifters and having shifter kids and a shifter mate.

She twined her hand into Dan's, and together, as a team, they went upstairs to see if they could help.

∼

If you enjoyed this book, please join my mailing list! You'll receive emails when I release a new book, and free story epilogues in which you can see what the couples get up to after their books.

http://www.zoechant.com/join-my-mailing-list/

And don't miss more mythic shifters in **_Stoneskin Dragon_**, #1 in a new **_Bodyguard Shifters_** spinoff series!

A NOTE FROM ZOE CHANT

Thank you for buying my book! I hope you enjoyed it. If you'd like to be emailed when I release my next book, please click here to be added to my mailing list: http://www.zoechant.com/join-my-mailing-list/. You can also visit my webpage at zoechant.com or follow me on Facebook or Twitter.

For this book, I asked readers in my Facebook group to submit cute kid stories that I might use in the book (with details changed, of course!). I got a wonderful deluge of stories - thank you so much! I had so much fun reading all of them! The ones that I ended up using were from Norma (kid covered in baby powder - there were also similar stories from two other moms, Carrie and Shay, so I guess a lot of parents can probably relate!), and the baby oil sliding races were from Ashley.

If you want to join in the fun, help me decide similar things for future books and have a chance at free ARCs, please join my VIP Readers Group on Facebook!

Also, please consider reviewing *Babysitter Bear,* even if

A NOTE FROM ZOE CHANT

you only write a line or two. I appreciate all reviews, whether positive or negative.

Cover art: © Depositphoto.com

ALSO BY ZOE CHANT

Stone Shifters

Stoneskin Dragon

Stonewing Guardian

Stoneheart Lion (forthcoming)

Bodyguard Shifters

Bearista

Pet Rescue Panther

Bear in a Bookshop

Day Care Dragon

Bull in a Tea Shop

Dancer Dragon

Babysitter Bear

There is a convenient boxed set of the first four books.

Bears of Pinerock County

Sheriff Bear

Bad Boy Bear

Alpha Rancher Bear

Mountain Guardian Bear

Hired Bear

A Pinerock Christmas

Boxed Set #1 (collects Books 1-3)

Boxed Set #2 (collects Books 4-6)

And more ... see my website for a full list at zoechant.com!

If you enjoyed this book, you might also like my paranormal romance and sci-fi romance written as Lauren Esker!

Shifter Agents

Handcuffed to the Bear

Guard Wolf

Dragon's Luck

Tiger in the Hot Zone

Shifter Agents Boxed Set #1

(Collecting *Handcuffed to the Bear, Guard Wolf,* and *Dragon's Luck*)

Standalone Paranormal Romance

Wolf in Sheep's Clothing

Keeping Her Pride

Warriors of Galatea

Metal Wolf

Metal Dragon

Metal Pirate

Printed in Great Britain
by Amazon